# The Listerdale Mystery

## and Other Stories

**HarperCollins***Publishers*

HarperCollins*Publishers* Ltd
1 London Bridge Street
London SE1 9GF

www.harpercollins.co.uk

HarperCollins*Publishers*
1st Floor, Watermarque Building, Ringsend Road
Dublin 4, Ireland

This paperback edition 2016

11

First published in Great Britain by
Collins, The Crime Club 1934

*The Listerdale Mystery*™ is a trade mark of Agatha Christie Limited
and Agatha Christie® and the Agatha Christie Signature are
registered trade marks of Agatha Christie Limited in the UK and elsewhere.
Copyright © 1934 Agatha Christie Limited. All rights reserved.
www.agathachristie.com

A catalogue record for this book is
available from the British Library

ISBN 978-0-00-819643-1 (PB)
ISBN 978-0-00-825551-0 (POD PB)

Set in Sabon LT Std by Palimpsest Book Production Limited,
Falkirk, Stirlingshire

Printed and bound in the UK using 100% renewable electricity
at CPI Group (UK) Ltd

MIX
Paper from
responsible sources
FSC
www.fsc.org
FSC™ C007454

We hope you enjoy this book. Please return or renew it by the due date.

You can renew it at www.norfolk.gov.uk/libraries or by using our free library app.

Otherwise you can phone 0344 800 8020 - please have your library card and PIN ready.

You can sign up for email reminders too.

NORFOLK ITEM

30129 088 546 081

NORFOLK COUNTY COUNCIL
LIBRARY AND INFORMATION SERVICE

## Mysteries

The Man in the Brown
  Suit
The Secret of Chimneys
The Seven Dials Mystery
The Mysterious Mr
  Quin
The Sittaford Mystery
The Hound of Death
The Listerdale Mystery
Why Didn't They Ask
  Evans?
Parker Pyne Investigates
Murder Is Easy
And Then There Were
  None
Towards Zero
Death Comes as the End
Sparkling Cyanide
Crooked House
They Came to Baghdad
Destination Unknown
Spider's Web *
The Unexpected Guest *
Ordeal by Innocence
The Pale Horse
Endless Night
Passenger To Frankfurt
Problem at Pollensa Bay
While the Light Lasts

## Poirot

The Mysterious Affair at
  Styles
The Murder on the
  Links
Poirot Investigates
The Murder of Roger
  Ackroyd
The Big Four
The Mystery of the Blue
  Train
Black Coffee *
Peril at End House

Lord Edgware Dies
Murder on the Orient
  Express
Three-Act Tragedy
Death in the Clouds
The ABC Murders
Murder in Mesopotamia
Cards on the Table
Murder in the Mews
Dumb Witness
Death on the Nile
Appointment with Death
Hercule Poirot's
  Christmas
Sad Cypress
One, Two, Buckle My
  Shoe
Evil Under the Sun
Five Little Pigs
The Hollow
The Labours of Hercules
Taken at the Flood
Mrs McGinty's Dead
After the Funeral
Hickory Dickory Dock
Dead Man's Folly
Cat Among the Pigeons
The Adventure of the
  Christmas Pudding
The Clocks
Third Girl
Hallowe'en Party
Elephants Can
  Remember
Poirot's Early Cases
Curtain: Poirot's Last
  Case

## Marple

The Murder at the
  Vicarage
The Thirteen Problems
The Body in the Library
The Moving Finger

A Murder Is Announced
They Do It with Mirrors
A Pocket Full of Rye
4.50 from Paddington
The Mirror Crack'd
  from Side to Side
A Caribbean Mystery
At Bertram's Hotel
Nemesis
Sleeping Murder
Miss Marple's Final Cases

## Tommy & Tuppence

The Secret Adversary
Partners in Crime
N or M?
By the Pricking of My
  Thumbs
Postern of Fate

## Published as Mary
  Westmacott

Giant's Bread
Unfinished Portrait
Absent in the Spring
The Rose and the Yew
  Tree
A Daughter's a Daughter
The Burden

## Memoirs

An Autobiography
Come, Tell Me How You
  Live
The Grand Tour

## Play and Stories

Akhnaton
The Mousetrap and
  Other Plays
The Floating Admiral †
Star Over Bethlehem
Hercule Poirot and the
  Greenshore Folly

* novelized by Charles Osborne      † contributor

# CONTENTS

# The Listerdale Mystery

Mrs St Vincent was adding up figures. Once or twice she sighed, and her hand stole to her aching forehead. She had always disliked arithmetic. It was unfortunate that nowadays her life should seem to be composed entirely of one particular kind of sum, the ceaseless adding together of small necessary items of expenditure making a total that never failed to surprise and alarm her.

Surely it couldn't come to *that!* She went back over the figures. She had made a trifling error in the pence, but otherwise the figures were correct.

Mrs St Vincent sighed again. Her headache by now was very bad indeed. She looked up as the door opened and her daughter Barbara came into the room. Barbara St Vincent was a very pretty girl, she had her mother's delicate features, and the same proud turn of the head, but her eyes were dark instead of blue, and she had a different mouth, a sulky red mouth not without attraction.

'Oh! Mother,' she cried. 'Still juggling with those horrid old accounts? Throw them all into the fire.'

'We must know where we are,' said Mrs St Vincent uncertainly.

The girl shrugged her shoulders.

'We're always in the same boat,' she said dryly. 'Damned hard up. Down to the last penny as usual.'

Mrs St Vincent sighed.

'I wish—' she began, and then stopped.

'I must find something to do,' said Barbara in hard tones. 'And find it quickly. After all, I have taken that shorthand and typing course. So have about one million other girls from all I can see! "What experience?" "None, but—" "Oh! thank you, good-morning. We'll let you know." But they never do! I must find some other kind of a job—*any* job.'

'Not yet, dear,' pleaded her mother. 'Wait a little longer.'

Barbara went to the window and stood looking out with unseeing eyes that took no note of the dingy line of houses opposite.

'Sometimes,' she said slowly, 'I'm sorry Cousin Amy took me with her to Egypt last winter. Oh! I know I had fun—about the only fun I've ever had or am likely to have in my life. I *did* enjoy myself—enjoyed myself thoroughly. But it was very unsettling. I mean—coming back to *this*.'

She swept a hand round the room. Mrs St Vincent followed it with her eyes and winced. The room was typical of cheap furnished lodgings. A dusty aspidistra, showily ornamental furniture, a gaudy wallpaper faded in patches. There were signs that the personality of the tenants had struggled with that of the landlady; one or two pieces of good china, much cracked and mended, so that their saleable value was *nil*, a piece of embroidery thrown over the back of the sofa, a water colour sketch of a young girl in the fashion of twenty years ago; near enough still to Mrs St Vincent not to be mistaken.

'It wouldn't matter,' continued Barbara, 'if we'd never known anything else. But to think of Ansteys—'

She broke off, not trusting herself to speak of that dearly loved home which had belonged to the St Vincent family for centuries and which was now in the hands of strangers.

'If only father—hadn't speculated—and borrowed—'

'My dear,' said Mrs St Vincent, 'your father was never, in any sense of the word, a business man.'

She said it with a graceful kind of finality, and Barbara came over and gave her an aimless sort of kiss, as she murmured, 'Poor old Mums. I won't say anything.'

Mrs St Vincent took up her pen again, and bent over her desk. Barbara went back to the window. Presently the girl said:

'Mother. I heard from—from Jim Masterton this morning. He wants to come and see me.'

Mrs St Vincent laid down her pen and looked up sharply.

'Here?' she exclaimed.

'Well, we can't ask him to dinner at the Ritz very well,' sneered Barbara.

Her mother looked unhappy. Again she looked round the room with innate distaste.

'You're right,' said Barbara. 'It's a disgusting place. Genteel poverty! Sounds all right—a white-washed cottage, in the country, shabby chintzes of good design, bowls of roses, crown Derby tea service that you wash up yourself. That's what it's like in books. In real life, with a son starting on the bottom rung of office life, it means London. Frowsy landladies, dirty children on the stairs, fellow-lodgers who always seem to be half-castes, haddocks for breakfasts that aren't quite—quite and so on.'

'If only—' began Mrs St Vincent. 'But, really, I'm beginning to be afraid we can't afford even this room much longer.'

'That means a bed-sitting room—horror!—for you and me,' said Barbara. 'And a cupboard under the tiles for Rupert. And when Jim comes to call, I'll receive him in that dreadful room downstairs with tabbies all round the walls knitting, and staring at us, and coughing that dreadful kind of gulping cough they have!'

There was a pause.

'Barbara,' said Mrs St Vincent at last. 'Do you—I mean—would you—?'

She stopped, flushing a little.

'You needn't be delicate, Mother,' said Barbara. 'Nobody is nowadays. Marry Jim, I suppose you mean? I would like a shot if he asked me. But I'm so awfully afraid he won't.'

'Oh! Barbara, dear.'

'Well, it's one thing seeing me out there with Cousin Amy, moving (as they say in novelettes) in the best society. He *did* take a fancy to me. Now he'll come here and see me in *this*! And he's a funny creature, you know, fastidious and old-fashioned. I—I rather like him for that. It reminds me of Ansteys and the village—everything a hundred

4

years behind the times, but so—so—oh! I don't know—so fragrant. Like lavender!'

She laughed, half-ashamed of her eagerness. Mrs St Vincent spoke with a kind of earnest simplicity.

'I should like you to marry Jim Masterton,' she said. 'He is—one of us. He is very well off, also, but that I don't mind about so much.'

'I do,' said Barbara. 'I'm sick of being hard up.'

'But, Barbara, it isn't—'

'Only for that? No. I do really. I—oh! Mother, can't you *see* I do?'

Mrs St Vincent looked very unhappy.

'I wish he could see you in your proper setting, darling,' she said wistfully.

'Oh, well!' said Barbara. 'Why worry? We might as well try and be cheerful about things. Sorry I've had such a grouch. Cheer up, darling.'

She bent over her mother, kissed her forehead lightly, and went out. Mrs St Vincent, relinquishing all attempts at finance, sat down on the uncomfortable sofa. Her thoughts ran round in circles like squirrels in a cage.

'One may say what one likes, appearances *do* put a man off. Not later—not if they were really engaged. He'd know then what a sweet, dear girl she is. But it's so easy for young people to take the tone of their surroundings. Rupert, now, he's quite different from what he used to be. Not that I want my children to be stuck up. That's not it a bit. But I should hate it if Rupert got engaged to that dreadful girl in the tobacconist's. I daresay she may be a very nice girl, really. But she's not our kind.

It's all so difficult. Poor little Babs. If I could do anything—anything. But where's the money to come from? We've sold everything to give Rupert his start. We really can't even afford this.'

To distract herself Mrs St Vincent picked up the *Morning Post*, and glanced down the advertisements on the front page. Most of them she knew by heart. People who wanted capital, people who had capital and were anxious to dispose of it on note of hand alone, people who wanted to buy teeth (she always wondered why), people who wanted to sell furs and gowns and who had optimistic ideas on the subject of price.

Suddenly she stiffened to attention. Again and again she read the printed words.

'To gentlepeople only. Small house in Westminster, exquisitely furnished, offered to those who would really care for it. Rent purely nominal. No agents.'

A very ordinary advertisement. She had read many the same or—well, nearly the same. Nominal rent, that was where the trap lay.

Yet, since she was restless and anxious to escape from her thoughts she put on her hat straightaway, and took a convenient bus to the address given in the advertisement.

It proved to be that of a firm of house-agents. Not a new bustling firm—a rather decrepit, old-fashioned place. Rather timidly she produced the advertisement, which she had torn out, and asked for particulars.

The white-haired old gentleman who was attending to her stroked his chin thoughtfully.

'Perfectly. Yes, perfectly, madam. That house, the house

mentioned in the advertisement is No 7 Cheviot Place. You would like an order?'

'I should like to know the rent first?' said Mrs St Vincent.

'Ah! the rent. The exact figure is not settled, but I can assure you that it is purely nominal.'

'Ideas of what is purely nominal can vary,' said Mrs St Vincent.

The old gentleman permitted himself to chuckle a little.

'Yes, that's an old trick—an old trick. But you can take my word for it, it isn't so in this case. Two or three guineas a week, perhaps, not more.'

Mrs St Vincent decided to have the order. Not, of course, that there was any real likelihood of her being able to afford the place. But, after all, she might just *see* it. There must be some grave disadvantage attaching to it, to be offered at such a price.

But her heart gave a little throb as she looked up at the outside of 7 Cheviot Place. A gem of a house. Queen Anne, and in perfect condition! A butler answered the door, he had grey hair and little side-whiskers, and the meditative calm of an archbishop. A kindly archbishop, Mrs St Vincent thought.

He accepted the order with a benevolent air.

'Certainly, madam. I will show you over. The house is ready for occupation.'

He went before her, opening doors, announcing rooms.

'The drawing-room, the white study, a powder closet through here, madam.'

It was perfect—a dream. The furniture all of the period,

each piece with signs of wear, but polished with loving care. The loose rugs were of beautiful dim old colours. In each room were bowls of fresh flowers. The back of the house looked over the Green Park. The whole place radiated an old-world charm.

The tears came into Mrs St Vincent's eyes, and she fought them back with difficulty. So had Ansteys looked—Ansteys . . .

She wondered whether the butler had noticed her emotion. If so, he was too much the perfectly trained servant to show it. She liked these old servants, one felt safe with them, at ease. They were like friends.

'It is a beautiful house,' she said softly. 'Very beautiful. I am glad to have seen it.'

'Is it for yourself alone, madam?'

'For myself and my son and daughter. But I'm afraid—'

She broke off. She wanted it so dreadfully—so dreadfully.

She felt instinctively that the butler understood. He did not look at her, as he said in a detached impersonal way:

'I happen to be aware, madam, that the owner requires above all, suitable tenants. The rent is of no importance to him. He wants the house to be tenanted by someone who will really care for and appreciate it.'

'I should appreciate it,' said Mrs St Vincent in a low voice.

She turned to go.

'Thank you for showing me over,' she said courteously.

'Not at all, madam.'

He stood in the doorway, very correct and upright as

she walked away down the street. She thought to herself: 'He knows. He's sorry for me. He's one of the old lot too. He'd like *me* to have it—not a labour member, or a button manufacturer! We're dying out, our sort, but we hang together.'

In the end she decided not to go back to the agents. What was the good? She could afford the rent—but there were servants to be considered. There would have to be servants in a house like that.

The next morning a letter lay by her plate. It was from the house-agents. It offered her the tenancy of 7 Cheviot Place for six months at two guineas a week, and went on: 'You have, I presume, taken into consideration the fact that the servants are remaining at the landlord's expense? It is really a unique offer.'

It was. So startled was she by it, that she read the letter out. A fire of questions followed and she described her visit of yesterday.

'Secretive little Mums!' cried Barbara. 'Is it really so lovely?'

Rupert cleared his throat, and began a judicial cross-questioning.

'There's something behind all this. It's fishy if you ask me. Decidedly fishy.'

'So's my egg,' said Barbara wrinkling her nose. 'Ugh! Why should there be something behind it? That's just like you, Rupert, always making mysteries out of nothing. It's those dreadful detective stories you're always reading.'

'The rent's a joke,' said Rupert. 'In the city,' he added

importantly, 'one gets wise to all sorts of queer things. I tell you, there's something very fishy about this business.'

'Nonsense,' said Barbara. 'House belongs to a man with lots of money, he's fond of it, and he wants it lived in by decent people whilst he's away. Something of that kind. Money's probably no object to him.'

'What did you say the address was?' asked Rupert of his mother.

'Seven Cheviot Place.'

'Whew!' He pushed back his chair. 'I say, this is exciting. That's the house Lord Listerdale disappeared from.'

'Are you sure?' asked Mrs St Vincent doubtfully.

'Positive. He's got a lot of other houses all over London, but this is the one he lived in. He walked out of it one evening saying he was going to his club, and nobody ever saw him again. Supposed to have done a bunk to East Africa or somewhere like that, but nobody knows why. Depend upon it, he was murdered in that house. You say there's a lot of panelling?'

'Ye-es,' said Mrs St Vincent faintly: 'but—'

Rupert gave her no time. He went on with immense enthusiasm.

'Panelling! There you are. Sure to be a secret recess somewhere. Body's been stuffed in there and has been there ever since. Perhaps it was embalmed first.'

'Rupert, dear, don't talk nonsense,' said his mother.

'Don't be a double-dyed idiot,' said Barbara. 'You've been taking that peroxide blonde to the pictures too much.'

Rupert rose with dignity—such dignity as his lanky and awkward age allowed, and delivered a final ultimatum.

'You take that house, Mums. *I'll* ferret out the mystery. You see if I don't.'

Rupert departed hurriedly, in fear of being late at the office.

The eyes of the two women met.

'Could we, Mother?' murmured Barbara tremulously. 'Oh! if we could.'

'The servants,' said Mrs St Vincent pathetically, 'would *eat*, you know. I mean, of course, one would want them to—but that's the drawback. One can so easily—just do without things—when it's only oneself.'

She looked piteously at Barbara, and the girl nodded.

'We must think it over,' said the mother.

But in reality her mind was made up. She had seen the sparkle in the girl's eyes. She thought to herself: 'Jim Masterton *must* see her in proper surroundings. This is a chance—a wonderful chance. I must take it.'

She sat down and wrote to the agents accepting their offer.

'Quentin, where did the lilies come from? I really can't buy expensive flowers.'

'They were sent up from King's Cheviot, madam. It has always been the custom here.'

The butler withdrew. Mrs St Vincent heaved a sigh of relief. What would she do without Quentin? He made everything so *easy*. She thought to herself, 'It's too good to last. I shall wake up soon, I know I shall, and find it's been all a dream. I'm so *happy* here—two months already, and it's passed like a flash.'

Life indeed had been astonishingly pleasant. Quentin, the butler, had displayed himself the autocrat of 7 Cheviot Place. 'If you will leave everything to me, madam,' he had said respectfully. 'You will find it the best way.'

Each week, he brought her the housekeeping books, their totals astonishingly low. There were only two other servants, a cook and a housemaid. They were pleasant in manner, and efficient in their duties, but it was Quentin who ran the house. Game and poultry appeared on the table sometimes, causing Mrs St Vincent solicitude. Quentin reassured her. Sent up from Lord Listerdale's country seat, King's Cheviot, or from his Yorkshire moor. 'It has always been the custom, madam.'

Privately Mrs St Vincent doubted whether the absent Lord Listerdale would agree with those words. She was inclined to suspect Quentin of usurping his master's authority. It was clear that he had taken a fancy to them, and that in his eyes nothing was too good for them.

Her curiosity aroused by Rupert's declaration, Mrs St Vincent had made a tentative reference to Lord Listerdale when she next interviewed the house-agent. The white-haired old gentleman had responded immediately.

Yes, Lord Listerdale was in East Africa, had been there for the last eighteen months.

'Our client is rather an eccentric man,' he had said, smiling broadly. 'He left London in a most unconventional manner, as you may perhaps remember? Not a word to anyone. The newspapers got hold of it. There were actually inquiries on foot at Scotland Yard. Luckily news was received from Lord Listerdale himself from East Africa. He invested his cousin, Colonel Carfax, with power of attorney. It is the latter who conducts all Lord Listerdale's affairs. Yes, rather eccentric, I fear. He has always been a great traveller in the wilds—it is quite on the cards that he may not return for years to England, though he is getting on in years.'

'Surely he is not so very old,' said Mrs St Vincent, with a sudden memory of a bluff, bearded face, rather like an Elizabethan sailor, which she had once noticed in an illustrated magazine.

'Middle-aged,' said the white-haired gentleman. 'Fifty-three, according to Debrett.'

This conversation Mrs St Vincent had retailed to Rupert with the intention of rebuking that young gentleman.

Rupert, however, was undismayed.

'It looks fishier than ever to me,' he had declared. 'Who's this Colonel Carfax? Probably comes into the title if anything happens to Listerdale. The letter from East Africa was probably forged. In three years, or whatever it is, this Carfax will presume death, and take the title. Meantime, he's got all the handling of the estate. *Very* fishy, I call it.'

He had condescended graciously to approve the house. In his leisure moments he was inclined to tap the panelling and make elaborate measurements for the possible location of a secret room, but little by little his interest in the mystery of Lord Listerdale abated. He was also less enthusiastic on the subject of the tobacconist's daughter. Atmosphere tells.

To Barbara the house had brought great satisfaction. Jim Masterton had come home, and was a frequent visitor. He and Mrs St Vincent got on splendidly together, and he said something to Barbara one day that startled her.

'This house is a wonderful setting for your mother, you know.'

'For *Mother*?'

'Yes. It was made for her! She belongs to it in an extraordinary way. You know there's something queer about this house altogether, something uncanny and haunting.'

'Don't get like Rupert,' Barbara implored him. 'He is convinced that the wicked Colonel Carfax murdered Lord Listerdale and hid his body under the floor.'

Masterton laughed.

'I admire Rupert's detective zeal. No, I didn't mean anything of *that* kind. But there's something in the air, some atmosphere that one doesn't quite understand.'

They had been three months in Cheviot Place when Barbara came to her mother with a radiant face.

'Jim and I—we're engaged. Yes—last night. Oh, Mother! It all seems like a fairy tale come true.'

'Oh, my dear! I'm so glad—so glad.'

Mother and daughter clasped each other close.

'You know Jim's almost as much in love with you as he is with me,' said Barbara at last, with a mischievous laugh.

Mrs St Vincent blushed very prettily.

'He is,' persisted the girl. 'You thought this house would make such a beautiful setting for me, and all the time it's really a setting for *you*. Rupert and I don't quite belong here. You do.'

'Don't talk nonsense, darling.'

'It's not nonsense. There's a flavour of enchanted castle about it, with you as an enchanted princess and Quentin as—as—oh! a benevolent magician.'

Mrs St Vincent laughed and admitted the last item.

Rupert received the news of his sister's engagement very calmly.

'I thought there was something of the kind in the wind,' he observed sapiently.

He and his mother were dining alone together; Barbara was out with Jim.

Quentin placed the port in front of him, and withdrew noiselessly.

'That's a rum old bird,' said Rupert, nodding towards the closed door. 'There's something odd about him, you know, something—'

'Not fishy?' interrupted Mrs St Vincent, with a faint smile.

'Why, Mother, how did you know what I was going to say?' demanded Rupert in all seriousness.

'It's rather a word of yours, darling. You think everything is fishy. I suppose you have an idea that it was Quentin who did away with Lord Listerdale and put him under the floor?'

'Behind the panelling,' corrected Rupert. 'You always get things a little bit wrong, Mother. No, I've inquired about that. Quentin was down at King's Cheviot at the time.'

Mrs St Vincent smiled at him, as she rose from the table

and went up to the drawing-room. In some ways Rupert was a long time growing up.

Yet a sudden wonder swept over her for the first time as to Lord Listerdale's reasons for leaving England so abruptly. There must be something behind it, to account for that sudden decision. She was still thinking the matter over when Quentin came in with the coffee tray, and she spoke out impulsively.

'You have been with Lord Listerdale a long time, haven't you, Quentin?'

'Yes, madam; since I was a lad of twenty-one. That was in the late Lord's time. I started as third footman.'

'You must know Lord Listerdale very well. What kind of a man is he?'

The butler turned the tray a little, so that she could help herself to sugar more conveniently, as he replied in even unemotional tones:

'Lord Listerdale was a very selfish gentleman, madam: with no consideration for others.'

He removed the tray and bore it from the room. Mrs St Vincent sat with her coffee cup in her hand, and a puzzled frown on her face. Something struck her as odd in the speech apart from the views it expressed. In another minute it flashed home to her.

Quentin had used the word '*was*' not 'is'. But then, he must think—must believe—She pulled herself up. She was as bad as Rupert! But a very definite uneasiness assailed her. Afterwards she dated her first suspicions from that moment.

With Barbara's happiness and future assured, she had

time to think her own thoughts, and against her will, they began to centre round the mystery of Lord Listerdale. What was the real story? Whatever it was Quentin knew something about it. Those had been odd words of his—'a very selfish gentleman—no consideration for others.' What lay behind them? He had spoken as a judge might speak, detachedly and impartially.

Was Quentin involved in Lord Listerdale's disappearance? Had he taken an active part in any tragedy there might have been? After all, ridiculous as Rupert's assumption had seemed at the time, that single letter with its power of attorney coming from East Africa was—well, open to suspicion.

But try as she would, she could not believe any real evil of Quentin. Quentin, she told herself over and over again, was *good*—she used the word as simply as a child might have done. Quentin was *good*. But he knew something!

She never spoke with him again of his master. The subject was apparently forgotten. Rupert and Barbara had other things to think of, and there were no further discussions.

It was towards the end of August that her vague surmises crystallized into realities. Rupert had gone for a fortnight's holiday with a friend who had a motor-cycle and trailer. It was some ten days after his departure that Mrs St Vincent was startled to see him rush into the room where she sat writing.

'Rupert!' she exclaimed.

'I know, Mother. You didn't expect to see me for another three days. But something's happened. Anderson—my pal, you know—didn't much care where he went, so I suggested having a look in at King's Cheviot—'

'King's Cheviot? But why—?'

'You know perfectly well, Mother, that I've always scented something fishy about things here. Well, I had a look at the old place—it's let, you know—nothing there. Not that I actually expected to find anything—I was just nosing round, so to speak.'

Yes, she thought. Rupert was very like a dog at this moment. Hunting in circles for something vague and unde-fined, led by instinct, busy and happy.

'It was when we were passing through a village about eight or nine miles away that it happened—that I saw him, I mean.'

'Saw whom?'

'Quentin—just going into a little cottage. Something fishy here, I said to myself, and we stopped the bus, and I went back. I rapped on the door and he himself opened it.'

'But I don't understand. Quentin hasn't been away—'

'I'm coming to that, Mother. If you'd only listen, and not interrupt. It was Quentin, and it wasn't Quentin, if you know what I mean.'

Mrs St Vincent clearly did not know, so he elucidated matters further.

'It was Quentin all right, but it wasn't *our* Quentin. It was the real man.'

'Rupert!'

'You listen. I was taken in myself at first, and said: "It is Quentin, isn't it?" And the old johnny said: "Quite right, sir, that is my name. What can I do for you?" And then I saw that it wasn't our man, though it was precious like him, voice and all. I asked a few questions, and it all came out. The old chap hadn't an idea of anything fishy being on. He'd been butler to Lord Listerdale all right, and was retired on a pension and given this cottage just about the time that Lord Listerdale was supposed to have gone off to Africa. You see where that leads us. This man's an impostor—he's playing the part of Quentin for purposes of his own. My theory is that he came up to town that evening, pretending to be the butler from King's Cheviot, got an interview with Lord Listerdale, killed him and hid his body behind the panelling. It's an old house, there's sure to be a secret recess—'

'Oh, don't let's go into all that again,' interrupted Mrs St Vincent wildly. 'I can't bear it. Why should he—that's what I want to know—why? *If* he did such a thing—which I don't believe for one minute, mind you—what was the *reason* for it all?'

'You're right,' said Rupert. 'Motive—that's important. Now I've made inquiries. Lord Listerdale had a lot of house property. In the last two days I've discovered that practically every one of these houses of his has been let in the last eighteen months to people like ourselves for a merely nominal rent— *and with the proviso that the servants should remain*. And in every case Quentin himself—the man calling himself Quentin, I mean—has been there for part of the time as butler. That looks as though there were something—jewels, or papers— secreted in one of Lord Listerdale's houses, and the gang doesn't know which. I'm assuming a gang, but of course this fellow Quentin may be in it single-handed. There's a—'

Mrs St Vincent interrupted him with a certain amount of determination:

'Rupert! Do stop talking for one minute. You're making my head spin. Anyway, what you are saying is nonsense—about gangs and hidden papers.'

'There's another theory,' admitted Rupert. 'This Quentin may be someone that Lord Listerdale has injured. The real butler told me a long story about a man called Samuel Lowe—an under-gardener he was, and about the same height and build as Quentin himself. He'd got a grudge against Listerdale—'

Mrs St Vincent started.

'With no consideration for others.' The words came back to her mind in their passionless, measured accents. Inadequate words, but what might they not stand for?

In her absorption she hardly listened to Rupert. He made a rapid explanation of something that she did not take in, and went hurriedly from the room.

Then she woke up. Where had Rupert gone? What was he going to do? She had not caught his last words. Perhaps he was going for the police. In that case . . .

She rose abruptly and rang the bell. With his usual promptness, Quentin answered it.

'You rang, madam?'

'Yes. Come in, please, and shut the door.'

The butler obeyed, and Mrs St Vincent was silent a moment whilst she studied him with earnest eyes.

She thought: 'He's been kind to me—nobody knows how kind. The children wouldn't understand. This wild story of Rupert's may be all nonsense—on the other hand, there may—

yes, there may—be something in it. Why should one judge? One can't *know*. The rights and wrongs of it, I mean . . . And I'd stake my life—yes, I would!—on his being a good man.'

Flushed and tremulous, she spoke.

'Quentin, Mr Rupert has just got back. He has been down to King's Cheviot—to a village near there—'

She stopped, noticing the quick start he was not able to conceal.

'He has—seen someone,' she went on in measured accents.

She thought to herself: 'There—he's warned. At any rate, he's warned.'

After that first quick start, Quentin had resumed his unruffled demeanour, but his eyes were fixed on her face, watchful and keen, with something in them she had not seen there before. They were, for the first time, the eyes of a man and not of a servant.

He hesitated for a minute, then said in a voice which also had subtly changed:

'Why do you tell me this, Mrs St Vincent?'

Before she could answer, the door flew open and Rupert strode into the room. With him was a dignified middle-aged man with little side-whiskers and the air of a benevolent archbishop. *Quentin!*

'Here he is,' said Rupert. 'The real Quentin. I had him outside in the taxi. Now, Quentin, look at this man and tell me—is he Samuel Lowe?'

It was for Rupert a triumphant moment. But it was short-lived, almost at once he scented something wrong. For while the real Quentin was looking abashed and highly

21

uncomfortable the second Quentin was smiling, a broad smile of undisguised enjoyment.

He slapped his embarrassed duplicate on the back.

'It's all right, Quentin. Got to let the cat out of the bag some time, I suppose. You can tell 'em who I am.'

The dignified stranger drew himself up.

'This, sir,' he announced, in a reproachful tone, 'is my master, Lord Listerdale, sir.'

The next minute beheld many things. First, the complete collapse of the cocksure Rupert. Before he knew what was happening, his mouth still open from the shock of the discovery, he found himself being gently manoeuvred towards the door, a friendly voice that was, and yet was not, familiar in his ear.

'It's quite all right, my boy. No bones broken. But I want a word with your mother. Very good work of yours, to ferret me out like this.'

He was outside on the landing gazing at the shut door. The real Quentin was standing by his side, a gentle stream of explanation flowing from his lips. Inside the room Lord Listerdale was fronting Mrs St Vincent.

'Let me explain—if I can! I've been a selfish devil all my life—the fact came home to me one day. I thought I'd try a little altruism for a change, and being a fantastic kind of fool, I started my career fantastically. I'd sent subscriptions to odd things, but I felt the need of doing something—well, something *personal*. I've been sorry always for the class that can't beg, that must suffer in silence—poor gentlefolk. I have a lot of house property. I conceived the idea of leasing these houses to people who—well, needed and appreciated them. Young couples with their way to make, widows with sons and daughters starting in the world. Quentin has been more than butler to me, he's a friend. With his consent and assistance I borrowed his personality. I've always had a talent for acting. The idea came to me on my way to the club one night, and I went straight off to talk it over with Quentin. When I found they were making a fuss about my disappearance, I arranged that a letter should come from me in East Africa. In it, I gave full instructions to my cousin, Maurice Carfax. And—well, that's the long and short of it.'

He broke off rather lamely, with an appealing glance at Mrs St Vincent. She stood very straight, and her eyes met his steadily.

'It was a kind plan,' she said. 'A very unusual one, and one that does you credit. I am—most grateful. But—of course, you understand that we cannot stay?'

'I expected that,' he said. 'Your pride won't let you accept what you'd probably style "charity".'

'Isn't that what it is?' she asked steadily.

'No,' he answered. 'Because I ask something in exchange.'

'Something?'

'Everything.' His voice rang out, the voice of one accustomed to dominate.

'When I was twenty-three,' he went on, 'I married the girl I loved. She died a year later. Since then I have been very lonely. I have wished very much I could find a certain lady—the lady of my dreams . . .'

'Am I that?' she asked, very low. 'I am so old—so faded.'

He laughed.

'Old? You are younger than either of your children. Now I am old, if you like.'

But her laugh rang out in turn. A soft ripple of amusement.

'You? You are a boy still. A boy who loves to dress up.'

She held out her hands and he caught them in his.

# Philomel Cottage

'Goodbye, darling.'

'Goodbye, sweetheart.'

Alix Martin stood leaning over the small rustic gate, watching the retreating figure of her husband as he walked down the road in the direction of the village.

Presently he turned a bend and was lost to sight, but Alix still stayed in the same position, absent-mindedly smoothing a lock of the rich brown hair which had blown across her face, her eyes far away and dreamy.

Alix Martin was not beautiful, nor even, strictly speaking, pretty. But her face, the face of a woman no longer in her first youth, was irradiated and softened until her former colleagues of the old office days would hardly have recognized her. Miss Alex King had been a trim business-like young woman, efficient, slightly brusque in manner, obviously capable and matter-of-fact.

Alix had graduated in a hard school. For fifteen years, from the age of eighteen until she was thirty-three, she had kept herself (and for seven years of the time an invalid mother) by her work as a shorthand typist. It was the struggle for existence which had hardened the soft lines of her girlish face.

True, there had been romance—of a kind—Dick Windyford, a fellow-clerk. Very much of a woman at heart, Alix had always known without seeming to know that he cared. Outwardly they had been friends, nothing more. Out of his slender salary Dick had been hard put to it to provide for the schooling of a younger brother. For the moment he could not think of marriage.

And then suddenly deliverance from daily toil had come to the girl in the most unexpected manner. A distant cousin had died, leaving her money to Alix—a few thousand pounds, enough to bring in a couple of hundred a year. To Alix it was freedom, life, independence. Now she and Dick need wait no longer.

But Dick reacted unexpectedly. He had never directly spoken of his love to Alix; now he seemed less inclined to do so than ever. He avoided her, became morose and gloomy. Alix was quick to realize the truth. She had become a woman of means. Delicacy and pride stood in the way of Dick's asking her to be his wife.

She liked him none the worse for it, and was indeed deliberating as to whether she herself might not take the first step, when for the second time the unexpected descended upon her.

She met Gerald Martin at a friend's house. He fell violently in love with her and within a week they were engaged. Alix, who had always considered herself 'not the falling-in-love kind', was swept clean off her feet.

Unwittingly she had found the way to arouse her former

lover. Dick Windyford had come to her stammering with rage and anger.

'The man's a perfect stranger to you! You know nothing about him!'

'I know that I love him.'

'How can you know—in a week?'

'It doesn't take everyone eleven years to find out that they're in love with a girl,' cried Alix angrily.

His face went white.

'I've cared for you ever since I met you. I thought that you cared also.'

Alix was truthful.

'I thought so too,' she admitted. 'But that was because I didn't know what love was.'

Then Dick had burst out again. Prayers, entreaties, even threats—threats against the man who had supplanted him. It was amazing to Alix to see the volcano that existed beneath the reserved exterior of the man she had thought she knew so well.

Her thoughts went back to that interview now, on this sunny morning, as she leant on the gate of the cottage. She had been married a month, and she was idyllically happy. Yet, in the momentary absence of the husband who was everything to her, a tinge of anxiety invaded her perfect happiness. And the cause of that anxiety was Dick Windyford.

Three times since her marriage she had dreamed the same dream. The environment differed, but the main facts were always the same. *She saw her husband lying dead and Dick Windyford standing over him, and she knew clearly and distinctly that his was the hand which had dealt the fatal blow.*

But horrible though that was, there was something more horrible still—horrible, that was, on awakening, for in the dream it seemed perfectly natural and inevitable. *She, Alix Martin, was glad that her husband was dead*; she stretched out grateful hands to the murderer, sometimes she thanked him. The dream always ended the same way, with herself clasped in Dick Windyford's arms.

She had said nothing of this dream to her husband, but secretly it had perturbed her more than she liked to admit. Was it a warning—a warning against Dick Windyford?

Alix was roused from her thoughts by the sharp ringing of the telephone bell from within the house. She entered the cottage and picked up the receiver. Suddenly she swayed, and put out a hand against the wall.

'Who did you say was speaking?'

'Why, Alix, what's the matter with your voice? I wouldn't have known it. It's Dick.'

'Oh!' said Alix. 'Oh! Where—where are you?'

'At the Traveller's Arms—that's the right name, isn't it? Or don't you even know of the existence of your village pub? I'm on my holiday—doing a bit of fishing here. Any objection to my looking you two good people up this evening after dinner?'

'No,' said Alix sharply. 'You mustn't come.'

There was a pause, and then Dick's voice, with a subtle alteration in it, spoke again.

'I beg your pardon,' he said formally. 'Of course I won't bother you—'

Alix broke in hastily. He must think her behaviour too extraordinary. It *was* extraordinary. Her nerves must be all to pieces.

'I only meant that we were—engaged tonight,' she explained, trying to make her voice sound as natural as possible. 'Won't you—won't you come to dinner tomorrow night?'

But Dick evidently noticed the lack of cordiality in her tone.

'Thanks very much,' he said, in the same formal voice, 'but I may be moving on any time. Depends if a pal of mine turns up or not. Goodbye, Alix.' He paused, and then added hastily, in a different tone: 'Best of luck to you, my dear.'

Alix hung up the receiver with a feeling of relief.

'He mustn't come here,' she repeated to herself. 'He mustn't come here. Oh, what a fool I am! To imagine myself into a state like this. All the same, I'm glad he's not coming.'

She caught up a rustic rush hat from a table, and passed out into the garden again, pausing to look up at the name carved over the porch: Philomel Cottage.

'Isn't it a very fanciful name?' she had said to Gerald once before they were married. He had laughed.

'You little Cockney,' he had said, affectionately. 'I don't believe you have ever heard a nightingale. I'm glad you haven't. Nightingales should sing only for lovers. We'll hear them together on a summer's evening outside our own home.'

And at the remembrance of how they had indeed heard them, Alix, standing in the doorway of her home, blushed happily.

It was Gerald who had found Philomel Cottage. He had come to Alix bursting with excitement. He had found the very spot for them—unique—a gem—the chance of a lifetime. And when Alix had seen it she too was captivated. It was true that the situation was rather lonely—they were two miles from the nearest village—but the cottage itself was so exquisite with its old-world appearance, and its solid comfort of bathrooms, hot-water system, electric light, and telephone, that she fell a victim to its charm immediately. And then a hitch occurred. The owner, a rich man who had made it his whim, declined to let it. He would only sell.

Gerald Martin, though possessed of a good income, was unable to touch his capital. He could raise at most a thousand pounds. The owner was asking three. But Alix, who had set her heart on the place, came to the rescue. Her own capital was easily realized, being in bearer bonds. She would contribute half of it to the purchase of the home. So Philomel Cottage became their very own, and never for a minute had Alix regretted the choice. It was true that servants did not appreciate the rural solitude—indeed, at the moment they had none at all—but Alix, who had been starved of domestic life, thoroughly enjoyed cooking dainty little meals and looking after the house.

The garden, which was magnificently stocked with flowers, was attended by an old man from the village who came twice a week.

As she rounded the corner of the house, Alix was surprised to see the old gardener in question busy over the flower-beds. She was surprised because his days for work were Mondays and Fridays, and today was Wednesday.

'Why, George, what are you doing here?' she asked, as she came towards him.

The old man straightened up with a chuckle, touching the brim of an aged cap.

'I thought as how you'd be surprised, ma'am. But 'tis this way. There be a fête over to Squire's on Friday, and I sez to myself, I sez, neither Mr Martin nor yet his good lady won't take it amiss if I comes for once on a Wednesday instead of a Friday.'

'That's quite all right,' said Alix. 'I hope you'll enjoy yourself at the fête.'

'I reckon to,' said George simply. 'It's a fine thing to be able to eat your fill and know all the time as it's not you as is paying for it. Squire allus has a proper sit-down tea for 'is tenants. Then I thought too, ma'am, as I might as well see you before you goes away so as to learn your wishes for the borders. You have no idea when you'll be back, ma'am, I suppose?'

'But I'm not going away.'

George stared.

'Bain't you going to Lunnon tomorrow?'

'No. What put such an idea into your head?'

George jerked his head over his shoulder.

'Met Maister down to village yesterday. He told me you was both going away to Lunnon tomorrow, and it was uncertain when you'd be back again.'

'Nonsense,' said Alix, laughing. 'You must have misunderstood him.'

All the same, she wondered exactly what it could have been that Gerald had said to lead the old man into such a curious mistake. Going to London? She never wanted to go to London again.

'I hate London,' she said suddenly and harshly.

'Ah!' said George placidly. 'I must have been mistook somehow, and yet he said it plain enough, it seemed to me. I'm glad you're stopping on here. I don't hold with all this gallivanting about, and I don't think nothing of Lunnon. *I've* never needed to go there. Too many moty cars—that's the trouble nowadays. Once people have got a moty car, blessed if they can stay still anywheres. Mr Ames, wot used to have this house—nice peaceful sort of gentleman he was until he bought one of them things. Hadn't had it a month before he put up this cottage for sale. A tidy lot he'd spent on it too, with taps in all the bedrooms, and the electric light and all. "You'll never see your money back," I sez to him. "But," he sez to me, "I'll get every penny of two thousand pounds for this house." And, sure enough, he did.'

'He got three thousand,' said Alix, smiling.

'Two thousand,' repeated George. 'The sum he was asking was talked of at the time.'

'It really was three thousand,' said Alix.

'Ladies never understand figures,' said George, unconvinced. 'You'll not tell me that Mr Ames had the face to stand up to you and say three thousand brazen-like in a loud voice?'

'He didn't say it to me,' said Alix; 'he said it to my husband.'

George stooped again to his flower-bed.

'The price was two thousand,' he said obstinately.

Alix did not trouble to argue with him. Moving to one of the farther beds, she began to pick an armful of flowers.

As she moved with her fragrant posy towards the house, Alix noticed a small dark-green object peeping from between some leaves in one of the beds. She stooped and picked it up, recognizing it for her husband's pocket diary.

She opened it, scanning the entries with some amusement. Almost from the beginning of their married life she had realized that the impulsive and emotional Gerald had the uncharacteristic virtues of neatness and method. He was extremely fussy about meals being punctual, and always planned his day ahead with the accuracy of a timetable.

Looking through the diary, she was amused to notice the entry on the date of May 14th: 'Marry Alix St Peter's 2.30.'

'The big silly,' murmured Alix to herself, turning the pages. Suddenly she stopped.

'"Wednesday, June 18th"—why, that's today.'

In the space for that day was written in Gerald's neat, precise hand: '9 p.m.' Nothing else. What had Gerald planned to do at 9 p.m.? Alix wondered. She smiled to herself as she realized that had this been a story, like those she had so often read, the diary would doubtless have furnished her with some sensational revelation. It would have had in it for certain the name of another woman. She fluttered the back pages idly. There were dates, appointments, cryptic references to business deals, but only one woman's name—her own.

Yet as she slipped the book into her pocket and went on with her flowers to the house, she was aware of a vague uneasiness. Those words of Dick Windyford's recurred to her almost as though he had been at her elbow repeating them: 'The man's a perfect stranger to you. You know nothing about him.'

It was true. What did she know about him? After all, Gerald was forty. In forty years there must have been women in his life . . .

Alix shook herself impatiently. She must not give way to these thoughts. She had a far more instant preoccupation to deal with. Should she, or should she not, tell her husband that Dick Windyford had rung her up?

There was the possibility to be considered that Gerald might have already run across him in the village. But in that case he would be sure to mention it to her immediately upon his return, and matters would be taken out of her hands. Otherwise—what? Alix was aware of a distinct desire to say nothing about it.

If she told him, he was sure to suggest asking Dick Windyford to Philomel Cottage. Then she would have to explain that Dick had proposed himself, and that she had made an excuse to prevent his coming. And when he asked her why she had done so, what could she say?

Tell him her dream? But he would only laugh—or worse, see that she attached an importance to it which he did not.

In the end, rather shamefacedly, Alix decided to say nothing. It was the first secret she had ever kept from her husband, and the consciousness of it made her feel ill at ease.

When she heard Gerald returning from the village shortly before lunch, she hurried into the kitchen and pretended to be busy with the cooking so as to hide her confusion.

It was evident at once that Gerald had seen nothing of Dick Windyford. Alix felt at once relieved and embarrassed. She was definitely committed now to a policy of concealment.

It was not until after their simple evening meal, when they were sitting in the oak-beamed living-room with the windows thrown open to let in the sweet night air scented with the perfume of the mauve and white stocks outside, that Alix remembered the pocket diary.

'Here's something you've been watering the flowers with,' she said, and threw it into his lap.

'Dropped it in the border, did I?'

'Yes; I know all your secrets now.'

'Not guilty,' said Gerald, shaking his head.

'What about your assignation at nine o'clock tonight?'

'Oh! that—' he seemed taken aback for a moment; then he smiled as though something afforded him particular amusement. 'It's an assignation with a particularly nice girl,

Alix. She's got brown hair and blue eyes, and she's very like you.'

'I don't understand,' said Alix, with mock severity. 'You're evading the point.'

'No, I'm not. As a matter of fact, that's a reminder that I'm going to develop some negatives tonight, and I want you to help me.'

Gerald Martin was an enthusiastic photographer. He had a somewhat old-fashioned camera, but with an excellent lens, and he developed his own plates in a small cellar which he had had fitted up as a dark-room.

'And it must be done at nine o'clock precisely,' said Alix teasingly.

Gerald looked a little vexed.

'My dear girl,' he said, with a shade of testiness in his manner, 'one should always plan a thing for a definite time. Then one gets through one's work properly.'

Alix sat for a minute or two in silence, watching her husband as he lay in his chair smoking, his dark head flung back and the clear-cut lines of his clean-shaven face showing up against the sombre background. And suddenly, from some unknown source, a wave of panic surged over her, so that she cried out before she could stop herself, 'Oh, Gerald, I wish I knew more about you!'

Her husband turned an astonished face upon her.

'But, my dear Alix, you do know all about me. I've told you of my boyhood in Northumberland, of my life in South Africa, and these last ten years in Canada which have brought me success.'

'Oh! business!' said Alix scornfully.

Gerald laughed suddenly.

'I know what you mean—love affairs. You women are all the same. Nothing interests you but the personal element.'

Alix felt her throat go dry, as she muttered indistinctly: 'Well, but there must have been—love affairs. I mean—if I only knew—'

There was silence again for a minute or two. Gerald Martin was frowning, a look of indecision on his face. When he spoke it was gravely, without a trace of his former bantering manner.

'Do you think it wise, Alix—this—Bluebeard's chamber business? There have been women in my life; yes, I don't deny it. You wouldn't believe me if I denied it. But I can swear to you truthfully that not one of them meant anything to me.'

There was a ring of sincerity in his voice which comforted the listening wife.

'Satisfied, Alix?' he asked, with a smile. Then he looked at her with a shade of curiosity.

'What has turned your mind on to these unpleasant subjects tonight of all nights?'

Alix got up, and began to walk about restlessly.

'Oh, I don't know,' she said. 'I've been nervy all day.'

'That's odd,' said Gerald, in a low voice, as though speaking to himself. 'That's very odd.'

'Why is it odd?'

'Oh, my dear girl, don't flash out at me so. I only said it was odd, because, as a rule, you're so sweet and serene.'

Alix forced a smile.

'Everything's conspired to annoy me today,' she confessed. 'Even old George had got some ridiculous idea into his head that we were going away to London. He said you had told him so.'

'Where did you see him?' asked Gerald sharply.

'He came to work today instead of Friday.'

'Damned old fool,' said Gerald angrily.

Alix stared in surprise. Her husband's face was convulsed with rage. She had never seen him so angry. Seeing her astonishment Gerald made an effort to regain control of himself.

'Well, he is a damned old fool,' he protested.

'What can you have said to make him think that?'

'I? I never said anything. At least—oh, yes, I remember; I made some weak joke about being "off to London in the morning," and I suppose he took it seriously. Or else he didn't hear properly. You undeceived him, of course?'

He waited anxiously for her reply.

'Of course, but he's the sort of old man who if once he gets an idea in his head—well, it isn't so easy to get it out again.'

Then she told him of George's insistence on the sum asked for the cottage.

Gerald was silent for a minute or two, then he said slowly:

'Ames was willing to take two thousand in cash and the remaining thousand on mortgage. That's the origin of that mistake, I fancy.'

'Very likely,' agreed Alix.

Then she looked up at the clock, and pointed to it with a mischievous finger.

'We ought to be getting down to it, Gerald. Five minutes behind schedule.'

A very peculiar smile came over Gerald Martin's face.

'I've changed my mind,' he said quietly; 'I shan't do any photography tonight.'

A woman's mind is a curious thing. When she went to bed that Wednesday night Alix's mind was contented and at rest. Her momentarily assailed happiness reasserted itself, triumphant as of yore.

But by the evening of the following day she realized that some subtle forces were at work undermining it. Dick Windyford had not rung up again, nevertheless she felt what she supposed to be his influence at work. Again and again those words of his recurred to her: '*The man's a perfect stranger. You know nothing about him.*' And with them came the memory of her husband's face, photographed clearly on her brain, as he said, 'Do you think it wise, Alix, this—Bluebeard's chamber business?' Why had he said that?

There had been warning in them—a hint of menace. It was as though he had said in effect: 'You had better not pry into my life, Alix. You may get a nasty shock if you do.'

By Friday morning Alix had convinced herself that there *had* been a woman in Gerald's life—a Bluebeard's chamber that he had sedulously sought to conceal from her. Her jealousy, slow to awaken, was now rampant.

Was it a woman he had been going to meet that night

39

at 9 p.m.? Was his story of photographs to develop a lie invented upon the spur of the moment?

Three days ago she would have sworn that she knew her husband through and through. Now it seemed to her that he was a stranger of whom she knew nothing. She remembered his unreasonable anger against old George, so at variance with his usual good-tempered manner. A small thing, perhaps, but it showed her that she did not really know the man who was her husband.

There were several little things required on Friday from the village. In the afternoon Alix suggested that she should go for them whilst Gerald remained in the garden; but somewhat to her surprise he opposed this plan vehemently, and insisted on going himself whilst she remained at home. Alix was forced to give way to him, but his insistence surprised and alarmed her. Why was he so anxious to prevent her going to the village?

Suddenly an explanation suggested itself to her which made the whole thing clear. Was it not possible that, whilst saying nothing to her, Gerald had indeed come across Dick Windyford? Her own jealousy, entirely dormant at the time of their marriage, had only developed afterwards. Might it not be the same with Gerald? Might he not be anxious to prevent her seeing Dick Windyford again? This explanation was so consistent with the facts, and so comforting to Alix's perturbed mind, that she embraced it eagerly.

Yet when tea-time had come and passed she was restless and ill at ease. She was struggling with a temptation that had assailed her ever since Gerald's departure. Finally, pacifying her conscience with the assurance that the room did need a thorough tidying, she went upstairs to her husband's dressing-room. She took a duster with her to keep up the pretence of housewifery.

'If I were only sure,' she repeated to herself. 'If I could only be *sure*.'

In vain she told herself that anything compromising would have been destroyed ages ago. Against that she argued that men do sometimes keep the most damning piece of evidence through an exaggerated sentimentality.

In the end Alix succumbed. Her cheeks burning with the shame of her action, she hunted breathlessly through packets of letters and documents, turned out the drawers, even went through the pockets of her husband's clothes. Only two drawers eluded her; the lower drawer of the chest of drawers and the small right-hand drawer of the writing-desk were both locked. But Alix was by now lost to all shame. In one of these drawers she was convinced that she would find evidence of this imaginary woman of the past who obsessed her.

She remembered that Gerald had left his keys lying carelessly on the sideboard downstairs. She fetched them and tried them one by one. The third key fitted the writing-table drawer. Alix pulled it open eagerly. There was a cheque-book and a wallet well stuffed with notes, and at the back of the drawer a packet of letters tied up with a piece of tape.

Her breath coming unevenly, Alix untied the tape. Then a deep burning blush overspread her face, and she dropped the letters back into the drawer, closing and relocking it. For the letters were her own, written to Gerald Martin before she married him.

She turned now to the chest of drawers, more with a wish to feel that she had left nothing undone than from any expectation of finding what she sought.

To her annoyance none of the keys on Gerald's bunch fitted the drawer in question. Not to be defeated, Alix went into the other rooms and brought back a selection of keys with her. To her satisfaction the key of the spare room wardrobe also fitted the chest of drawers. She unlocked the drawer and pulled it open. But there was nothing in it but a roll of newspaper clippings already dirty and discoloured with age.

Alix breathed a sigh of relief. Nevertheless, she glanced at the clippings, curious to know what subject had interested Gerald so much that he had taken the trouble to keep the dusty roll. They were nearly all American papers, dated some seven years ago, and dealing with the trial of the notorious swindler and bigamist, Charles Lemaitre. Lemaitre had been suspected of doing away with his women victims. A skeleton had been found beneath the floor of one of the houses he had rented, and most of the women he had 'married' had never been heard of again.

He had defended himself from the charges with consummate skill, aided by some of the best legal talent in the United States. The Scottish verdict of 'Not Proven' might perhaps have stated the case best. In its absence, he was found Not Guilty on the capital charge, though sentenced to a long term of imprisonment on the other charges preferred against him.

Alix remembered the excitement caused by the case at the time, and also the sensation aroused by the escape of

Lemaitre some three years later. He had never been recaptured. The personality of the man and his extraordinary power over women had been discussed at great length in the English papers at the time, together with an account of his excitability in court, his passionate protestations, and his occasional sudden physical collapses, due to the fact that he had a weak heart, though the ignorant accredited it to his dramatic powers.

There was a picture of him in one of the clippings Alix held, and she studied it with some interest—a long-bearded, scholarly-looking gentleman.

Who was it the face reminded her of? Suddenly, with a shock, she realized that it was Gerald himself. The eyes and brow bore a strong resemblance to his. Perhaps he had kept the cutting for that reason. Her eyes went on to the paragraph beside the picture. Certain dates, it seemed, had been entered in the accused's pocket-book, and it was contended that these were dates when he had done away with his victims. Then a woman gave evidence and identified the prisoner positively by the fact that he had a mole on his left wrist, just below the palm of the hand.

Alix dropped the papers and swayed as she stood. *On his left wrist, just below the palm, her husband had a small scar* . . .

The room whirled round her. Afterwards it struck her as strange that she should have leaped at once to such absolute certainty. Gerald Martin was Charles Lemaitre! She knew it, and accepted it in a flash. Disjointed fragments whirled through her brain, like pieces of a jigsaw puzzle fitting into place.

The money paid for the house—her money—her money only; the bearer bonds she had entrusted to his keeping. Even her dream appeared in its true significance. Deep down in her, her subconscious self had always feared Gerald Martin and wished to escape from him. And it was to Dick Windyford this self of hers had looked for help. That, too, was why she was able to accept the truth too easily, without doubt or hesitation. She was to have been another of Lemaitre's victims. Very soon, perhaps . . .

A half-cry escaped her as she remembered something. *Wednesday, 9 p.m.* The cellar, with the flagstones that were so easily raised! Once before he had buried one of his victims in a cellar. It had been all planned for Wednesday night. But to write it down beforehand in that methodical manner—insanity! No, it was logical. Gerald always made a memorandum of his engagements; murder was to him a business proposition like any other.

But what had saved her? What could possibly have saved her? Had he relented at the last minute? No. In a flash the answer came to her—*old George.*

She understood now her husband's uncontrollable anger. Doubtless he had paved the way by telling everyone he met that they were going to London the next day. Then George had come to work unexpectedly, had mentioned London to her, and she had contradicted the story. Too risky to do away with her that night, with old George repeating that conversation. But what an escape! If she had not happened to mention that trivial matter—Alix shuddered.

And then she stayed motionless as though frozen to stone. She had heard the creak of the gate into the road. *Her husband had returned.*

For a moment Alix stayed as though petrified, then she crept on tiptoe to the window, looking out from behind the shelter of the curtain.

Yes, it was her husband. He was smiling to himself and humming a little tune. In his hand he held an object which almost made the terrified girl's heart stop beating. It was a brand-new spade.

Alix leaped to a knowledge born of instinct. *It was to be tonight . . .*

But there was still a chance. Gerald, humming his little tune, went round to the back of the house.

Without hesitating a moment, she ran down the stairs and out of the cottage. But just as she emerged from the door, her husband came round the other side of the house.

'Hallo,' he said, 'where are you running off to in such a hurry?'

Alix strove desperately to appear calm and as usual. Her chance was gone for the moment, but if she was careful not to arouse his suspicions, it would come again later. Even now, perhaps . . .

'I was going to walk to the end of the lane and back,' she said in a voice that sounded weak and uncertain in her own ears.

'Right,' said Gerald. 'I'll come with you.'

'No—please, Gerald. I'm—nervy, headachy—I'd rather go alone.'

He looked at her attentively. She fancied a momentary suspicion gleamed in his eye.

'What's the matter with you, Alix? You're pale—trembling.'

'Nothing.' She forced herself to be brusque—smiling. 'I've got a headache, that's all. A walk will do me good.'

'Well, it's no good your saying you don't want me,' declared Gerald, with his easy laugh. 'I'm coming, whether you want me or not.'

She dared not protest further. If he suspected that she *knew* . . .

With an effort she managed to regain something of her normal manner. Yet she had an uneasy feeling that he looked at her sideways every now and then, as though not quite satisfied. She felt that his suspicions were not completely allayed.

When they returned to the house he insisted on her lying down, and brought some eau-de-cologne to bathe her temples. He was, as ever, the devoted husband. Alix felt herself as helpless as though bound hand and foot in a trap.

Not for a minute would he leave her alone. He went with her into the kitchen and helped her to bring in the simple cold dishes she had already prepared. Supper was a meal that choked her, yet she forced herself to eat, and even to appear gay and natural. She knew now that she was fighting for her life. She was alone with this man, miles from help, absolutely at his mercy. Her only chance was so to lull his suspicions that he would leave her alone for a few moments—long enough for her to get to the telephone in the hall and summon assistance. That was her only hope now.

A momentary hope flashed over her as she remembered how he had abandoned his plan before. Suppose she told him that Dick Windyford was coming up to see them that evening?

The words trembled on her lips—then she rejected them hastily. This man would not be baulked a second time. There was a determination, an elation, underneath his calm bearing that sickened her. She would only precipitate the crime. He would murder her there and then, and calmly ring up Dick Windyford with a tale of having been suddenly called away. Oh! if only Dick Windyford were coming to the house this evening! If Dick . . .

A sudden idea flashed into her mind. She looked sharply sideways at her husband as though she feared that he might read her mind. With the forming of a plan, her courage was reinforced. She became so completely natural in manner that she marvelled at herself.

She made the coffee and took it out to the porch where they often sat on fine evenings.

'By the way,' said Gerald suddenly, 'we'll do those photographs later.'

Alix felt a shiver run through her, but she replied non-chalantly, 'Can't you manage alone? I'm rather tired tonight.'

'It won't take long.' He smiled to himself. 'And I can promise you you won't be tired afterwards.'

The words seemed to amuse him. Alix shuddered. Now or never was the time to carry out her plan.

She rose to her feet.

'I'm just going to telephone to the butcher,' she announced nonchalantly. 'Don't you bother to move.'

'To the butcher? At this time of night?'

'His shop's shut, of course, silly. But he's in his house all right. And tomorrow's Saturday, and I want him to bring me some veal cutlets early, before someone else grabs them off him. The old dear will do anything for me.'

She passed quickly into the house, closing the door behind her. She heard Gerald say, 'Don't shut the door,' and was quick with her light reply, 'It keeps the moths out. I hate moths. Are you afraid I'm going to make love to the butcher, silly?'

Once inside, she snatched down the telephone receiver and gave the number of the Traveller's Arms. She was put through at once.

'Mr Windyford? Is he still there? Can I speak to him?'

Then her heart gave a sickening thump. The door was pushed open and her husband came into the hall.

'Do go away, Gerald,' she said pettishly. 'I hate anyone listening when I'm telephoning.'

He merely laughed and threw himself into a chair.

'Sure it really is the butcher you're telephoning to?' he quizzed.

Alix was in despair. Her plan had failed. In a minute Dick Windyford would come to the phone. Should she risk all and cry out an appeal for help?

And then, as she nervously depressed and released the little key in the receiver she was holding, which permits the voice to be heard or not heard at the other end, another plan flashed into her head.

'It will be difficult,' she thought to herself. 'It means keeping my head, and thinking of the right words, and not faltering for a moment, but I believe I could do it. I *must* do it.'

And at that minute she heard Dick Windyford's voice at the other end of the phone.

Alix drew a deep breath. Then she depressed the key firmly and spoke.

'*Mrs Martin speaking—from Philomel Cottage. Please come* (she released the key) tomorrow morning with six nice veal cutlets (she depressed the key again). *It's very important* (she released the key). Thank you so much, Mr Hexworthy: you won't mind my ringing you up so late. I hope, but those veal cutlets are really a matter of (she depressed the key again) *life or death* (she released it). Very well—tomorrow morning (she depressed it) *as soon as possible.*'

She replaced the receiver on the hook and turned to face her husband, breathing hard.

'So that's how you talk to your butcher, is it?' said Gerald.

'It's the feminine touch,' said Alix lightly.

She was simmering with excitement. He had suspected nothing. Dick, even if he didn't understand, would come.

She passed into the sitting-room and switched on the electric light. Gerald followed her.

'You seem very full of spirits now?' he said, watching her curiously.

'Yes,' said Alix. 'My headache's gone.'

She sat down in her usual seat and smiled at her husband

as he sank into his own chair opposite her. She was saved. It was only five and twenty past eight. Long before nine o'clock Dick would have arrived.

'I didn't think much of that coffee you gave me,' complained Gerald. 'It tasted very bitter.'

'It's a new kind I was trying. We won't have it again if you don't like it, dear.'

Alix took up a piece of needlework and began to stitch. Gerald read a few pages of his book. Then he glanced up at the clock and tossed the book away.

'Half-past eight. Time to go down to the cellar and start work.'

The sewing slipped from Alix's fingers.

'Oh, not yet. Let us wait until nine o'clock.'

'No, my girl—half-past eight. That's the time I fixed. You'll be able to get to bed all the earlier.'

'But I'd rather wait until nine.'

'You know when I fix a time I always stick to it. Come along, Alix. I'm not going to wait a minute longer.'

Alix looked up at him, and in spite of herself she felt a wave of terror slide over her. The mask had been lifted. Gerald's hands were twitching, his eyes were shining with excitement, he was continually passing his tongue over his dry lips. He no longer cared to conceal his excitement.

Alix thought, 'It's true—*he can't wait*—he's like a madman.'

He strode over to her, and jerked her on to her feet with a hand on her shoulder.

'Come on, my girl—or I'll carry you there.'

His tone was gay, but there was an undisguised ferocity

behind it that appalled her. With a supreme effort she jerked herself free and clung cowering against the wall. She was powerless. She couldn't get away—she couldn't do anything—and he was coming towards her.

'Now, Alix—'

'No—no.'

She screamed, her hands held out impotently to ward him off.

'Gerald—stop—I've got something to tell you, something to confess—'

He did stop.

'To confess?' he said curiously.

'Yes, to confess.' She had used the words at random, but she went on desperately, seeking to hold his arrested attention.

A look of contempt swept over his face.

'A former lover, I suppose,' he sneered.

'No,' said Alix. 'Something else. You'd call it, I expect—yes, you'd call it a crime.'

And at once she saw that she had struck the right note. Again his attention was arrested, held. Seeing that, her nerve came back to her. She felt mistress of the situation once more.

'You had better sit down again,' she said quietly.

She herself crossed the room to her old chair and sat down. She even stooped and picked up her needlework. But behind her calmness she was thinking and inventing feverishly: for the story she invented must hold his interest until help arrived.

'I told you,' she said slowly, 'that I had been a shorthand

51

typist for fifteen years. That was not entirely true. There were two intervals. The first occurred when I was twenty-two. I came across a man, an elderly man with a little property. He fell in love with me and asked me to marry him. I accepted. We were married.' She paused. 'I induced him to insure his life in my favour.'

She saw a sudden keen interest spring up in her husband's face, and went on with renewed assurance:

'During the war I worked for a time in a hospital dispensary. There I had the handling of all kinds of rare drugs and poisons.'

She paused reflectively. He was keenly interested now, not a doubt of it. The murderer is bound to have an interest in murder. She had gambled on that, and succeeded. She stole a glance at the clock. It was five and twenty to nine.

'There is one poison—it is a little white powder. A pinch of it means death. You know something about poisons perhaps?'

She put the question in some trepidation. If he did, she would have to be careful.

'No,' said Gerald: 'I know very little about them.'

She drew a breath of relief.

'You have heard of hyoscine, of course? This is a drug that acts much the same way, but is absolutely untraceable. Any doctor would give a certificate of heart failure. I stole a small quantity of this drug and kept it by me.'

She paused, marshalling her forces.

'Go on,' said Gerald.

'No. I'm afraid. I can't tell you. Another time.'

'Now,' he said impatiently. 'I want to hear.'

'We had been married a month. I was very good to my elderly husband, very kind and devoted. He spoke in praise of me to all the neighbours. Everyone knew what a devoted wife I was. I always made his coffee myself every evening. One evening, when we were alone together, I put a pinch of the deadly alkaloid in his cup—'

Alix paused, and carefully re-threaded her needle. She, who had never acted in her life, rivalled the greatest actress in the world at this moment. She was actually living the part of the cold-blooded poisoner.

'It was very peaceful. I sat watching him. Once he gasped a little and asked for air. I opened the window. Then he said he could not move from his chair. *Presently he died.*'

She stopped, smiling. It was a quarter to nine. Surely they would come soon.

'How much,' said Gerald, 'was the insurance money?'

'About two thousand pounds. I speculated with it, and lost it. I went back to my office work. But I never meant to remain there long. Then I met another man. I had stuck to my maiden name at the office. He didn't know I had been married before. He was a younger man, rather good-looking, and quite well-off. We were married quietly in Sussex. He didn't want to insure his life, but of course he made a will in my favour. He liked me to make his coffee myself just as my first husband had done.'

Alix smiled reflectively, and added simply, 'I make very good coffee.'

Then she went on:

'I had several friends in the village where we were living. They were very sorry for me, with my husband dying suddenly of heart failure one evening after dinner. I didn't quite like the doctor. I don't think he suspected me, but he was certainly very surprised at my husband's sudden death. I don't quite know why I drifted back to the office again. Habit, I suppose. My second husband left about four thousand pounds. I didn't speculate with it this time; I invested it. Then, you see—'

But she was interrupted. Gerald Martin, his face suffused with blood, half-choking, was pointing a shaking forefinger at her.

'The coffee—my God! the coffee!'

She stared at him.

'I understand now why it was bitter. You devil! You've been up to your tricks again.'

His hands gripped the arms of his chair. He was ready to spring upon her.

'You've poisoned me.'

Alix had retreated from him to the fireplace. Now, terrified, she opened her lips to deny—and then paused. In another minute he would spring upon her. She summoned all her strength. Her eyes held his steamy, compellingly.

'Yes,' she said. 'I poisoned you. Already the poison is working. At this minute you can't move from your chair— you can't move—'

If she could keep him there—even a few minutes . . .

Ah! what was that? Footsteps on the road. The creak of the gate. Then footsteps on the path outside. The outer door opening.

'*You can't move,*' she said again.

Then she slipped past him and fled headlong from the room to fall fainting into Dick Windyford's arms.

'My God! Alix,' he cried.

Then he turned to the man with him, a tall stalwart figure in policeman's uniform.

'Go and see what's been happening in that room.'

He laid Alix carefully down on a couch and bent over her.

'My little girl,' he murmured. 'My poor little girl. What have they been doing to you?'

Her eyelids fluttered and her lips just murmured his name.

Dick was aroused by the policeman's touching him on the arm.

'There's nothing in that room, sir, but a man sitting in a chair. Looks as though he'd had some kind of bad fright, and—'

'Yes?'

'Well, sir, he's—dead.'

They were startled by hearing Alix's voice. She spoke as though in some kind of dream, her eyes still closed.

'*And presently*,' she said, almost as though she were quoting from something, '*he died—*'

# The Girl in the Train

'And that's that!' observed George Rowland ruefully, as he gazed up at the imposing smoke-grimed façade of the building he had just quitted.

It might be said to represent very aptly the power of Money—and Money, in the person of William Rowland, uncle to the aforementioned George, had just spoken its mind very freely. In the course of a brief ten minutes, from being the apple of his uncle's eye, the heir to his wealth, and a young man with a promising business career in front of him, George had suddenly become one of the vast army of the unemployed.

'And in these clothes they won't even give me the dole,' reflected Mr Rowland gloomily, 'and as for writing poems and selling them at the door at twopence (or "what you care to give, lydy") I simply haven't got the brains.'

It was true that George embodied a veritable triumph of the tailor's art. He was exquisitely and beautifully arrayed. Solomon and the lilies of the field were simply not in it with George. But man cannot live by clothes alone—unless he has had some considerable training in the art—and Mr Rowland was painfully aware of the fact.

'And all because of that rotten show last night,' he reflected sadly.

The rotten show last night had been a Covent Garden Ball. Mr Rowland had returned from it at a somewhat late—or rather early—hour—as a matter of fact, he could not strictly say that he remembered returning at all. Rogers, his uncle's butler, was a helpful fellow, and could doubtless give more details on the matter. A splitting head, a cup of strong tea, and an arrival at the office at five minutes to twelve instead of half-past nine had precipitated the catastrophe. Mr Rowland, senior, who for twenty-four years had condoned and paid up as a tactful relative should, had suddenly abandoned these tactics and revealed himself in a totally new light. The inconsequence of George's replies (the young man's head was still opening and shutting like some mediæval instrument of the Inquisition) had displeased him still further. William Rowland was nothing if not thorough. He cast his nephew adrift upon the world in a few short succinct words, and then settled down to his interrupted survey of some oilfields in Peru.

George Rowland shook the dust of his uncle's office from off his feet, and stepped out into the City of London. George was a practical fellow. A good lunch, he considered, was essential to a review of the situation. He had it. Then he retraced his steps to the family mansion. Rogers opened the door. His well-trained face expressed no surprise at seeing George at this unusual hour.

'Good afternoon, Rogers. Just pack up my things for me, will you? I'm leaving here.'

'Yes, sir. Just for a short visit, sir?'

'For good, Rogers. I am going to the colonies this afternoon.'

'Indeed, sir?'

'Yes. That is, if there is a suitable boat. Do you know anything about the boats, Rogers?'

'Which colony were you thinking of visiting, sir?'

'I'm not particular. Any of 'em will do. Let's say Australia. What do you think of the idea, Rogers?'

Rogers coughed discreetly.

'Well, sir, I've certainly heard it said that there's room out there for anyone who really wants to work.'

Mr Rowland gazed at him with interest and admiration.

'Very neatly put, Rogers. Just what I was thinking myself. I shan't go to Australia—not today, at any rate. Fetch me an *A.B.C.*, will you? We will select something nearer at hand.'

Rogers brought the required volume. George opened it at random and turned the pages with a rapid hand.

'Perth—too far away—Putney Bridge—too near at hand. Ramsgate? I think not. Reigate also leaves me cold. Why— what an extraordinary thing! There's actually a place called Rowland's Castle. Ever heard of it, Rogers?'

'I fancy, sir, that you go there from Waterloo.'

'What an extraordinary fellow you are, Rogers. You know everything. Well, well, Rowland's Castle! I wonder what sort of a place it is.'

'Not much of a place, I should say, sir.'

'All the better; there'll be less competition. These quiet

little country hamlets have a lot of the old feudal spirit knocking about. The last of the original Rowlands ought to meet with instant appreciation. I shouldn't wonder if they elected me mayor in a week.'

He shut up the *A.B.C.* with a bang.

'The die is cast. Pack me a small suitcase, will you, Rogers? Also my compliments to the cook, and will she oblige me with the loan of the cat. Dick Whittington, you know. When you set out to become a Lord Mayor, a cat is essential.'

'I'm sorry, sir, but the cat is not available at the present moment.'

'How is that?'

'A family of eight, sir. Arrived this morning.'

'You don't say so. I thought its name was Peter.'

'So it is, sir. A great surprise to all of us.'

'A case of careless christening and the deceitful sex, eh? Well, well, I shall have to go catless. Pack up those things at once, will you?'

'Very good, sir.'

Rogers hesitated, then advanced a little farther into the room.

'You'll excuse the liberty, sir, but if I was you, I shouldn't take too much notice of anything Mr Rowland said this morning. He was at one of those city dinners last night, and—'

'Say no more,' said George. 'I understand.'

'And being inclined to gout—'

'I know, I know. Rather a strenuous evening for you, Rogers, with two of us, eh? But I've set my heart on distinguishing myself at Rowland's Castle—the cradle of my historic race—that would go well in a speech, wouldn't it? A wire to me there, or a discreet advertisement in the morning papers, will recall me at any time if a fricassée of veal is in preparation. And now—to Waterloo!—as Wellington said on the eve of the historic battle.'

Waterloo Station was not at its brightest and best that afternoon. Mr Rowland eventually discovered a train that would take him to his destination, but it was an undistinguished train, an unimposing train—a train that nobody seemed anxious to travel by. Mr Rowland had a first-class carriage to himself, up in the front of the train. A fog was descending in an indeterminate way over the metropolis, now it lifted, now it descended. The platform was deserted, and only the asthmatic breathing of the engine broke the silence.

And then, all of a sudden, things began to happen with bewildering rapidity.

A girl happened first. She wrenched open the door and jumped in, rousing Mr Rowland from something perilously near a nap, exclaiming as she did so: 'Oh! hide me—oh! please hide me.'

George was essentially a man of action—his not to reason why, his but to do and die, etc. There is only one place to hide in a railway carriage—under the seat. In seven seconds the girl was bestowed there, and George's suit-case, negligently standing on end, covered her retreat. None too soon. An infuriated face appeared at the carriage window.

'My niece! You have her here. I want my niece.'

George, a little breathless, was reclining in the corner,

deep in the sporting column of the evening paper, one-thirty edition. He laid it aside with the air of a man recalling himself from far away.

'I beg your pardon, sir?' he said politely.

'My niece—what have you done with her?'

Acting on the policy that attack is always better than defence, George leaped into action.

'What the devil do you mean?' he cried, with a very creditable imitation of his own uncle's manner.

The other paused a minute, taken aback by this sudden fierceness. He was a fat man, still panting a little as though he had run some way. His hair was cut *en brosse*, and he had a moustache of the Hohenzollern persuasion. His accents were decidedly guttural, and the stiffness of his carriage denoted that he was more at home in uniform than out of it. George had the true-born Briton's prejudice against foreigners—and an especial distaste for German-looking foreigners.

'What the devil do you mean, sir?' he repeated angrily.

'She came in here,' said the other. 'I saw her. What have you done with her?'

George flung aside the paper and thrust his head and shoulders through the window.

'So that's it, is it?' he roared. 'Blackmail. But you've tried it on the wrong person. I read all about you in the *Daily Mail* this morning. Here, guard, guard!'

Already attracted from afar by the altercation, that functionary came hurrying up.

'Here, guard,' said Mr Rowland, with that air of authority which the lower classes so adore. 'This fellow is

61

annoying me. I'll give him in charge for attempted blackmail if necessary. Pretends I've got his niece hidden in here. There's a regular gang of these foreigners trying this sort of thing on. It ought to be stopped. Take him away, will you? Here's my card if you want it.'

The guard looked from one to the other. His mind was soon made up. His training led him to despise foreigners, and to respect and admire well-dressed gentlemen who travelled first class.

He laid his hand on the shoulder of the intruder.

'Here,' he said, 'you come out of this.'

At this crisis the stranger's English failed him, and he plunged into passionate profanity in his native tongue.

'That's enough of that,' said the guard. 'Stand away, will you? She's due out.'

Flags were waved and whistles were blown. With an unwilling jerk the train drew out of the station.

George remained at his observation post until they were clear of the platform. Then he drew in his head, and picking up the suitcase tossed it into the rack.

'It's quite all right. You can come out,' he said reassuringly.

The girl crawled out.

'Oh!' she gasped. 'How can I thank you?'

'That's quite all right. It's been a pleasure, I assure you,' returned George nonchalantly.

He smiled at her reassuringly. There was a slightly puzzled look in her eyes. She seemed to be missing something to which she was accustomed. At that moment, she caught sight of herself in the narrow glass opposite, and gave a heartfelt gasp.

Whether the carriage cleaners do, or do not, sweep under the seats every day is doubtful. Appearances were against their doing so, but it may be that every particle of dirt and smoke finds its way there like a homing bird. George had hardly had time to take in the girl's appearance, so sudden had been her arrival, and so brief the space of time before she crawled into hiding, but it was certainly a trim and well-dressed young woman who had disappeared under the seat. Now her little red hat was crushed and dented, and her face was disfigured with long streaks of dirt.

'Oh!' said the girl.

She fumbled for her bag. George, with the tact of a true gentleman, looked fixedly out of the window and admired the streets of London south of the Thames.

'How can I thank you?' said the girl again.

Taking this as a hint that conversation might now be resumed, George withdrew his gaze, and made another polite disclaimer, but this time with a good deal of added warmth in his manner.

The girl was absolutely lovely! Never before, George told himself, had he seen such a lovely girl. The *empressement* of his manner became even more marked.

'I think it was simply splendid of you,' said the girl with enthusiasm.

'Not at all. Easiest thing in the world. Only too pleased been of use,' mumbled George.

'Splendid,' she reiterated emphatically.

It is undoubtedly pleasant to have the loveliest girl you have ever seen gazing into your eyes and telling you how splendid you are. George enjoyed it as much as anyone could.

Then there came a rather difficult silence. It seemed to dawn upon the girl that further explanation might be expected. She flushed a little.

'The awkward part of it is,' she said nervously, 'that I'm afraid I can't explain.'

She looked at him with a piteous air of uncertainty.

'You can't explain?'

'No.'

'How perfectly splendid!' said Mr Rowland with enthusiasm.

'I beg your pardon?'

'I said, "How perfectly splendid". Just like one of those books that keep you up all night. The heroine always says "I can't explain" in the first chapter. She explains in the last, of course, and there's never any real reason why she shouldn't have done so in the beginning—except that it would spoil the story. I can't tell you how pleased I am to be mixed up in a real mystery—I didn't know there were such things. I hope it's got something to do with secret documents of immense importance, and the Balkan express. I dote upon the Balkan express.'

The girl stared at him with wide, suspicious eyes.

'What makes you say the Balkan express?' she asked sharply.

'I hope I haven't been indiscreet,' George hastened to put in. 'Your uncle travelled by it, perhaps.'

'My uncle—' She paused, then began again. 'My uncle—'

'Quite so,' said George sympathetically. 'I've got an uncle

myself. Nobody should be held responsible for their uncles. Nature's little throwbacks—that's how I look at it.'

The girl began to laugh suddenly. When she spoke George was aware of the slight foreign inflection in her voice. At first he had taken her to be English.

'What a refreshing and unusual person you are, Mr—'

'Rowland. George to my friends.'

'My name is Elizabeth—'

She stopped abruptly.

'I like the name of Elizabeth,' said George, to cover her momentary confusion. 'They don't call you Bessie, or anything horrible like that, I hope?'

She shook her head.

'Well,' said George, 'now that we know each other, we'd better get down to business. If you'll stand up, Elizabeth, I'll brush down the back of your coat.'

She stood up obediently, and George was as good as his word.

'Thank you, Mr Rowland.'

'George. George to my friends, remember. And you can't come into my nice empty carriage, roll under the seat, induce me to tell lies to your uncle, and then refuse to be friends, can you?'

'Thank you, George.'

'That's better.'

'Do I look quite all right now?' asked Elizabeth, trying to see over her left shoulder.

'You look—oh! you look—you look all right,' said George, curbing himself sternly.

'It was all so sudden, you see,' explained the girl.

'It must have been.'

'He saw us in the taxi, and then at the station I just bolted in here knowing he was close behind me. Where is this train going to, by the way?'

'Rowland's Castle,' said George firmly.

The girl looked puzzled.

'Rowland's Castle?'

'Not at once, of course. Only after a good deal of stopping and slow going. But I confidently expect to be there before midnight. The old South-Western was a very reliable line—slow but sure—and I'm sure the Southern Railway is keeping up the old traditions.'

'I don't know that I want to go to Rowland's Castle,' said Elizabeth doubtfully.

'You hurt me. It's a delightful spot.'

'Have you ever been there?'

'Not exactly. But there are lots of other places you can go to, if you don't fancy Rowland's Castle. There's Woking, and Weybridge, and Wimbledon. The train is sure to stop at one or other of them.'

'I see,' said the girl. 'Yes, I can get out there, and perhaps motor back to London. That would be the best plan, I think.'

Even as she spoke, the train began to slow up. Mr Rowland gazed at her with appealing eyes.

'If I can do anything—'

'No, indeed. You've done a lot already.'

There was a pause, then the girl broke out suddenly:

'I—I wish I could explain. I—'

'For heaven's sake don't do that! It would spoil everything.

But look here, isn't there anything that I could do? Carry the secret papers to Vienna—or something of that kind? There always are secret papers. Do give me a chance.'

The train had stopped. Elizabeth jumped quickly out on to the platform. She turned and spoke to him through the window.

'Are you in earnest? Would you really do something for us—for me?'

'I'd do anything in the world for you, Elizabeth.'

'Even if I could give you no reasons?'

'Rotten things, reasons!'

'Even if it were—dangerous?'

'The more danger, the better.'

She hesitated a minute then seemed to make up her mind.

'Lean out of the window. Look down the platform as though you weren't really looking.' Mr Rowland endeavoured to comply with this somewhat difficult recommendation. 'Do you see that man getting in—with a small dark beard—light overcoat? Follow him, see what he does and where he goes.'

'Is that all?' asked Mr Rowland. 'What do I—?'

She interrupted him.

'Further instructions will be sent to you. Watch him—and guard this.' She thrust a small sealed packet into his hand. 'Guard it with your life. It's the key to everything.'

The train went on. Mr Rowland remained staring out of the window, watching Elizabeth's tall, graceful figure threading its way down the platform. In his hand he clutched the small sealed packet.

The rest of his journey was both monotonous and

uneventful. The train was a slow one. It stopped everywhere. At every station, George's head shot out of the window, in case his quarry should alight. Occasionally he strolled up and down the platform when the wait promised to be a long one, and reassured himself that the man was still there.

The eventual destination of the train was Portsmouth, and it was there that the black-bearded traveller alighted. He made his way to a small second-class hotel where he booked a room. Mr Rowland also booked a room.

The rooms were in the same corridor, two doors from each other. The arrangement seemed satisfactory to George. He was a complete novice in the art of shadowing, but was anxious to acquit himself well, and justify Elizabeth's trust in him.

At dinner George was given a table not far from that of his quarry. The room was not full, and the majority of the diners George put down as commercial travellers, quiet respectable men who ate their food with appetite. Only one man attracted his special notice, a small man with ginger hair and moustache and a suggestion of horsiness in his apparel. He seemed to be interested in George also, and suggested a drink and a game of billiards when the meal had come to a close. But George had just espied the black-bearded man putting on his hat and overcoat, and declined politely. In another minute he was out in the street, gaining fresh insight into the difficult art of shadowing. The chase was a long and a weary one—and in the end it seemed to lead nowhere. After twisting and turning through the streets of Portsmouth for about four miles, the man returned to the hotel, George hard upon his heels. A faint doubt assailed the latter. Was it possible that the man was aware of his presence? As he debated this point, standing in the hall, the outer door was pushed open, and the little ginger man entered. Evidently he, too, had been out for a stroll.

George was suddenly aware that the beauteous damsel in the office was addressing him.

'Mr Rowland, isn't it? Two gentlemen have called to see you. Two foreign gentlemen. They are in the little room at the end of the passage.'

Somewhat astonished, George sought the room in question. Two men who were sitting there, rose to their feet and bowed punctiliously.

'Mr Rowland? I have no doubt, sir, that you can guess our identity.'

George gazed from one to the other of them. The spokesman was the elder of the two, a grey-haired, pompous gentleman who spoke excellent English. The other was a tall, somewhat pimply young man, with a blond Teutonic cast of countenance which was not rendered more attractive by the fierce scowl which he wore at the present moment.

Somewhat relieved to find that neither of his visitors was the old gentleman he had encountered at Waterloo, George assumed his most debonair manner.

'Pray sit down, gentlemen. I'm delighted to make your acquaintance. How about a drink?'

The elder man held up a protesting hand.

'Thank you, Lord Rowland—not for us. We have but

a few brief moments—just time for you to answer a question.'

'It's very kind of you to elect me to the peerage,' said George. 'I'm sorry you won't have a drink. And what is this momentous question?'

'Lord Rowland, you left London in company with a certain lady. You arrived here alone. Where is the lady?'

George rose to his feet.

'I fail to understand the question,' he said coldly, speaking as much like the hero of a novel as he could. 'I have the honour to wish you good-evening, gentlemen.'

'But you do understand it. You understand it perfectly,' cried the younger man, breaking out suddenly. 'What have you done with Alexa?'

'Be calm, sir,' murmured the other. 'I beg of you to be calm.'

'I can assure you,' said George, 'that I know no lady of that name. There is some mistake.'

The older man was eyeing him keenly.

'That can hardly be,' he said drily. 'I took the liberty of examining the hotel register. You entered yourself as Mr G Rowland of Rowland's Castle.'

George was forced to blush.

'A—a little joke of mine,' he explained feebly.

'A somewhat poor subterfuge. Come, let us not beat about the bush. Where is Her Highness?'

'If you mean Elizabeth—'

With a howl of rage the young man flung himself forward again.

'Insolent pig-dog! To speak of her thus.'

'I am referring,' said the other slowly, 'as you very well know, to the Grand Duchess Anastasia Sophia Alexandra Marie Helena Olga Elizabeth of Catonia.'

'Oh!' said Mr Rowland helplessly.

He tried to recall all that he had ever known of Catonia. It was, as far as he remembered, a small Balkan kingdom, and he seemed to remember something about a revolution having occurred there. He rallied himself with an effort.

'Evidently we mean the same person,' he said cheerfully, 'only *I* call her Elizabeth.'

'You will give me satisfaction for that,' snarled the younger man. 'We will fight.'

'Fight?'

'A duel.'

'I never fight duels,' said Mr Rowland firmly.

'Why not?' demanded the other unpleasantly.

'I'm too afraid of getting hurt.'

'Aha! is that so? Then I will at least pull your nose for you.'

The young man advanced fiercely. Exactly what happened was difficult to see, but he described a sudden semi-circle in the air and fell to the ground with a heavy thud. He picked himself up in a dazed manner. Mr Rowland was smiling pleasantly.

'As I was saying,' he remarked, 'I'm always afraid of getting hurt. That's why I thought it well to learn ju-jitsu.'

There was a pause. The two foreigners looked doubtfully at this amiable looking young man, as though they suddenly realized that some dangerous quality lurked behind the pleasant nonchalance of his manner. The young Teuton was white with passion.

'You will repent this,' he hissed.

The older man retained his dignity.

'That is your last word, Lord Rowland? You refuse to tell us Her Highness's whereabouts?'

'I am unaware of them myself.'

'You can hardly expect me to believe that.'

'I am afraid you are of an unbelieving nature, sir.'

The other merely shook his head, and murmuring: 'This is not the end. You will hear from us again,' the two men took their leave.

George passed his hand over his brow. Events were proceeding at a bewildering rate. He was evidently mixed up in a first-class European scandal.

'It might even mean another war,' said George hopefully, as he hunted round to see what had become of the man with the black beard.

To his great relief, he discovered him sitting in a corner of the commercial-room. George sat down in another corner. In about three minutes the black-bearded man got up and went up to bed. George followed and saw him go into his room and close the door. George heaved a sigh of relief.

'I need a night's rest,' he murmured. 'Need it badly.'

Then a dire thought struck him. Supposing the black-bearded man had realized that George was on his trail? Supposing that he should slip away during the night whilst George himself was sleeping the sleep of the just? A few minutes' reflection suggested to Mr Rowland a way of dealing with his difficulty. He unravelled one of his socks till he got a good length of neutral-coloured wool, then creeping quietly out of his room, he pasted one end of the wool to the farther side of the stranger's door with stamp paper, carrying the wool across it and along to his own room. There he hung the end with a small silver bell—a relic of last night's entertainment. He surveyed these arrangements with a good deal of satisfaction. Should the black-bearded man attempt to leave his room George would be instantly warned by the ringing of the bell.

This matter disposed of, George lost no time in seeking his couch. The small packet he placed carefully under his pillow. As he did so, he fell into a momentary brown study. His thoughts could have been translated thus:

'Anastasia Sophia Marie Alexandra Olga Elizabeth. Hang it all, I've missed out one. I wonder now—'

He was unable to go to sleep immediately, being tantalized with his failure to grasp the situation. What was it all about? What was the connection between the escaping Grand Duchess, the sealed packet and the black-bearded man? What was the Grand Duchess escaping from? Were the foreigners aware that the sealed packet was in his possession? What was it likely to contain?

Pondering these matters, with an irritated sense that he was no nearer the solution, Mr Rowland fell asleep.

He was awakened by the faint jangle of a bell. Not one of those men who awake to instant action, it took him just a minute and a half to realize the situation. Then he jumped up, thrust on some slippers, and, opening the door with the utmost caution, slipped out into the corridor. A faint moving patch of shadow at the far end of the passage showed him the direction taken by his quarry. Moving as noiselessly as possible, Mr Rowland followed the trail. He was just in time to see the black-bearded man disappear into a bathroom. That was puzzling, particularly so as there was a bathroom just opposite his own room. Moving up close to the door, which was ajar, George peered through the crack. The man was on his knees by the side of the bath, doing something to the skirting board immediately behind it. He remained there for about five minutes, then he rose to his feet, and George beat a prudent retreat. Safe in the shadow of his own door, he watched the other pass and regain his own room.

'Good,' said George to himself. 'The mystery of the bathroom will be investigated tomorrow morning.'

He got into bed and slipped his hand under the pillow to assure himself that the precious packet was still there. In another minute, he was scattering the bedclothes in a panic. The packet was gone!

It was a sadly chastened George who sat consuming eggs and bacon the following morning. He had failed Elizabeth. He had allowed the precious packet she had entrusted to his charge to be taken from him, and the 'Mystery of the Bathroom' was miserably inadequate. Yes, undoubtedly George had made a mutt of himself.

After breakfast he strolled upstairs again. A chambermaid was standing in the passage looking perplexed.

'Anything wrong, my dear?' said George kindly.

'It's the gentleman here, sir. He asked to be called at half-past eight, and I can't get any answer and the door's locked.'

'You don't say so,' said George.

An uneasy feeling rose in his own breast. He hurried into his room. Whatever plans he was forming were instantly brushed aside by a most unexpected sight. There on the dressing-table was the little packet which had been stolen from him the night before!

George picked it up and examined it. Yes, it was undoubtedly the same. But the seals had been broken. After a minute's hesitation, he unwrapped it. If other people had seen its contents there was no reason why he should not see them also. Besides, it was possible that the contents had been abstracted. The unwound paper revealed a small cardboard box, such as jewellers use. George opened it. Inside, nestling on a bed of cotton wool, was a plain gold wedding ring.

He picked it up and examined it. There was no inscription inside—nothing whatever to mark it out from any other wedding ring. George dropped his head into his hands with a groan.

'Lunacy,' he murmured. 'That's what it is. Stark staring lunacy. There's no sense anywhere.'

Suddenly he remembered the chambermaid's statement, and at the same time he observed that there was a broad parapet outside the window. It was not a feat he would ordinarily have attempted, but he was so aflame with curiosity and anger that he was in the mood to make light of difficulties. He sprang upon the window sill. A few seconds later he was peering in at the window of the room occupied by the black-bearded man. The window was open and the room was empty. A little further along was a fire escape. It was clear how the quarry had taken his departure.

George jumped in through the window. The missing man's effects were still scattered about. There might be some clue amongst them to shed light on George's perplexities. He began to hunt about, starting with the contents of a battered kit-bag.

It was a sound that arrested his search—a very slight sound, but a sound indubitably in the room. George's glance leapt to the big wardrobe. He sprang up and wrenched open the door. As he did so, a man jumped out from it and went rolling over the floor locked in George's embrace. He was no mean antagonist. All George's special tricks availed very little. They fell apart at length in sheer exhaustion, and for the first time George saw who his adversary was. It was the little man with the ginger moustache.

'Who the devil are you?' demanded George.

For answer the other drew out a card and handed it to him. George read it aloud.

'Detective-Inspector Jarrold, Scotland Yard.'

'That's right, sir. And you'd do well to tell me all you know about this business.'

'I would, would I?' said George thoughtfully. 'Do you know, Inspector, I believe you're right. Shall we adjourn to a more cheerful spot?'

In a quiet corner of the bar George unfolded his soul. Inspector Jarrold listened sympathetically.

'Very puzzling, as you say, sir,' he remarked when George had finished. 'There's a lot as I can't make head or tail of myself, but there's one or two points I can clear up for you. I was here after Mardenberg (your black-bearded friend) and your turning up and watching him the way you did made me suspicious. I couldn't place you. I slipped into your room last night when you were out of it, and it was I who sneaked the little packet from under your pillow. When I opened it and found it wasn't what I was after, I took the first opportunity of returning it to your room.'

'That makes things a little clearer certainly,' said George thoughtfully. 'I seem to have made rather an ass of myself all through.'

'I wouldn't say that, sir. You did uncommon well for a beginner. You say you visited the bathroom this morning and took away what was concealed behind the skirting board?'

'Yes. But it's only a rotten love letter,' said George gloomily. 'Dash it all, I didn't mean to go nosing out the poor fellow's private life.'

'Would you mind letting me see it, sir?'

George took a folded letter from his pocket and passed it to the inspector. The latter unfolded it.

'As you say, sir. But I rather fancy that if you drew lines from one dotted *i* to another, you'd get a different result. Why, bless you, sir, this is a plan of the Portsmouth harbour defences.'

'What?'

'Yes. We've had our eye on the gentleman for some time. But he was too sharp for us. Got a woman to do most of the dirty work.'

'A woman?' said George, in a faint voice. 'What was her name?'

77

*Agatha Christie*

'She goes by a good many, sir. Most usually known as Betty Brighteyes. A remarkably good-looking young woman she is.'

'Betty—Brighteyes,' said George. 'Thank you, Inspector.'

'Excuse me, sir, but you're not looking well.'

'I'm not well. I'm very ill. In fact, I think I'd better take the first train back to town.'

The Inspector looked at his watch.

'That will be a slow train, I'm afraid, sir. Better wait for the express.'

'It doesn't matter,' said George gloomily. 'No train could be slower than the one I came down by yesterday.'

Seated once more in a first-class carriage, George leisurely perused the day's news. Suddenly he sat bolt upright and stared at the sheet in front of him.

'A romantic wedding took place yesterday in London when Lord Roland Gaigh, second son of the Marquis of Axminster, was married to the Grand Duchess Anastasia of Catonia. The ceremony was kept a profound secret. The Grand Duchess has been living in Paris with her uncle since the upheaval in Catonia. She met Lord Roland when he was secretary to the British Embassy in Catonia and their attachment dates from that time.'

'Well, I'm—'

Mr Rowland could not think of anything strong enough to express his feelings. He continued to stare into space. The train stopped at a small station and a lady got in. She sat down opposite him.

'Good morning, George,' she said sweetly.

'Good heavens!' cried George. 'Elizabeth!'

78

She smiled at him. She was, if possible, lovelier than ever.

'Look here,' cried George, clutching his head. 'For God's sake tell me. Are you the Grand Duchess Anastasia, or are you Betty Brighteyes?'

She stared at him.

'I'm not either. I'm Elizabeth Gaigh. I can tell you all about it now. And I've got to apologize too. You see, Roland (that's my brother) has always been in love with Alexa—'

'Meaning the Grand Duchess?'

'Yes, that's what the family call her. Well, as I say, Roland was always in love with her, and she with him. And then the revolution came, and Alexa was in Paris, and they were just going to fix it up when old Stürm, the chancellor, came along and insisted on carrying off Alexa and forcing her to marry Prince Karl, her cousin, a horrid pimply person—'

'I fancy I've met him,' said George.

'Whom she simply hates. And old Prince Osric, her uncle, forbade her to see Roland again. So she ran away to England, and I came up to town and met her, and we wired to Roland who was in Scotland. And just at the very last minute, when we were driving to the Registry Office in a taxi, whom should we meet in another taxi face to face, but old Prince Osric. Of course he followed us, and we were at our wits' end what to do because he'd have made the most fearful scene, and, anyway, he is her guardian. Then I had the brilliant idea of changing places. You can practically see nothing of a girl nowadays but the tip of her nose. I put on Alexa's red hat and brown wrap coat, and she put on my grey. Then we told the taxi to go to

Waterloo, and I skipped out there and hurried into the station. Old Osric followed the red hat all right, without a thought for the other occupant of the taxi sitting huddled up inside, but of course it wouldn't do for him to see my face. So I just bolted into your carriage and threw myself on your mercy.'

'I've got that all right,' said George. 'It's the rest of it.'

'I know. That's what I've got to apologize about. I hope you won't be awfully cross. You see, you looked so keen on its being a real mystery—like in books, that I really couldn't resist the temptation. I picked out a rather sinister looking man on the platform and told you to follow him. And then I thrust the parcel on you.'

'Containing a wedding ring.'

'Yes. Alexa and I bought that, because Roland wasn't due to arrive from Scotland until just before the wedding. And of course I knew that by the time I got to London they wouldn't want it—they would have had to use a curtain ring or something.'

'I see,' said George. 'It's like all these things—so simple when you know! Allow me, Elizabeth.'

He stripped off her left glove, and uttered a sigh of relief at the sight of the bare third finger.

'That's all right,' he remarked. 'That ring won't be wasted after all.'

'Oh!' cried Elizabeth; 'but I don't know anything about you.'

'You know how nice I am,' said George. 'By the way, it has just occurred to me, you are the Lady Elizabeth Gaigh, of course.'

'Oh! George, are you a snob?'

'As a matter of fact, I am, rather. My best dream was one where King George borrowed half a crown from me to see him over the week-end. But I was thinking of my uncle—the one from whom I am estranged. He's a frightful snob. When he knows I'm going to marry you, and that we'll have a title in the family, he'll make me a partner at once!'

'Oh! George, is he very rich?'

'Elizabeth, are you mercenary?'

'Very. I adore spending money. But I was thinking of Father. Five daughters, full of beauty and blue blood. He's just yearning for a rich son-in-law.'

'H'm,' said George. 'It will be one of those marriages made in Heaven and approved on earth. Shall we live at Rowland's Castle? They'd be sure to make me Lord Mayor with you for a wife. Oh! Elizabeth, darling, it's probably contravening the company's by-laws, but I simply must kiss you!'

# Sing a Song of Sixpence

Sir Edward Palliser, K.C., lived at No 9 Queen Anne's Close. Queen Anne's Close is a *cul-de-sac*. In the very heart of Westminster it manages to have a peaceful old-world atmosphere far removed from the turmoil of the twentieth century. It suited Sir Edward Palliser admirably.

Sir Edward had been one of the most eminent criminal barristers of his day and now that he no longer practised at the Bar he had amused himself by amassing a very fine criminological library. He was also the author of a volume of Reminiscences of Eminent Criminals.

On this particular evening Sir Edward was sitting in front of his library fire sipping some very excellent black coffee, and shaking his head over a volume of Lombroso. Such ingenious theories and so completely out of date.

The door opened almost noiselessly and his well-trained manservant approached over the thick pile carpet, and murmured discreetly:

'A young lady wishes to see you, sir.'

'A young lady?'

Sir Edward was surprised. Here was something quite

out of the usual course of events. Then he reflected that it might be his niece, Ethel—but no, in that case Armour would have said so.

He inquired cautiously.

'The lady did not give her name?'

'No, sir, but she said she was quite sure you would wish to see her.'

'Show her in,' said Sir Edward Palliser. He felt pleasurably intrigued.

A tall, dark girl of close on thirty, wearing a black coat and skirt, well cut, and a little black hat, came to Sir Edward with outstretched hand and a look of eager recognition on her face. Armour withdrew, closing the door noiselessly behind him.

'Sir Edward—you do know me, don't you? I'm Magdalen Vaughan.'

'Why, of course.' He pressed the outstretched hand warmly.

He remembered her perfectly now. That trip home from America on the *Siluric*! This charming child—for she had been little more than a child. He had made love to her, he remembered, in a discreet elderly man-of-the-world fashion. She had been so adorably young—so eager—so full of admiration and hero worship—just made to captivate the heart of a man nearing sixty. The remembrance brought additional warmth into the pressure of his hand.

'This is most delightful of you. Sit down, won't you.' He arranged an armchair for her, talking easily and evenly, wondering all the time why she had come. When at last he brought the easy flow of small talk to an end, there was a silence.

Her hand closed and unclosed on the arm of the chair, she moistened her lips. Suddenly she spoke—abruptly.

'Sir Edward—I want you to help me.'

He was surprised and murmured mechanically:

'Yes?'

She went on, speaking more intensely:

'You said that if ever I needed help—that if there was anything in the world you could do for me—you would do it.'

Yes, he *had* said that. It was the sort of thing one did say—particularly at the moment of parting. He could recall the break in his voice—the way he had raised her hand to his lips.

'*If there is ever anything I can do—remember, I mean it . . .*'

Yes, one said that sort of thing . . . But very, very rarely did one have to fulfil one's words! And certainly not after—how many?—nine or ten years. He flashed a quick glance at her—she was still a very good-looking girl, but she had lost what had been to him her charm—that look of dewy untouched youth. It was a more interesting face now, perhaps—a younger man might have thought so—but Sir Edward was far from feeling the tide of warmth and emotion that had been his at the end of that Atlantic voyage.

His face became legal and cautious. He said in a rather brisk way:

'Certainly, my dear young lady. I shall be delighted to do anything in my power—though I doubt if I can be very helpful to anyone in these days.'

If he was preparing his way of retreat she did not notice it. She was of the type that can only see one thing at a time and what she was seeing at this moment was her own need. She took Sir Edward's willingness to help for granted.

'We are in terrible trouble, Sir Edward.'

'*We*? You are married?'

'No—I meant my brother and I. Oh! and William and Emily too, for that matter. But I must explain. I have—I had an aunt—Miss Crabtree. You may have read about her in the papers. It was horrible. She was killed— murdered.'

'Ah!' A flash of interest lit up Sir Edward's face. 'About a month ago, wasn't it?'

The girl nodded.

'Rather less than that—three weeks.'

'Yes, I remember. She was hit on the head in her own house. They didn't get the fellow who did it.'

Again Magdalen Vaughan nodded.

'They didn't get the man—I don't believe they ever will get the man. You see—there mightn't be any man to get.'

'What?'

'Yes—it's awful. Nothing's come out about it in the papers. But that's what the police think. They *know* nobody came to the house that night.'

'You mean—?'

'That it's one of us four. It *must* be. They don't know which—and *we* don't know which . . . *We don't know*. And we sit there every day looking at each other surreptitiously and wondering. Oh! if only it could have been someone from outside—but I don't see how it can . . .'

Sir Edward stared at her, his interest arising.

'You mean that the members of the family are under suspicion?'

'Yes, that's what I mean. The police haven't said so, of course. They've been quite polite and nice. But they've ransacked the house, they've questioned us all, and Martha again and again . . . And because they don't know which, they're holding their hand. I'm so frightened—so horribly frightened . . .'

'My dear child. Come now, surely you are exaggerating.'

'I'm not. It's one of us four—it must be.'

'Who are the four to whom you refer?'

Magdalen sat up straight and spoke more composedly.

'There's myself and Matthew. Aunt Lily was our great aunt. She was my grandmother's sister. We've lived with her ever since we were fourteen (we're twins, you know). Then there was William Crabtree. He was her nephew— her brother's child. He lived there too, with his wife Emily.'

'She supported them?'

'More or less. He has a little money of his own, but he's not strong and has to live at home. He's a quiet, dreamy sort of man. I'm sure it would have been impossible for him to have—oh!—it's awful of me to think of it even!'

'I am still very far from understanding the position. Perhaps you would not mind running over the facts—if it does not distress you too much.'

'Oh! no—I want to tell you. And it's all quite clear in my mind still—horribly clear. We'd had tea, you understand,

and we'd all gone off to do things of our own. I to do some dressmaking, Matthew to type an article—he does a little journalism; William to do his stamps. Emily hadn't been down to tea. She'd taken a headache powder and was lying down. So there we were, all of us, busy and occupied. And when Martha went in to lay supper at half-past seven, there Aunt Lily was—dead. Her head—oh! it's horrible—all crushed in.'

'The weapon was found, I think?'

'Yes. It was a heavy paperweight that always lay on the table by the door. The police tested it for fingerprints, but there were none. It had been wiped clean.'

'And your first surmise?'

'We thought of course it was a burglar. There were two or three drawers of the bureau pulled out, as though a thief had been looking for something. Of course we thought it was a burglar! And then the police came—and they said she had been dead at least an hour, and asked Martha who had been to the house, and Martha said nobody. And all the windows were fastened on the inside, and there seemed no signs of anything having been tampered with. And then they began to ask us questions . . .'

She stopped. Her breast heaved. Her eyes, frightened and imploring, sought Sir Edward's in search of reassurance.

'For instance, who benefited by your aunt's death?'

'That's simple. We all benefit equally. She left her money to be divided in equal shares among the four of us.'

'And what was the value of her estate?'

'The lawyer told us it will come to about eighty thousand pounds after the death duties are paid.'

Sir Edward opened his eyes in some slight surprise.

'That is quite a considerable sum. You knew, I suppose, the total of your aunt's fortune?'

Magdalen shook her head.

'No—it came quite as a surprise to us. Aunt Lily was always terribly careful about money. She kept just the one servant and always talked a lot about economy.'

Sir Edward nodded thoughtfully. Magdalen leaned forward a little in her chair.

'You will help me—you will?'

Her words came to Sir Edward as an unpleasant shock just at the moment when he was becoming interested in her story for its own sake.

'My dear young lady—what can I possibly do? If you want good legal advice, I can give you the name—'

She interrupted him.

'Oh! I don't want that sort of thing! I want you to help me personally—as a friend.'

'That's very charming of you, but—'

'I want you to come to our house. I want you to ask questions. I want you to see and judge for yourself.'

'But my dear young—'

'Remember, you promised. Anywhere—any time—you said, if I wanted help . . .'

Her eyes, pleading yet confident, looked into his. He felt ashamed and strangely touched. That terrific sincerity of hers, that absolute belief in an idle promise, ten years old, as a sacred binding thing. How many men had not said those self-same words—a *cliché* almost!—and how few of them had ever been called upon to make good.

He said rather weakly: 'I'm sure there are many people who could advise you better than I could.'

'I've got lots of friends—naturally.' (He was amused by the naïve self-assurance of that.) 'But you see, none of them are clever. Not like you. You're used to questioning people. And with all your experience you must *know*.'

'Know what?'

'Whether they're innocent or guilty.'

He smiled rather grimly to himself. He flattered himself that on the whole he usually *had* known! Though, on many occasions, his private opinion had not been that of the jury.

Magdalen pushed back her hat from her forehead with a nervous gesture, looked round the room, and said:

'How quiet it is here. Don't you sometimes long for some noise?'

The *cul-de-sac*! All unwittingly her words, spoken at random, touched him on the raw. A *cul-de-sac*. Yes, but there was always a way out—the way you had come—the way back into the world . . . Something impetuous and youthful stirred in him. Her simple trust appealed to the best side of his nature—and the condition of her problem appealed to something else—the innate criminologist in him. He wanted to see these people of whom she spoke. He wanted to form his own judgement.

He said: 'If you are really convinced I can be of any use . . . Mind, I guarantee nothing.'

He expected her to be overwhelmed with delight, but she took it very calmly.

'I knew you would do it. I've always thought of you as a real friend. Will you come back with me now?'

'No. I think if I pay you a visit tomorrow it will be more satisfactory. Will you give me the name and address of Miss Crabtree's lawyer? I may want to ask him a few questions.'

She wrote it down and handed it to him. Then she got up and said rather shyly:

'I—I'm really most awfully grateful. Goodbye.'

'And your own address?'

'How stupid of me. 18 Palatine Walk, Chelsea.'

It was three o'clock on the following afternoon when Sir Edward Palliser approached 18 Palatine Walk with a sober, measured tread. In the interval he had found out several things. He had paid a visit that morning to Scotland Yard, where the Assistant Commissioner was an old friend of his, and he had also had an interview with the late Miss Crabtree's lawyer. As a result he had a clearer vision of the circumstances. Miss Crabtree's arrangements in regard to money had been somewhat peculiar. She never made use of a cheque-book. Instead she was in the habit of writing to her lawyer and asking him to have a certain sum in five-pound notes waiting for her. It was nearly always the same sum. Three hundred pounds four times a year. She came to fetch it herself in a four-wheeler which she regarded as the only safe means of conveyance. At other times she never left the house.

At Scotland Yard Sir Edward learned that the question of finance had been gone into very carefully. Miss Crabtree had been almost due for her next instalment of money. Presumably the previous three hundred had been spent—or almost spent. But this was exactly the point that had not been easy to ascertain. By checking the household expenditure, it was soon evident that Miss Crabtree's expenditure per quarter fell a good deal short of three hundred pounds. On the other hand she was in the habit of sending five-pound notes away to needy friends or relatives. Whether there had been much or little money in the house at the time of her death was a debatable point. None had been found.

It was this particular point which Sir Edward was revolving in his mind as he approached Palatine Walk.

The door of the house (which was a non-basement one) was opened to him by a small elderly woman with an alert gaze. He was shown into a big double room on the left of the small hallway and there Magdalen came to him. More clearly than before, he saw the traces of nervous strain in her face.

'You told me to ask questions, and I have come to do so,' said Sir Edward, smiling as he shook hands. 'First of all I want to know who last saw your aunt and exactly what time that was?'

'It was after tea—five o'clock. Martha was the last person with her. She had been paying the books that afternoon, and brought Aunt Lily the change and the accounts.'

'You trust Martha?'

'Oh, absolutely. She was with Aunt Lily for—oh! thirty years, I suppose. She's honest as the day.'

Sir Edward nodded.

'Another question. Why did your cousin, Mrs Crabtree, take a headache powder?'

'Well, because she had a headache.'

'Naturally, but was there any particular reason why she *should* have a headache?'

'Well, yes, in a way. There was rather a scene at lunch. Emily is very excitable and highly strung. She and Aunt Lily used to have rows sometimes.'

'And they had one at lunch?'

'Yes. Aunt Lily was rather trying about little things. It all started out of nothing—and then they were at it hammer and tongs—with Emily saying all sorts of things she couldn't possibly have meant—that she'd leave the house and never come back—that she was grudged every mouthful she ate—oh! all sorts of silly things. And Aunt Lily said the sooner she and her husband packed their boxes and went the better. But it all meant nothing, really.'

'Because Mr and Mrs Crabtree couldn't afford to pack up and go?'

'Oh, not only that. William was fond of Aunt Emily. He really was.'

'It wasn't a day of quarrels by any chance?'

Magdalen's colour heightened.

'You mean me? The fuss about my wanting to be a mannequin?'

'Your aunt wouldn't agree?'

'No.'

'Why did you want to be a mannequin, Miss Magdalen? Does the life strike you as a very attractive one?'

'No, but anything would be better than going on living here.'

'Yes, then. But now you will have a comfortable income, won't you?'

'Oh! yes, it's quite different *now*.'

She made the admission with the utmost simplicity.

He smiled but pursued the subject no further. Instead he said: 'And your brother? Did he have a quarrel too?'

'Matthew? Oh, no.'

'Then no one can say he had a motive for wishing his aunt out of the way?'

He was quick to seize on the momentary dismay that showed in her face.

'I forgot,' he said casually. 'He owed a good deal of money, didn't he?'

'Yes; poor old Matthew.'

'Still, that will be all right now.'

'Yes—' She sighed. 'It *is* a relief.'

And still she saw nothing! He changed the subject hastily.

'Your cousins and your brother are at home?'

'Yes; I told them you were coming. They are all so anxious to help. Oh, Sir Edward—I feel, somehow, that you are going to find out that everything is all right—that none of us had anything to do with it—that, after all, it *was* an outsider.'

'I can't do miracles. I may be able to find out the truth, but I can't make the truth be what you want it to be.'

'Can't you? I feel that you could do anything—anything.'

She left the room. He thought, disturbed, 'What did she mean by that? Does she want me to suggest a line of defence? For whom?'

His meditations were interrupted by the entrance of a man about fifty years of age. He had a naturally powerful frame, but stooped slightly. His clothes were untidy and his hair carelessly brushed. He looked good-natured but vague.

'Sir Edward Palliser? Oh, how do you do. Magdalen sent me along. It's very good of you, I'm sure, to wish to help us. Though I don't think anything will ever be really discovered. I mean, they won't catch the fellow.'

'You think it was a burglar then—someone from outside?'

'Well, it must have been. It couldn't be one of the family. These fellows are very clever nowadays, they climb like cats and they get in and out as they like.'

'Where were you, Mr Crabtree, when the tragedy occurred?'

'I was busy with my stamps—in my little sitting-room upstairs.'

'You didn't hear anything?'

'No—but then I never do hear anything when I'm absorbed. Very foolish of me, but there it is.'

'Is the sitting-room you refer to over this room?'

'No, it's at the back.'

Again the door opened. A small fair woman entered. Her hands were twitching nervously. She looked fretful and excited.

'William, why didn't you wait for me? I said "wait".'

'Sorry, my dear, I forgot. Sir Edward Palliser—my wife.'

'How do you do, Mrs Crabtree? I hope you don't mind my coming here to ask a few questions. I know how anxious you must all be to have things cleared up.'

'Naturally. But I can't tell you anything—can I, William?

I was asleep—on my bed—I only woke up when Martha screamed.'

Her hands continued to twitch.

'Where is your room, Mrs Crabtree?'

'It's over this. But I didn't hear anything—how could I? I was asleep.'

He could get nothing out of her but that. She knew nothing—she had heard nothing—she had been asleep. She reiterated it with the obstinacy of a frightened woman. Yet Sir Edward knew very well that it might easily be— probably was—the bare truth.

He excused himself at last—said he would like to put a few questions to Martha. William Crabtree volunteered to take him to the kitchen. In the hall, Sir Edward nearly collided with a tall dark young man who was striding towards the front door.

'Mr Matthew Vaughan?'

'Yes—but look here, I can't wait. I've got an appointment.'

'Matthew!' It was his sister's voice from the stairs. 'Oh! Matthew, you promised—'

'I know, sis. But I can't. Got to meet a fellow. And, anyway, what's the good of talking about the damned thing over and over again. We have enough of that with the police. I'm fed up with the whole show.'

The front door banged. Mr Matthew Vaughan had made his exit.

Sir Edward was introduced into the kitchen. Martha was ironing. She paused, iron in hand. Sir Edward shut the door behind him.

'Miss Vaughan has asked me to help her,' he said. 'I hope you won't object to my asking you a few questions.'

She looked at him, then shook her head.

'None of them did it, sir. I know what you're thinking, but it isn't so. As nice a set of ladies and gentlemen as you could wish to see.'

'I've no doubt of it. But their niceness isn't what we call evidence, you know.'

'Perhaps not, sir. The law's a funny thing. But there is evidence—as you call it, sir. None of them could have done it without *my* knowing.'

'But surely—'

'I know what I'm talking about sir. There, listen to that—'

'That' was a creaking sound above their heads.

'The stairs, sir. Every time anyone goes up or down, the stairs creak something awful. It doesn't matter how quiet you go. Mrs Crabtree, she was lying on her bed, and Mr Crabtree was fiddling about with them wretched stamps of his, and Miss Magdalen she was up above again working her machine, and if any one of those three had come down the stairs I should have known it. And they didn't!'

She spoke with a positive assurance which impressed the barrister. He thought: 'A good witness. She'd carry weight.'

'You mightn't have noticed.'

'Yes, I would. I'd have noticed without noticing, so to speak. Like you notice when a door shuts and somebody goes out.'

Sir Edward shifted his ground.

'That is three of them acounted for, but there is a fourth. Was Mr Matthew Vaughan upstairs also?'

'No, but he was in the little room downstairs. Next door. And he was typewriting. You can hear it plain in here. His machine never stopped for a moment. Not for a moment, sir, I can swear to it. A nasty irritating tap-tapping noise it is, too.'

Sir Edward paused a minute.

'It was you who found her, wasn't it?'

'Yes, sir, it was. Lying there with blood on her poor hair. And no one hearing a sound on account of the tap-tapping of Mr Matthew's typewriter.'

'I understand you are positive that no one came into the house?'

'How could they, sir, without my knowing? The bell rings in here. And there's only the one door.'

He looked at her straight in the face.

'You were attached to Miss Crabtree?'

A warm glow—genuine—unmistakable—came into her face.

'Yes, indeed, I was, sir. But for Miss Crabtree—well, I'm getting on and I don't mind speaking of it now. I got into trouble, sir, when I was a girl, and Miss Crabtree stood by me—took me back into her service, she did, when it was all over. I'd have died for her—I would indeed.'

Sir Edward knew sincerity when he heard it. Martha was sincere.

'As far as you know, no one came to the door—?'

'No one could have come.'

'I said as far as *you* know. But if Miss Crabtree had

been expecting someone—if she opened the door to that
someone herself . . .'

'Oh!' Martha seemed taken aback.

'That's possible, I suppose?' Sir Edward urged.

'It's possible—yes—but it isn't very likely. I mean . . .'

She was clearly taken aback. She couldn't deny and yet
she wanted to do so. Why? Because she knew that the truth
lay elsewhere. Was that it? The four people in the house—
one of them guilty? Did Martha want to shield that guilty
party? *Had* the stairs creaked? Had someone come stealthily
down and did Martha know who that someone was?

She herself was honest—Sir Edward was convinced of
that.

He pressed his point, watching her.

'Miss Crabtree might have done that, I suppose? The
window of that room faces the street. She might have seen
whoever it was she was waiting for from the window and
gone out into the hall and let him—or her—in. She might
even have wished that no one should see the person.'

Martha looked troubled. She said at last reluctantly:

'Yes, you may be right, sir. I never thought of that. That
she was expecting a gentleman—yes, it well might be.'

It was though she began to perceive advantages in the
idea.

'You were the last person to see her, were you not?'

'Yes, sir. After I'd cleared away the tea. I took the
receipted books to her and the change from the money
she'd given me.'

'Had she given the money to you in five-pound notes?'

'A five-pound note, sir,' said Martha in a shocked voice.

'The book never came up as high as five pounds. I'm very careful.'

'Where did she keep her money?'

'I don't rightly know, sir. I should say that she carried it about with her—in her black velvet bag. But of course she may have kept it in one of the drawers in her bedroom that were locked. She was very fond of locking up things, though prone to lose her keys.'

Sir Edward nodded.

'You don't know how much money she had—in five-pound notes, I mean?'

'No, sir, I couldn't say what the exact amount was.'

'And she said nothing to you that could lead you to believe that she was expecting anybody?'

'No, sir.'

'You're quite sure? What exactly did she say?'

'Well,' Martha considered, 'she said the butcher was nothing more than a rogue and a cheat, and she said I'd had in a quarter of a pound of tea more than I ought, and she said Mrs Crabtree was full of nonsense for not liking to eat margarine, and she didn't like one of the sixpences I'd brought her back—one of the new ones with oak leaves on it—she said it was bad, and I had a lot of trouble to convince her. And she said—oh, that the fishmonger had sent haddocks instead of whitings, and had I told him about it, and I said I had—and, really, I think that's all, sir.'

Martha's speech had made the deceased lady loom clear to Sir Edward as a detailed description would never have done. He said casually:

'Rather a difficult mistress to please, eh?'

'A bit fussy, but there, poor dear, she didn't often get out, and staying cooped up she had to have something to amuse herself like. She was pernickety but kind hearted—never a beggar sent away from the door without something. Fussy she may have been, but a real charitable lady.'

'I am glad, Martha, that she leaves one person to regret her.'

The old servant caught her breath.

'You mean—oh, but they were all fond of her—really—underneath. They all had words with her now and again, but it didn't mean anything.'

Sir Edward lifted his head. There was a creak above.

'That's Miss Magdalen coming down.'

'How do you know?' he shot at her.

The old woman flushed. 'I know her step,' she muttered.

Sir Edward left the kitchen rapidly. Martha had been right. Magdalen had just reached the bottom stair. She looked at him hopefully.

'Not very far on as yet,' said Sir Edward, answering her look, and added, 'You don't happen to know what letters your aunt received on the day of her death?'

'They are all together. The police have been through them, of course.'

She led the way to the big double drawing-room, and unlocking a drawer took out a large black velvet bag with an old-fashioned silver clasp.

'This is Aunt's bag. Everything is in here just as it was on the day of her death. I've kept it like that.'

Sir Edward thanked her and proceeded to turn out the

contents of the bag on the table. It was, he fancied, a fair specimen of an eccentric elderly lady's handbag.

There was some odd silver change, two ginger nuts, three newspaper cuttings about Joanna Southcott's box, a trashy printed poem about the unemployed, an *Old Moore's Almanack*, a large piece of camphor, some spectacles and three letters. A spidery one from someone called 'Cousin Lucy', a bill for mending a watch, and an appeal from a charitable institution.

Sir Edward went through everything very carefully, then repacked the bag and handed it to Magdalen with a sigh.

'Thank you, Miss Magdalen. I'm afraid there isn't much there.'

He rose, observed that from the window you commanded a good view of the front door steps, then took Magdalen's hand in his.

'You are going?'

'Yes.'

'But it's—it's going to be all right?'

'Nobody connected with the law ever commits himself to a rash statement like that,' said Sir Edward solemnly, and made his escape.

He walked along the street lost in thought. The puzzle was there under his hand—and he had not solved it. It needed something—some little thing. Just to point the way.

A hand fell on his shoulder and he started. It was Matthew Vaughan, somewhat out of breath.

'I've been chasing you, Sir Edward. I want to apologize. For my rotten manners half an hour ago. But I've not got the best temper in the world, I'm afraid. It's awfully good of you to bother about this business. Please ask me whatever you like. If there's anything I can do to help—'

Suddenly Sir Edward stiffened. His glance was fixed—not on Matthew—but across the street. Somewhat bewildered, Matthew repeated:

'If there's anything I can do to help—'

'You have already done it, my dear young man,' said Sir Edward. 'By stopping me at this particular spot and so fixing my attention on something I might otherwise have missed.'

He pointed across the street to a small restaurant opposite.

'*The Four and Twenty Blackbirds?*' asked Matthew in a puzzled voice.

'Exactly.'

'It's an odd name—but you get quite decent food there, I believe.'

'I shall not take the risk of experimenting,' said Sir Edward. 'Being further from my nursery days than you are, my friend, I probably remember my nursery rhymes better. There is a classic that runs thus, if I remember rightly:

*Sing a song of sixpence, a pocket full of rye,*
*Four and twenty blackbirds, baked in a pie*

—and so on. The rest of it does not concern us.'

He wheeled round sharply.

'Where are you going?' asked Matthew Vaughan.

'Back to your house, my friend.'

They walked there in silence, Matthew Vaughan shooting

puzzled glances at his companion. Sir Edward entered, strode to a drawer, lifted out a velvet bag and opened it. He looked at Matthew and the young man reluctantly left the room.

Sir Edward tumbled out the silver change on the table. Then he nodded. His memory had not been at fault.

He got up and rang the bell, slipping something into the palm of his hand as he did so.

Martha answered the bell.

'You told me, Martha, if I remember rightly, that you had a slight altercation with your late mistress over one of the new sixpences.'

'Yes, sir.'

'Ah! but the curious thing is, Martha, that among this loose change, there is no new sixpence. There are two sixpences, but they are both old ones.'

She stared at him in a puzzled fashion.

'You see what that means? *Someone did come to the house that evening—someone to whom your mistress gave sixpence* . . . I think she gave it him in exchange for this . . .'

With a swift movement, he shot his hand forward, holding out the doggerel verse about unemployment.

One glance at her face was enough.

'The game is up, Martha—you see, I know. You may as well tell me everything.'

She sank down on a chair—the tears raced down her face.

'It's true—it's true—the bell didn't ring properly—I wasn't sure, and then I thought I'd better go and see. I got to the door just as he struck her down. The roll of five-pound notes was on the table in front of her—it was the sight of them as made him do it—that and thinking she was alone in the house as she'd let him in. I couldn't scream. I was too paralysed and then he turned—and I saw it was my boy . . .

'Oh, he's been a bad one always. I gave him all the money I could. He's been in gaol twice. He must have come around to see me, and then Miss Crabtree, seeing as I didn't answer the door, went to answer it herself, and he was taken aback and pulled out one of those unemployment leaflets, and the mistress being kind of charitable, told him to come in and got out a sixpence. And all the time that roll of notes was lying on the table where it had been when I was giving her the change. And the devil got into my Ben and he got behind her and struck her down.'

'And then?' asked Sir Edward.

'Oh, sir, what could I do? My own flesh and blood. His father was a bad one, and Ben takes after him—but he was my own son. I hustled him out, and I went back to the kitchen and I went to lay for supper at the usual time. Do you think it was very wicked of me, sir? I tried to tell you no lies when you was asking me questions.'

Sir Edward rose.

'My poor woman,' he said with feeling in his voice, 'I am very sorry for you. All the same, the law will have to take its course, you know.'

'He's fled the country, sir. I don't know where he is.'

'There's a chance, then, that he may escape the gallows, but don't build upon it. Will you send Miss Magdalen to me.'

'Oh, Sir Edward. How wonderful of you—how wonderful you are,' said Magdalen when he had finished his brief recital. 'You've saved us all. How can I ever thank you?'

Sir Edward smiled down at her and patted her hand gently. He was very much the great man. Little Magdalen had been very charming on the *Siluric*. That bloom of seventeen—wonderful! She had completely lost it now, of course.

'Next time you need a friend—' he said.

'I'll come straight to you.'

'No, no,' cried Sir Edward in alarm. 'That's just what I don't want you to do. Go to a younger man.'

He extricated himself with dexterity from the grateful household and hailing a taxi sank into it with a sigh of relief.

Even the charm of a dewy seventeen seemed doubtful.

It could not really compare with a really well-stocked library on criminology.

The taxi turned into Queen Anne's Close.

His *cul-de-sac*.

# The Manhood of Edward Robinson

*'With a swing of his mighty arms, Bill lifted her right off her feet, crushing her to his breast. With a deep sigh she yielded her lips in such a kiss as he had never dreamed of—'*

With a sigh, Mr Edward Robinson put down *When Love is King* and stared out of the window of the underground train. They were running through Stamford Brook. Edward Robinson was thinking about Bill. Bill was the real hundred per cent he-man beloved of lady novelists. Edward envied him his muscles, his rugged good looks and his terrific passions. He picked up the book again and read the description of the proud Marchesa Bianca (she who had yielded her lips). So ravishing was her beauty, the intoxication of her was so great, that strong men went down before her like ninepins, faint and helpless with love.

'Of course,' said Edward to himself, 'it's all bosh, this sort of stuff. All bosh, it is. And yet, I wonder—'

His eyes looked wistful. Was there such a thing as a

world of romance and adventure somewhere? Were there women whose beauty intoxicated? Was there such a thing as love that devoured one like a flame?

'This is real life, this is,' said Edward. 'I've got to go on the same just like all the other chaps.'

On the whole, he supposed, he ought to consider himself a lucky young man. He had an excellent berth—a clerkship in a flourishing concern. He had good health, no one dependent upon him, and he was engaged to Maud.

But the mere thought of Maud brought a shadow over his face. Though he would never have admitted it, he was afraid of Maud. He loved her—yes—he still remembered the thrill with which he had admired the back of her white neck rising out of the cheap four and elevenpenny blouse on the first occasion they had met. He had sat behind her at the cinema, and the friend he was with had known her and had introduced them. No doubt about it, Maud was very superior. She was good-looking and clever and very lady-like, and she was always right about everything. The kind of girl, everyone said, who would make such an excellent wife.

Edward wondered whether the Marchesa Bianca would have made an excellent wife. Somehow, he doubted it. He couldn't picture the voluptuous Bianca, with her red lips and her swaying form, tamely sewing on buttons, say, for the virile Bill. No, Bianca was Romance, and this was real life. He and Maud would be very happy together. She had so much common sense . . .

But all the same, he wished that she wasn't quite so—well, sharp in manner. So prone to 'jump upon him'.

It was, of course, her prudence and her common sense which made her do so. Maud was very sensible. And, as a rule, Edward was very sensible too, but sometimes—He had wanted to get married this Christmas, for instance. Maud had pointed out how much more prudent it would be to wait a while—a year or two, perhaps. His salary was not large. He had wanted to give her an expensive ring— she had been horror stricken, and had forced him to take it back and exchange it for a cheaper one. Her qualities were all excellent qualities, but sometimes Edward wished that she had more faults and less virtues. It was her virtues that drove him to desperate deeds.

For instance—

A blush of guilt overspread his face. He had got to tell her—and tell her soon. His secret guilt was already making him behave strangely. Tomorrow was the first of three days' holiday, Christmas Eve, Christmas Day and Boxing Day. She had suggested that he should come round and spend the day with her people, and in a clumsy foolish manner, a manner that could not fail to arouse her suspicions, he had managed to get out of it—had told a long, lying story about a pal of his in the country with whom he had promised to spend the day.

And there was no pal in the country. There was only his guilty secret.

Three months ago, Edward Robinson, in company with a few hundred thousand other young men, had gone in for a competition in one of the weekly papers. Twelve girls' names had to be arranged in order of popularity. Edward had had a brilliant idea. His own preference was sure to be wrong—he had noticed that in several similar competitions. He wrote down the twelve names arranged in his own order of merit, then he wrote them down again this time placing one from the top and one from the bottom of the list alternately.

When the result was announced, Edward had got eight right out of the twelve, and was awarded the first prize of £500. This result, which might easily be ascribed to luck, Edward persisted in regarding as the direct outcome of his 'system.' He was inordinately proud of himself.

The next thing was, what do do with the £500? He knew very well what Maud would say. Invest it. A nice little nest egg for the future. And, of course, Maud would be quite right, he knew that. But to win money as the result of a competition is an entirely different feeling from anything else in the world.

Had the money been left to him as a legacy, Edward would have invested it religiously in Conversion Loan or Savings Certificates as a matter of course. But money that one has achieved by a mere stroke of the pen, by a lucky and unbelievable chance, comes under the same heading as a child's sixpence—'for your very own—to spend as you like'.

And in a certain rich shop which he passed daily on his way to the office, was the unbelievable dream, a small two-seater car, with a long shining nose, and the price clearly displayed on it—£465.

'If I were rich,' Edward had said to it, day after day. 'If I were rich, I'd have you.'

And now he was—if not rich—at least possessed of a

lump sum of money sufficient to realize his dream. That car, that shining alluring piece of loveliness, was his if he cared to pay the price.

He had meant to tell Maud about the money. Once he had told her, he would have secured himself against temptation. In face of Maud's horror and disapproval, he would never have the courage to persist in his madness. But, as it chanced, it was Maud herself who clinched the matter. He had taken her to the cinema—and to the best seats in the house. She had pointed out to him, kindly but firmly, the criminal folly of his behaviour—wasting good money—three and sixpence against two and fourpence, when one saw just as well from the latter places.

Edward took her reproaches in sullen silence. Maud felt contentedly that she was making an impression. Edward could not be allowed to continue in these extravagant ways. She loved Edward, but she realized that he was weak—hers the task of being ever at hand to influence him in the way he should go. She observed his worm-like demeanour with satisfaction.

Edward was indeed worm-like. Like worms, he turned. He remained crushed by her words, but it was at that precise minute that he made up his mind to buy the car.

'Damn it,' said Edward to himself. 'For once in my life, I'll do what I like. Maud can go hang!'

And the very next morning he had walked into that palace of plate glass, with its lordly inmates in their glory of gleaming enamel and shimmering metal, and with an insouciance that surprised himself, he bought the car. It was the easiest thing in the world, buying a car!

It had been his for four days now. He had gone about, outwardly calm, but inwardly bathed in ecstasy. And to Maud he had as yet breathed no word. For four days, in his luncheon hour, he had received instruction in the handling of the lovely creature. He was an apt pupil.

Tomorrow, Christmas Eve, he was to take her out into the country. He had lied to Maud, and he would lie again if need be. He was enslaved body and soul by his new possession. It stood to him for Romance, for Adventure, for all the things that he had longed for and had never had. Tomorrow, he and his mistress would take the road together. They would rush through the keen cold air, leaving the throb and fret of London far behind—out into the wide clear spaces . . .

At this moment, Edward, though he did not know it, was very near to being a poet.

Tomorrow—

He looked down at the book in his hand—*When Love is King*. He laughed and stuffed it into his pocket. The car, and the red lips of the Marchesa Bianca, and the amazing prowess of Bill seemed all mixed up together. Tomorrow—

The weather, usually a sorry jade to those who count upon her, was kindly disposed towards Edward. She gave him the day of his dreams, a day of glittering frost, and pale-blue sky, and a primrose-yellow sun.

So, in a mood of high adventure, of dare-devil wickedness, Edward drove out of London. There was trouble at Hyde Park Corner, and a sad *contretemps* at Putney Bridge, there was much protesting of gears, and a frequent

111

jarring of brakes, and much abuse was freely showered upon Edward by the drivers of other vehicles. But for a novice he did not acquit himself so badly, and presently he came out on to one of those fair wide roads that are the joy of the motorist. There was little congestion on this particular road today. Edward drove on and on, drunk with his mastery over this creature of the gleaming sides, speeding through the cold white world with the elation of a god.

It was a delirious day. He stopped for lunch at an old-fashioned inn, and again later for tea. Then reluctantly he turned homewards—back again to London, to Maud, to the inevitable explanation, recriminations . . .

He shook off the thought with a sigh. Let tomorrow look after itself. He still had today. And what could be more fascinating than this? Rushing through the darkness with the headlights searching out the way in front. Why, this was the best of all!

He judged that he had no time to stop anywhere for dinner. This driving through the darkness was a ticklish business. It was going to take longer to get back to London than he had thought. It was just eight o'clock when he passed through Hindhead and came out upon the rim of the Devil's Punch Bowl. There was moonlight, and the snow that had fallen two days ago was still unmelted.

He stopped the car and stood staring. What did it matter if he didn't get back to London until midnight? What did it matter if he never got back? He wasn't going to tear himself away from this at once.

He got out of the car, and approached the edge. There

was a path winding down temptingly near him. Edward yielded to the spell. For the next half-hour he wandered deliriously in a snowbound world. Never had he imagined anything quite like this. And it was his, his very own, given to him by his shining mistress who waited for him faithfully on the road above.

He climbed up again, got into the car and drove off, still a little dizzy from that discovery of sheer beauty which comes to the most prosaic men once in a while.

Then, with a sigh, he came to himself, and thrust his hand into the pocket of the car where he had stuffed an additional muffler earlier in the day.

But the muffler was no longer there. The pocket was empty. No, not completely empty—there was something scratchy and hard—like pebbles.

Edward thrust his hand deep down. In another minute he was staring like a man bereft of his senses. The object that he held in his hand, dangling from his fingers, with the moonlight striking a hundred fires from it, was a diamond necklace.

Edward stared and stared. But there was no doubting possible. A diamond necklace worth probably thousands of pounds (for the stones were large ones) had been casually reposing in the side-pocket of the car.

But who had put it there? It had certainly not been there when he started from town. Someone must have come along when he was walking about in the snow, and deliberately thrust it in. But why? Why choose *his* car? Had the owner of the necklace made a mistake? Or was it—could it possibly be—a *stolen* necklace?

*Agatha Christie*

And then, as all these thoughts went whirling through his brain, Edward suddenly stiffened and went cold all over. *This was not his car.*

It was very like it, yes. It was the same brilliant shade of scarlet—red as the Marchesa Bianca's lips—it had the same long and gleaming nose, but by a thousand small signs, Edward realized that it was not his car. Its shining newness was scarred here and there, it bore signs, faint but unmistakeable, of wear and tear. In that case . . .

Edward, without more ado, made haste to turn the car. Turning was not his strong point. With the car in reverse, he invariably lost his head and twisted the wheel the wrong way. Also, he frequently became entangled between the accelerator and the foot brake with disastrous results. In the end, however, he succeeded, and straightaway the car began purring up the hill again.

Edward remembered that there had been another car standing some little distance away. He had not noticed it particularly at the time. He had returned from his walk by a different path from that by which he had gone down into the hollow. This second path had brought him out on the road immediately behind, as he had thought, his own car. It must really have been the other one.

In about ten minutes he was once more at the spot where he had halted. But there was now no car at all by the roadside. Whoever had owned this car must now have gone off in Edward's—he also, perhaps, misled by the resemblance.

Edward took out the diamond necklace from his pocket and let it run through his fingers perplexedly.

114

What to do next? Run on to the nearest police station? Explain the circumstances, hand over the necklace, and give the number of his own car.

By the by, what was the number of his car? Edward thought and thought, but for the life of him he couldn't remember. He felt a cold sinking sensation. He was going to look the most utter fool at the police station. There was an eight in it, that was all that he could remember. Of course, it didn't really matter—at least . . . He looked uncomfortably at the diamonds. Supposing they should think—oh, but they wouldn't—and yet again they might—that he had stolen the car and the diamonds? Because, after all, when one came to think of it, would anyone in their senses thrust a valuable diamond necklace carelessly into the open pocket of a car?

Edward got out and went round to the back of the motor. Its number was XRI0061. Beyond the fact that that was certainly not the number of his car, it conveyed nothing to him. Then he set to work systematically to search all the pockets. In the one where he had found the diamonds he made a discovery—a small scrap of paper with some words pencilled on it. By the light of the headlights, Edward read them easily enough.

'*Meet me, Greane, corner of Salter's Lane, ten o'clock.*'

He remembered the name Greane. He had seen it on a sign-post earlier in the day. In a minute, his mind was made up. He would go to this village, Greane, find Salter's Lane, meet the person who had written the note, and explain the circumstances. That would be much better than looking a fool in the local police station.

He started off almost happily. After all, this was an adventure. This was the sort of thing that didn't happen every day. The diamond necklace made it exciting and mysterious.

He had some little difficulty in finding Greane, and still more difficulty in finding Salter's Lane, but after knocking up two cottages, he succeeded.

Still, it was a few minutes after the appointed hour when he drove cautiously along a narrow road, keeping a sharp look-out on the left-hand side where he had been told Salter's Lane branched off.

He came upon it quite suddenly round a bend, and even as he drew up, a figure came forward out of the darkness.

'At last!' a girl's voice cried. 'What an age you've been, Gerald!'

As she spoke, the girl stepped right into the glare of the headlights, and Edward caught his breath. She was the most glorious creature he had ever seen.

She was quite young, with hair black as night, and wonderful scarlet lips. The heavy cloak that she wore swung open, and Edward saw that she was in full evening dress—a kind of flame-coloured sheath, outlining her perfect body. Round her neck was a row of exquisite pearls.

Suddenly the girl started.

'Why,' she cried; 'it isn't Gerald.'

'No,' said Edward hastily. 'I must explain.' He took the diamond necklace from his pocket and held it out to her. 'My name is Edward—'

He got no further, for the girl clapped her hands and broke in:

'Edward, of course! I am so glad. But that idiot Jimmy told me over the phone that he was sending Gerald along with the car. It's awfully sporting of you to come. I've been dying to meet you. Remember I haven't seen you since I was six years old. I see you've got the necklace all right. Shove it in your pocket again. The village policeman might come along and see it. Brrr, it's cold as ice waiting here! Let me get in.'

As though in a dream Edward opened the door, and she sprang lightly in beside him. Her furs swept his cheek, and an elusive scent, like that of violets after rain, assailed his nostrils.

He had no plan, no definite thought even. In a minute, without conscious volition, he had yielded himself to the adventure. She had called him Edward—what matter if he were the wrong Edward? She would find him out soon enough. In the meantime, let the game go on. He let in the clutch and they glided off.

Presently the girl laughed. Her laugh was just as wonderful as the rest of her.

'It's easy to see you don't know much about cars. I suppose they don't have them out there?'

'I wonder where "out there" is?' thought Edward. Aloud he said, 'Not much.'

'Better let me drive,' said the girl. 'It's tricky work finding your way round these lanes until we get on the main road again.'

He relinquished his place to her gladly. Presently they

were humming through the night at a pace and with a recklessness that secretly appalled Edward. She turned her head towards him.

'I like pace. Do you? You know—you're not a bit like Gerald. No one would ever take you to be brothers. You're not a bit like what I imagined, either.'

'I suppose,' said Edward, 'that I'm so completely ordinary. Is that it?'

'Not ordinary—different. I can't make you out. How's poor old Jimmy? Very fed up, I suppose?'

'Oh, Jimmy's all right,' said Edward.

'It's easy enough to say that—but it's rough luck on him having a sprained ankle. Did he tell you the whole story?'

'Not a word. I'm completely in the dark. I wish you'd enlighten me.'

'Oh, the thing worked like a dream. Jimmy went in at the front door, togged up in his girl's clothes. I gave him a minute or two, and then shinned up to the window. Agnes Larella's maid was there laying out Agnes's dress and jewels, and all the rest. Then there was a great yell downstairs, and the squib went off, and everyone shouted fire. The maid dashed out, and I hopped in, helped myself to the necklace, and was out and down in a flash, and out of the place by the back way across the Punch Bowl. I shoved the necklace and the notice where to pick me up in the pocket of the car in passing. Then I joined Louise at the hotel, having shed my snow boots of course. Perfect alibi for me. She'd no idea I'd been out at all.'

'And what about Jimmy?'

'Well, you know more about that than I do.'

'He didn't tell me anything,' said Edward easily.

'Well, in the general rag, he caught his foot in his skirt and managed to sprain it. They had to carry him to the car, and the Larellas' chauffeur drove him home. Just fancy if the chauffeur had happened to put his hand in the pocket!'

Edward laughed with her, but his mind was busy. He understood the position more or less now. The name of Larella was vaguely familiar to him—it was a name that spelt wealth. This girl, and an unknown man called Jimmy, had conspired together to steal the necklace, and had succeeded. Owing to his sprained ankle and the presence of the Larellas' chauffeur Jimmy had not been able to look in the pocket of the car before telephoning to the girl— probably had had no wish to do so. But it was almost certain that the other unknown 'Gerald' would do so at any early opportunity. And in it, he would find Edward's muffler!

'Good going,' said the girl.

A tram flashed past them, they were on the outskirts of London. They flashed in and out of the traffic. Edward's heart stood in his mouth. She was a wonderful driver, this girl, but she took risks!

Quarter of an hour later they drew up before an imposing house in a frigid square.

'We can shed some of our clothing here,' said the girl, 'before we go on to Ritson's.'

'Ritson's?' queried Edward. He mentioned the famous night-club almost reverently.

'Yes, didn't Gerald tell you?'

'He did not,' said Edward grimly. 'What about my clothes?'

She frowned.

'Didn't they tell you *anything*? We'll rig you up somehow. We've got to carry this through.'

A stately butler opened the door and stood aside to let them enter.

'Mr Gerald Champneys rang up, your ladyship. He was very anxious to speak to you, but he wouldn't leave a message.'

'I bet he was anxious to speak to her,' said Edward to himself. 'At any rate, I know my full name now. Edward Champneys. But who is she? Your ladyship, they called her. What does she want to steal a necklace for? Bridge debts?'

In the *feuilletons* which he occasionally read, the beautiful and titled heroine was always driven desperate by bridge debts.

Edward was led away by the stately butler, and delivered over to a smooth-mannered valet. A quarter of an hour later he rejoined his hostess in the hall, exquisitely attired in evening clothes made in Savile Row which fitted him to a nicety.

Heavens! What a night!

They drove in the car to the famous Ritson's. In common with everyone else Edward had read scandalous paragraphs concerning Ritson's. Anyone who was anyone turned up at Ritson's sooner or later. Edward's only fear was that someone who knew the real Edward Champneys might turn up. He consoled himself by the reflection that the real man had evidently been out of England for some years.

Sitting at a little table against the wall, they sipped cocktails. Cocktails! To the simple Edward they represented the quintessence of the fast life. The girl, wrapped in a wonderful embroidered shawl, sipped nonchalantly. Suddenly she dropped the shawl from her shoulders and rose.

'Let's dance.'

Now the one thing that Edward could do to perfection was to dance. When he and Maud took the floor together at the Palais de Danse, lesser lights stood still and watched in admiration.

'I nearly forgot,' said the girl suddenly. 'The necklace?'

She held out her hand. Edward, completely bewildered, drew it from his pocket and gave it to her. To his utter amazement, she coolly clasped it round her neck. Then she smiled up at him intoxicatingly.

'Now,' she said softly, 'we'll dance.'

They danced. And in all Ritson's nothing more perfect could be seen.

Then, as at length they returned to their table, an old gentleman with a would-be rakish air accosted Edward's companion.

'Ah! Lady Noreen, always dancing! Yes, yes. Is Captain Folliot here tonight?'

'Jimmy's taken a toss—racked his ankle.'

'You don't say so? How did that happen?'

'No details as yet.'

She laughed and passed on.

Edward followed, his brain in a whirl. He knew now. Lady Noreen Elliot, the famous Lady Noreen herself, perhaps the most talked of girl in England. Celebrated for her beauty, for her daring—the leader of that set known as the Bright Young People. Her engagement to Captain James Folliot, V.C., of the Household Cavalry, had been recently announced.

But the necklace? He still couldn't understand the necklace. He must risk giving himself away, but know he must.

As they sat down again, he pointed to it.

'Why that, Noreen?' he said. 'Tell me why?'

She smiled dreamily, her eyes far away, the spell of the dance still holding her.

'It's difficult for you to understand, I suppose. One gets so tired of the same thing—always the same thing. Treasure hunts were all very well for a while, but one gets used to everything. "Burglaries" were my idea. Fifty pounds entrance fee, and lots to be drawn. This is the third. Jimmy and I drew Agnes Larella. You know the rules? Burglary to be carried out within three days and the loot to be worn for at least an hour in a public place, or you forfeit your stake and a hundred-pound fine. It's rough luck on Jimmy spraining his ankle, but we'll scoop the pool all right.'

'I see,' said Edward, drawing a deep breath. 'I see.'

Noreen rose suddenly, pulling her shawl round her.

'Drive me somewhere in the car. Down to the docks. Somewhere horrible and exciting. Wait a minute—' She reached up and unclasped the diamonds from her neck.

'You'd better take these again. I don't want to be murdered for them.'

They went out of Ritson's together. The car stood in a small by-street, narrow and dark. As they turned the corner towards it, another car drew up to the curb, and a young man sprang out.

'Thank the Lord, Noreen, I've got hold of you at last,' he cried. 'There's the devil to pay. That ass Jimmy got off with the wrong car. God knows where those diamonds are at this minute. We're in the devil of a mess.'

Lady Noreen stared at him.

'What do you mean? We've got the diamonds—at least Edward has.'

'Edward?'

'Yes.' She made a slight gesture to indicate the figure by her side.

'It's I who am in the devil of a mess,' thought Edward. 'Ten to one this is brother Gerald.'

The young man stared at him.

'What do you mean?' he said slowly. 'Edward's in Scotland.'

'Oh!' cried the girl. She stared at Edward. 'Oh!'

Her colour came and went.

'So you,' she said, in a low voice, 'are the real thing?'

It took Edward just one minute to grasp the situation. There was awe in the girl's eyes—was it, could it be—admiration? Should he explain? Nothing so tame! He would play up to the end.

He bowed ceremoniously.

'I have to thank you, Lady Noreen,' he said, in the best highwayman manner, 'for a most delightful evening.'

One quick look he cast at the car from which the other had just alighted. A scarlet car with a shining bonnet. His car!

'And I will wish you good-evening.'

One quick spring and he was inside, his foot on the clutch. The car started forward. Gerald stood paralysed, but the girl was quicker. As the car slid past she leapt for it, alighting on the running board.

The car swerved, shot blindly round the corner and pulled up. Noreen, still panting from her spring, laid her hand on Edward's arm.

'You must give it me—oh, you must give it me. I've got to return it to Agnes Larella. Be a sport—we've had a good evening together—we've danced—we've been—pals. Won't you give it to me? To *me*?'

A woman who intoxicated you with her beauty. There were such women then . . .

Also, Edward was only too anxious to get rid of the necklace. It was a heaven-sent opportunity for a *beau geste*.

He took it from his pocket and dropped it into her outstretched hand.

'We've been—pals,' he said.

'Ah!' Her eyes smouldered—lit up.

Then surprisingly she bent her head to him. For a moment he held her, her lips against his . . .

Then she jumped off. The scarlet car sped forward with a great leap.

Romance!

Adventure!

At twelve o'clock on Christmas Day, Edward Robinson strode into the tiny drawing-room of a house in Clapham with the customary greeting of 'Merry Christmas'.

Maud, who was rearranging a piece of holly, greeted him coldly.

'Have a good day in the country with that friend of yours?' she inquired.

'Look here,' said Edward. 'That was a lie I told you. I won a competition—£500, and I bought a car with it. I didn't tell you because I knew you'd kick up a row about it. That's the first thing. I've bought the car and there's nothing more to be said about it. The second thing is this—I'm not going to hang about for years. My prospects are quite good enough and I mean to marry you next month. See?'

'Oh!' said Maud faintly.

Was this—could this be—*Edward* speaking in this masterful fashion?

'Will you?' said Edward. 'Yes or no?'

She gazed at him, fascinated. There was awe and admiration in her eyes, and the sight of that look was intoxicating to Edward. Gone was that patient motherliness which had roused him to exasperation.

So had the Lady Noreen looked at him last night. But the Lady Noreen had receded far away, right into the region of Romance, side by side with the Marchesa Bianca. This was the Real Thing. This was his woman.

'Yes or no?' he repeated, and drew a step nearer.

'Ye—ye-es,' faltered Maud. 'But, oh, Edward, what has happened to you? You're quite different today.'

'Yes,' said Edward. 'For twenty-four hours I've been a man instead of a worm—and, by God, it pays!'

He caught her in his arms almost as Bill the superman might have done.

'Do you love me, Maud? Tell me, do you love me?'

'Oh, Edward!' breathed Maud. 'I adore you . . .'

# *Accident*

'. . . And I tell you this—it's the same woman—not a doubt of it!'

Captain Haydock looked into the eager, vehement face of his friend and sighed. He wished Evans would not be so positive and so jubilant. In the course of a career spent at sea, the old sea captain had learned to leave things that did not concern him well alone. His friend, Evans, late C.I.D. Inspector, had a different philosophy of life. 'Acting on information received—' had been his motto in early days, and he had improved upon it to the extent of finding out his own information. Inspector Evans had been a very smart, wide-awake officer, and had justly earned the promotion which had been his. Even now, when he had retired from the force, and had settled down in the country cottage of his dreams, his professional instinct was still active.

'Don't often forget a face,' he reiterated complacently. 'Mrs Anthony—yes, it's Mrs Anthony right enough. When you said Mrs Merrowdene—I knew her at once.'

Captain Haydock stirred uneasily. The Merrowdenes were his nearest neighbours, barring Evans himself, and this identifying of Mrs Merrowdene with a former heroine of a *cause célèbre* distressed him.

'It's a long time ago,' he said rather weakly.

'Nine years,' said Evans, accurately as ever. 'Nine years and three months. You remember the case?'

'In a vague sort of way.'

'Anthony turned out to be an arsenic eater,' said Evans, 'so they acquitted her.'

'Well, why shouldn't they?'

'No reason in the world. Only verdict they could give on the evidence. Absolutely correct.'

'Then that's all right,' said Haydock. 'And I don't see what we're bothering about.'

'Who's bothering?'

'I thought you were.'

'Not at all.'

'The thing's over and done with,' summed up the captain. 'If Mrs Merrowdene at one time of her life was unfortunate enough to be tried and acquitted for murder—'

'It's not usually considered unfortunate to be acquitted,' put in Evans.

'You know what I mean,' said Captain Haydock irritably. 'If the poor lady has been through that harrowing experience, it's no business of ours to rake it up, is it?'

Evans did not answer.

'Come now, Evans. The lady was innocent—you've just said so.'

'I didn't say she was innocent. I said she was acquitted.'

'It's the same thing.'

'Not always.'

Captain Haydock, who had commenced to tap his pipe out against the side of his chair, stopped, and sat up with a very alert expression.

'Hallo—allo—allo,' he said. 'The wind's in that quarter, is it? You think she wasn't innocent?'

'I wouldn't say that. I just—don't know. Anthony was in the habit of taking arsenic. His wife got it for him. One day, by mistake, he takes far too much. Was the mistake his or his wife's? Nobody could tell, and the jury very properly gave her the benefit of the doubt. That's all quite right and I'm not finding fault with it. All the same—I'd like to *know*.'

Captain Haydock transferred his attention to his pipe once more.

'Well,' he said comfortably. 'It's none of our business.'

'I'm not so sure . . .'

'But surely—'

'Listen to me a minute. This man, Merrowdene—in his laboratory this evening, fiddling round with tests—you remember—'

'Yes. He mentioned Marsh's test for arsenic. Said *you* would know all about it—it was in *your* line—and chuckled. He wouldn't have said that if he'd thought for one moment—'

Evans interrupted him.

'You mean he wouldn't have said that if he *knew*. They've been married how long—six years you told me? I bet you anything he has no idea his wife is the once notorious Mrs Anthony.'

'And he will certainly not know it from me,' said Captain Haydock stiffly.

129

Evans paid no attention, but went on:

'You interrupted me just now. After Marsh's test, Merrowdene heated a substance in a test-tube, the metallic residue he dissolved in water and then precipitated it by adding silver nitrate. That was a test for chlorates. A neat unassuming little test. But I chanced to read these words in a book that stood open on the table:

"$H_2SO_4$ *decomposes chlorates with evolution of* $CL_4O_2$. *If heated, violent explosions occur; the mixture ought therefore to be kept cool and only very small quantities used.*"'

Haydock stared at his friend.

'Well, what about it?'

'Just this. In my profession we've got tests too—tests for murder. There's adding up the facts—weighing them, dissecting the residue when you've allowed for prejudice and the general inaccuracy of witnesses. But there's another test of murder—one that is fairly accurate, but rather—dangerous! *A murderer is seldom content with one crime.* Give him time, and a lack of suspicion, and he'll commit another. You catch a man—has he murdered his wife or hasn't he?—perhaps the case isn't very black against him. Look into his past—if you find that he's had several wives—and that they've all died shall we say—rather curiously?—then you *know*! I'm not speaking *legally*, you understand. I'm speaking of *moral* certainty. Once you *know*, you can go ahead looking for evidence.'

'Well?'

'I'm coming to the point. That's all right if there *is* a past to look into. But suppose you catch your murderer at his or her first crime? Then that test will be one from which you get no reaction. But suppose the prisoner is acquitted—starting life under another name. Will or will not the murderer repeat the crime?'

'That's a horrible idea!'

'Do you still say it's none of our business?'

'Yes, I do. You've no reason to think that Mrs Merrowdene is anything but a perfectly innocent woman.'

The ex-inspector was silent for a moment. Then he said slowly:

'I told you that we looked into her past and found nothing. That's not quite true. There was a stepfather. As a girl of eighteen she had a fancy for some young man—and her stepfather exerted his authority to keep them apart. She and her stepfather went for a walk along a rather dangerous part of the cliff. There was an accident—the stepfather went too near the edge—it gave way, and he went over and was killed.'

'You don't think—'

'It was an accident. *Accident!* Anthony's overdose of arsenic was an accident. She'd never have been tried if it hadn't transpired that there was another man—he sheered off, by the way. Looked as though he weren't satisfied even if the jury were. I tell you, Haydock, where that woman is concerned I'm afraid of another—accident!'

The old captain shrugged his shoulders.

'It's been nine years since that affair. Why should there be another "accident", as you call it, now?'

131

'I didn't say now. I said some day or other. If the necessary motive arose.'

Captain Haydock shrugged his shoulders.

'Well, I don't know how you're going to guard against that.'

'Neither do I,' said Evans ruefully.

'I should leave well alone,' said Captain Haydock. 'No good ever came of butting into other people's affairs.'

But that advice was not palatable to the ex-inspector. He was a man of patience but determination. Taking leave of his friend, he sauntered down to the village, revolving in his mind the possibilities of some kind of successful action.

Turning into the post office to buy some stamps, he ran into the object of his solicitude, George Merrowdene. The ex-chemistry professor was a small dreamy-looking man, gentle and kindly in manner, and usually completely absent-minded. He recognized the other and greeted him amicably, stooping to recover the letters that the impact had caused him to drop on the ground. Evans stooped also and, more rapid in his movements than the other, secured them first, handing them back to their owner with an apology.

He glanced down at them in doing so, and the address on the topmost suddenly awakened all his suspicions anew. It bore the name of a well-known insurance firm.

Instantly his mind was made up. The guileless George Merrowdene hardly realized how it came about that he and the ex-inspector were strolling down the village together, and still less could he have said how it came about that the conversation should come round to the subject of life insurance.

Evans had no difficulty in attaining his object. Merrowdene of his own accord volunteered the information that he had just insured his life for his wife's benefit, and asked Evans's opinion of the company in question.

'I made some rather unwise investments,' he explained. 'As a result my income has diminished. If anything were to happen to me, my wife would be left very badly off. This insurance will put things right.'

'She didn't object to the idea?' inquired Evans casually. 'Some ladies do, you know. Feel it's unlucky—that sort of thing.'

'Oh, Margaret is very practical,' said Merrowdene, smiling. 'Not at all superstitious. In fact, I believe it was her idea originally. She didn't like my being so worried.'

Evans had got the information he wanted. He left the other shortly afterwards, and his lips were set in a grim line. The late Mr Anthony had insured his life in his wife's favour a few weeks before his death.

Accustomed to rely on his instincts, he was perfectly sure in his own mind. But how to act was another matter. He wanted, not to arrest a criminal red-handed, but to prevent a crime being committed, and that was a very different and a very much more difficult thing.

All day he was very thoughtful. There was a Primrose League Fête that afternoon held in the grounds of the local squire, and he went to it, indulging in the penny dip, guessing the weight of a pig, and shying at coconuts all with the same look of abstracted concentration on his face.

He even indulged in half a crown's worth of Zara, the Crystal Gazer, smiling a little to himself as he did so, remembering his own activities against fortune-tellers in his official days.

He did not pay very much heed to her sing-song droning voice—till the end of a sentence held his attention.

'. . . And you will very shortly—very shortly indeed—be engaged on a matter of life or death . . . Life or death to one person.'

'Eh—what's that?' he asked abruptly.

'A decision—you have a decision to make. You must be very careful—very, very careful . . . If you were to make a mistake—the smallest mistake—'

'Yes?'

The fortune-teller shivered. Inspector Evans knew it was all nonsense, but he was nevertheless impressed. 'I warn you—*you must not make a mistake*. If you do, I see the result clearly—a death . . .'

Odd, damned odd. A death. Fancy her lighting upon that!

'If I make a mistake a death will result? Is that it?'

'Yes.'

'In that case,' said Evans, rising to his feet and handing over half a crown, 'I mustn't make a mistake, eh?'

He spoke lightly enough, but as he went out of the tent, his jaw set determinedly. Easy to say—not so easy to be sure of doing. He mustn't make a slip. A life, a vulnerable human life depended on it.

And there was no one to help him. He looked across at the figure of his friend Haydock in the distance. No help

134

there. 'Leave things alone,' was Haydock's motto. And that wouldn't do here.

Haydock was talking to a woman. She moved away from him and came towards Evans and the inspector recognized her. It was Mrs Merrowdene. On an impulse he put himself deliberately in her path.

Mrs Merrowdene was rather a fine-looking woman. She had a broad serene brow, very beautiful brown eyes, and a placid expression. She had the look of an Italian madonna which she heightened by parting her hair in the middle and looping it over her ears. She had a deep rather sleepy voice.

She smiled up at Evans, a contented welcoming smile.

'I thought it was you, Mrs Anthony—I mean Mrs Merrowdene,' he said glibly.

He made the slip deliberately, watching her without seeming to do so. He saw her eyes widen, heard the quick intake of her breath. But her eyes did not falter. She gazed at him steadily and proudly.

'I was looking for my husband,' she said quietly. 'Have you seen him anywhere about?'

'He was over in that direction when I last saw him.'

They went side by side in the direction indicated, chatting quietly and pleasantly. The inspector felt his admiration mounting. What a woman! What self-command. What wonderful poise. A remarkable woman—and a very dangerous one. He felt sure—a very dangerous one.

He still felt very uneasy, though he was satisfied with his initial step. He had let her know that he recognized her. That would put her on her guard. She would not dare attempt anything rash. There was the question of Merrowdene. If he could be warned . . .

They found the little man absently contemplating a china doll which had fallen to his share in the penny dip. His wife suggested going home and he agreed eagerly. Mrs Merrowdene turned to the inspector:

'Won't you come back with us and have a quiet cup of tea, Mr Evans?'

Was there a faint note of challenge in her voice? He thought there was.

'Thank you, Mrs Merrowdene. I should like to very much.'

They walked there, talking together of pleasant ordinary things. The sun shone, a breeze blew gently, everything around them was pleasant and ordinary.

Their maid was out at the fête, Mrs Merrowdene explained, when they arrived at the charming old-world cottage. She went into her room to remove her hat, returning to set out tea and boil the kettle on a little silver lamp. From a shelf near the fireplace she took three small bowls and saucers.

'We have some very special Chinese tea,' she explained. 'And we always drink it in the Chinese manner—out of bowls, not cups.'

She broke off, peered into a bowl and exchanged it for another with an exclamation of annoyance.

'George—it's too bad of you. You've been taking these bowls again.'

'I'm sorry, dear,' said the professor apologetically. 'They're such a convenient size. The ones I ordered haven't come.'

'One of these days you'll poison us all,' said his wife with a half-laugh. 'Mary finds them in the laboratory and brings them back here, and never troubles to wash them out unless they've anything very noticeable in them. Why, you were using one of them for potassium cyanide the other day. Really, George, it's frightfully dangerous.'

Merrowdene looked a little irritated.

'Mary's no business to remove things from the laboratory. She's not to touch anything there.'

'But we often leave our teacups there after tea. How is she to know? Be reasonable, dear.'

The professor went into his laboratory, murmuring to himself, and with a smile Mrs Merrowdene poured boiling water on the tea and blew out the flame of the little silver lamp.

Evans was puzzled. Yet a glimmering of light penetrated to him. For some reason or other, Mrs Merrowdene was showing her hand. Was this to be the 'accident'? Was she speaking of all this so as deliberately to prepare her alibi beforehand? So that when, one day, the 'accident' happened, he would be forced to give evidence in her favour. Stupid of her, if so, because before that—

Suddenly he drew in his breath. She had poured the tea into the three bowls. One she set before him, one before herself, the other she placed on a little table by the fire near the chair her husband usually sat in, and it was as she placed this last one on the table that a little strange smile curved round her lips. It was the smile that did it.

*He knew!*

A remarkable woman—a dangerous woman. No

waiting—no preparation. This afternoon—this very afternoon—with him here as witness. The boldness of it took his breath away.

It was clever—it was damnably clever. He would be able to prove nothing. She counted on his not suspecting—simply because it was 'so soon'. A woman of lightning rapidity of thought and action.

He drew a deep breath and leaned forward.

'Mrs Merrowdene, I'm a man of queer whims. Will you be very kind and indulge me in one of them?'

She looked inquiring but unsuspicious.

He rose, took the bowl from in front of her and crossed to the little table where he substituted it for the other. This other he brought back and placed in front of her.

'I want to see you drink this.'

Her eyes met his. They were steady, unfathomable. The colour slowly drained from her face.

She stretched out her hand, raised the cup. He held his breath. Supposing all along he had made a mistake.

She raised it to her lips—at the last moment, with a shudder, she leant forward and quickly poured it into a pot containing a fern. Then she sat back and gazed at him defiantly.

He drew a long sigh of relief, and sat down again.

'Well?' she said.

Her voice had altered. It was slightly mocking—defiant.

He answered her soberly and quietly:

'You are a very clever woman, Mrs Merrowdene. I think you understand me. There must be no—repetition. You know what I mean?'

'I know what you mean.'

Her voice was even, devoid of expression. He nodded his head, satisfied. She was a clever woman, and she didn't want to be hanged.

'To your long life and to that of your husband,' he said significantly, and raised his tea to his lips.

Then his face changed. It contorted horribly . . . he tried to rise—to cry out . . . His body stiffened—his face went purple. He fell back sprawling over his chair—his limbs convulsed.

Mrs Merrowdene leaned forward, watching him. A little smile crossed her lips. She spoke to him—very softly and gently.

'You made a mistake, Mr Evans. You thought I wanted to kill George . . . How stupid of you—how very stupid.'

She sat there a minute longer looking at the dead man, the third man who had threatened to cross her path and separate her from the man she loved.

Her smile broadened. She looked more than ever like a madonna. Then she raised her voice and called:

'George, George! . . . Oh, do come here! I'm afraid there's been the most dreadful accident . . . Poor Mr Evans . . .'

# Jane in Search of a Job

Jane Cleveland rustled the pages of the *Daily Leader* and sighed. A deep sigh that came from the innermost recesses of her being. She looked with distaste at the marble-topped table, the poached egg on toast which reposed on it, and the small pot of tea. Not because she was not hungry. That was far from being the case. Jane was extremely hungry. At that moment she felt like consuming a pound and a half of well-cooked beefsteak, with chip potatoes, and possibly French beans. The whole washed down with some more exciting vintage than tea.

But young women whose exchequers are in a parlous condition cannot be choosers. Jane was lucky to be able to order a poached egg and a pot of tea. It seemed unlikely that she would be able to do so tomorrow. That is unless—

She turned once more to the advertisement columns of the *Daily Leader*. To put it plainly, Jane was out of a job, and the position was becoming acute. Already the genteel lady who presided over the shabby boarding-house was looking askance at this particular young woman.

'And yet,' said Jane to herself, throwing up her chin

indignantly, which was a habit of hers, 'and yet I'm intelligent and good-looking and well educated. What more does anyone want?'

According to the *Daily Leader*, they seemed to want shorthand typists of vast experience, managers for business houses with a little capital to invest, ladies to share in the profits of poultry farming (here again a little capital was required), and innumerable cooks, housemaids and parlourmaids—particularly parlourmaids.

'I wouldn't mind being a parlourmaid,' said Jane to herself. 'But there again, no one would take me without experience. I could go somewhere, I dare say, as a Willing Young Girl—but they don't pay willing young girls anything to speak of.'

She sighed again, propped the paper up in front of her, and attacked the poached egg with all the vigour of healthy youth.

When the last mouthful had been despatched, she turned the paper, and studied the Agony and Personal column whilst she drank her tea. The Agony column was always the last hope.

Had she but possessed a couple of thousand pounds, the thing would have been easy enough. There were at least seven unique opportunities—all yielding not less than three thousand a year. Jane's lip curled a little.

'If I had two thousand pounds,' she murmured, 'it wouldn't be easy to separate me from it.'

She cast her eyes rapidly down to the bottom of the column and ascended with the ease born of long practice.

There was the lady who gave such wonderful prices for

cast-off clothing. 'Ladies' wardrobes inspected at their own dwellings.' There were gentlemen who bought ANYTHING—but principally TEETH. There were ladies of title going abroad who would dispose of their furs at a ridiculous figure. There was the distressed clergyman and the hard-working widow, and the disabled officer, all needing sums varying from fifty pounds to two thousand. And then suddenly Jane came to an abrupt halt. She put down her teacup and read the advertisement through again.

'There's a catch in it, of course,' she murmured. 'There always is a catch in these sort of things. I shall have to be careful. But still—'

The advertisement which so intrigued Jane Cleveland ran as follows:

*If a young lady of twenty-five to thirty years of age, eyes dark blue, very fair hair, black lashes and brows, straight nose, slim figure, height five feet seven inches, good mimic and able to speak French, will call at 7 Endersleigh Street, between 5 and 6 p.m., she will hear of something to her advantage.*

'Guileless Gwendolen, or why girls go wrong,' murmured Jane. 'I shall certainly have to be careful. But there are too many specifications, really, for that sort of thing. I wonder now . . . Let us overhaul the catalogue.'

She proceeded to do so.

'Twenty-five to thirty—I'm twenty-six. Eyes dark blue, that's right. Hair very fair—black lashes and brows—all OK. Straight nose? Ye-es—straight enough, anyway. It doesn't hook or turn up. And I've got a slim figure—slim even for nowadays. I'm only five feet six inches—but I could wear high heels. I *am* a good mimic—nothing wonderful, but I can copy people's voices, and I speak French like an angel or a Frenchwoman. In fact, I'm absolutely the goods. They ought to tumble over themselves with delight when I turn up. Jane Cleveland, go in and win.'

Resolutely Jane tore out the advertisement and placed it in her handbag. Then she demanded her bill, with a new briskness in her voice.

At ten minutes to five Jane was reconnoitring in the neighbourhood of Endersleigh Street. Endersleigh Street itself is a small street sandwiched between two larger streets in the neighbourhood of Oxford Circus. It is drab, but respectable.

No 7 seemed in no way different from the neighbouring houses. It was composed like they were of offices. But looking up at it, it dawned upon Jane for the first time that she was not the only blue-eyed, fair-haired, straight-nosed, slim-figured girl of between twenty-five and thirty years of age. London was evidently full of such girls, and forty or fifty of them at least were grouped outside No 7 Endersleigh Street.

'Competition,' said Jane. 'I'd better join the queue quickly.'

She did so, just as three more girls turned the corner of the street. Others followed them. Jane amused herself by taking stock of her immediate neighbours. In each case she managed to find something wrong—fair eyelashes instead of dark, eyes more grey than blue, fair hair that owed its fairness to art and not to Nature, interesting variations in noses, and figures that only an all-embracing charity could have described as slim. Jane's spirits rose.

'I believe I've got as good an all-round chance as anyone,' she murmured to herself. 'I wonder what it's all about? A beauty chorus, I hope.'

The queue was moving slowly but steadily forward. Presently a second stream of girls began, issuing from inside the house. Some of them tossed their heads, some of them smirked.

'Rejected,' said Jane, with glee. 'I hope to goodness they won't be full up before I get in.'

And still the queue of girls moved forwards. There were anxious glances in tiny mirrors, and a frenzied powdering of noses. Lipsticks were brandished freely.

'I wish I had a smarter hat,' said Jane to herself sadly.

At last it was her turn. Inside the door of the house was a glass door at one side, with the legend, Messrs. Cuthbertsons, inscribed on it. It was through this glass door that the applicants were passing one by one. Jane's turn came. She drew a deep breath and entered.

Inside was an outer office, obviously intended for clerks. At the end was another glass door. Jane was directed to pass through this, and did so. She found herself in a smaller room. There was a big desk in it, and behind the desk was a keen-eyed man of middle age with a thick rather foreign-looking moustache. His glance swept over Jane, then he pointed to a door on the left.

'Wait in there, please,' he said crisply.

Jane obeyed. The apartment she entered was already occupied. Five girls sat there, all very upright and all glaring at each other. It was clear to Jane that she had been included amongst the likely candidates, and her spirits rose. Nevertheless, she was forced to admit that these five girls were equally eligible with herself as far as the terms of the advertisement went.

The time passed. Streams of girls were evidently passing through the inner office. Most of them were dismissed through another door giving on the corridor, but every now and then a recruit arrived to swell the select assembly. At half-past six there were fourteen girls assembled there.

Jane heard a murmur of voices from the inner office, and then the foreign-looking gentleman, whom she had nicknamed in her mind 'the Colonel' owing to the military character of his moustache, appeared in the doorway.

'I will see you ladies one at a time, if you please,' he announced. 'In the order in which you arrived, please.'

Jane was, of course, the sixth on the list. Twenty minutes elapsed before she was called in. 'The Colonel' was standing with his hands behind his back. He put her through a rapid catechism, tested her knowledge of French, and measured her height.

'It is possible, mademoiselle,' he said in French, 'that you may suit. I do not know. But it is possible.'

'What is this post, if I may ask?' said Jane bluntly.

He shrugged his shoulders.

'That I cannot tell you as yet. If you are chosen—then you shall know.'

'This seems very mysterious,' objected Jane. 'I couldn't possibly take up anything without knowing all about it. Is it connected with the stage, may I ask?'

'The stage? Indeed, no.'

'Oh!' said Jane, rather taken aback.

He was looking at her keenly.

'You have intelligence, yes? And discretion?'

'I've quantities of intelligence and discretion,' said Jane calmly. 'What about the pay?'

'The pay will amount to two thousand pounds—for a fortnight's work.'

'Oh!' said Jane faintly.

She was too taken aback by the munificence of the sum named to recover all at once.

The Colonel resumed speaking.

'One other young lady I have already selected. You and she are equally suitable. There may be others I have not yet seen. I will give you instruction as to your further proceedings. You know Harridge's Hotel?'

Jane gasped. Who in England did not know Harridge's Hotel? That famous hostelry situated modestly in a by-street of Mayfair, where notabilities and royalties arrived and departed as a matter of course. Only this morning Jane had read of the arrival of the Grand Duchess Pauline of Ostrova. She had come over to open a big bazaar in aid of Russian refugees, and was, of course, staying at Harridge's.

'Yes,' said Jane, in answer to the Colonel's question.

'Very good. Go there. Ask for Count Streptitch. Send up your card—you have a card?'

Jane produced one. The Colonel took it from her and inscribed in the corner a minute P. He handed the card back to her.

'That ensures that the count will see you. He will understand that you come from me. The final decision lies with him—and another. If he considers you suitable, he will explain matters to you, and you can accept or decline his proposal. Is that satisfactory?'

'Perfectly satisfactory,' said Jane.

'So far,' she murmured to herself as she emerged into the street, 'I can't see the catch. And yet, there must be one. There's no such thing as money for nothing. It must be crime! There's nothing else left.'

Her spirits rose. In moderation Jane did not object to crime. The papers had been full lately of the exploits of various girl bandits. Jane had seriously thought of becoming one if all else failed.

She entered the exclusive portals of Harridge's with slight trepidation. More than ever, she wished that she had a new hat.

But she walked bravely up to the bureau and produced her card, and asked for Count Streptitch without a shade of hesitation in her manner. She fancied that the clerk looked at her rather curiously. He took the card, however, and gave it to a small page boy with some low-voiced instructions which Jane did not catch. Presently the page returned, and Jane was invited to accompany him. They went up in the lift and along a corridor to some big double doors where the page knocked. A moment later Jane found herself in a big room, facing a tall thin man with a fair beard, who was holding her card in a languid white hand.

'Miss Jane Cleveland,' he read slowly. 'I am Count Streptitch.'

His lips parted suddenly in what was presumably intended to be a smile, disclosing two rows of white even teeth. But no effect of merriment was obtained.

'I understand that you applied in answer to our advertisement,' continued the count. 'The good Colonel Kranin sent you on here.'

'He *was* a colonel,' thought Jane, pleased with her perspicacity, but she merely bowed her head.

'You will pardon me if I ask you a few questions?'

He did not wait for a reply, but proceeded to put Jane through a catechism very similar to that of Colonel Kranin. Her replies seemed to satisfy him. He nodded his head once or twice.

'I will ask you now, mademoiselle, to walk to the door and back again slowly.'

'Perhaps they want me to be a mannequin,' thought Jane, as she complied. 'But they wouldn't pay two thousand pounds to a mannequin. Still, I suppose I'd better not ask questions yet awhile.'

Count Streptitch was frowning. He tapped on the table with his white fingers. Suddenly he rose, and opening the door of an adjoining room, he spoke to someone inside.

He returned to his seat, and a short middle-aged lady came through the door, closing it behind her. She was plump and extremely ugly, but had nevertheless the air of being a person of importance.

'Well, Anna Michaelovna,' said the count. 'What do you think of her?'

The lady looked Jane up and down much as though the

girl had been a waxwork at a show. She made no pretence of any greeting.

'She might do,' she said at length. 'Of actual likeness in the real sense of the word, there is very little. But the figure and the colouring are very good, better than any of the others. What do you think of it, Feodor Alexandrovitch?'

'I agree with you, Anna Michaelovna.'

'Does she speak French?'

'Her French is excellent.'

Jane felt more and more of a dummy. Neither of these strange people appeared to remember that she was a human being.

'But will she be discreet?' asked the lady, frowning heavily at the girl.

'This is the Princess Poporensky,' said Count Streptitch to Jane in French. 'She asks whether you can be discreet?'

Jane addressed her reply to the princess.

'Until I have had the position explained to me, I can hardly make promises.'

'It is just what she says there, the little one,' remarked the lady. 'I think she is intelligent, Feodor Alexandrovitch—more intelligent than the others. Tell me, little one, have you also courage?'

'I don't know,' said Jane, puzzled. 'I don't particularly like being hurt, but I can bear it.'

'Ah! that is not what I mean. You do not mind danger, no?'

'Oh!' said Jane. 'Danger! That's all right. I like danger.'

'And you are poor? You would like to earn much money?'

149

*Agatha Christie*

'Try me,' said Jane with something approaching enthusiasm.

Count Streptitch and Princess Poporensky exchanged glances. Then, simultaneously, they nodded.

'Shall I explain matters, Anna Michaelovna?' the former asked.

The princess shook her head.

'Her Highness wishes to do that herself.'

'It is unnecessary—and unwise.'

'Nevertheless those are her commands. I was to bring the girl in as soon as you had done with her.'

Streptitch shrugged his shoulders. Clearly he was not pleased. Equally clearly he had no intention of disobeying the edict. He turned to Jane.

'The Princess Poporensky will present you to Her Highness the Grand Duchess Pauline. Do not be alarmed.'

Jane was not in the least alarmed. She was delighted at the idea of being presented to a real live grand duchess. There was nothing of the Socialist about Jane. For the moment she had even ceased to worry about her hat.

The Princess Poporensky led the way, waddling along with a gait that she managed to invest with a certain dignity in spite of adverse circumstances. They passed through the adjoining room, which was a kind of ante-chamber, and the princess knocked upon a door in the farther wall. A voice from inside replied and the princess opened the door and passed in, Jane close upon her heels.

'Let me present to you, madame,' said the princess in a solemn voice, 'Miss Jane Cleveland.'

A young woman who had been sitting in a big armchair

at the other end of the room jumped up and ran forward. She stared fixedly at Jane for a minute or two, and then laughed merrily.

'But this is splendid, Anna,' she replied. 'I never imagined we should succeed so well. Come, let us see ourselves side by side.'

Taking Jane's arm, she drew the girl across the room, pausing before a full-length mirror which hung on the wall.

'You see?' she cried delightedly. 'It is a perfect match!'

Already, with her first glance at the Grand Duchess Pauline, Jane had begun to understand. The Grand Duchess was a young woman perhaps a year or two older than Jane. She had the same shade of fair hair, and the same slim figure. She was, perhaps, a shade taller. Now that they stood side by side, the likeness was very apparent. Detail for detail, the colouring was almost exactly the same.

The Grand Duchess clapped her hands. She seemed an extremely cheerful young woman.

'Nothing could be better,' she declared. 'You must congratulate Feodor Alexandrovitch for me, Anna. He has indeed done well.'

'As yet, madame,' murmured the princess, in a low voice, 'this young woman does not know what is required of her.'

'True,' said the Grand Duchess, becoming somewhat calmer in manner. 'I forgot. Well, I will enlighten her. Leave us together, Anna Michaelovna.'

'But, madame—'

'Leave us alone, I say.'

She stamped her foot angrily. With considerable reluctance

Anna Michaelovna left the room. The Grand Duchess sat down and motioned to Jane to do the same.

'They are tiresome, these old women,' remarked Pauline. 'But one has to have them. Anna Michaelovna is better than most. Now then, Miss—ah, yes, Miss Jane Cleveland. I like the name. I like you too. You are sympathetic. I can tell at once if people are sympathetic.'

'That's very clever of you, ma'am,' said Jane, speaking for the first time.

'I am clever,' said Pauline calmly. 'Come now, I will explain things to you. Not that there is much to explain. You know the history of Ostrova. Practically all of my family are dead—massacred by the Communists. I am, perhaps, the last of my line. I am a woman, I cannot sit upon the throne. You think they would let me be. But no, wherever I go attempts are made to assassinate me. Absurd, is it not? These vodka-soaked brutes never have any sense of proportion.'

'I see,' said Jane, feeling that something was required of her.

'For the most part I live in retirement—where I can take precautions, but now and then I have to take part in public ceremonies. While I am here, for instance, I have to attend several semi-public functions. Also in Paris on my way back. I have an estate in Hungary, you know. The sport there is magnificent.'

'Is it really?' said Jane.

'Superb. I adore sport. Also—I ought not to tell you this, but I shall because your face is so sympathetic—there are plans being made there—very quietly, you understand.

Altogether it is very important that I should not be assassinated during the next two weeks.'

'But surely the police—' began Jane.

'The police? Oh, yes, they are very good, I believe. And we too—we have our spies. It is possible that I shall be forewarned when the attempt is to take place. But then, again, I might not.'

She shrugged her shoulders.

'I begin to understand,' said Jane slowly. 'You want me to take your place?'

'Only on certain occasions,' said the Grand Duchess eagerly. 'You must be somewhere at hand, you understand? I may require you twice, three times, four times in the next fortnight. Each time it will be upon the occasion of some public function. Naturally in intimacy of any kind, you could not represent me.'

'Of course not,' agreed Jane.

'You will do very well indeed. It was clever of Feodor Alexandrovitch to think of an advertisement, was it not?'

'Supposing,' said Jane, 'that I get assassinated?'

The Grand Duchess shrugged her shoulders.

'There is the risk, of course, but according to our own secret information, they want to kidnap me, not kill me outright. But I will be quite honest—it is always possible that they might throw a bomb.'

'I see,' said Jane.

She tried to imitate the light-hearted manner of Pauline. She wanted very much to come to the question of money, but did not quite see how best to introduce the subject. But Pauline saved her the trouble.

'We will pay you well, of course,' she said carelessly. 'I cannot remember now exactly how much Feodor Alexandrovitch suggested. We were speaking in francs or kronen.'

'Colonel Kranin,' said Jane, 'said something about two thousand pounds.'

'That was it,' said Pauline, brightening. 'I remember now. It is enough, I hope? Or would you rather have three thousand?'

'Well,' said Jane, 'if it's all the same to you, I'd rather have three thousand.'

'You are business-like, I see,' said the Grand Duchess kindly. 'I wish I was. But I have no idea of money at all. What I want I have to have, that is all.'

It seemed to Jane a simple but admirable attitude of mind.

'And of course, as you say, there is danger,' Pauline continued thoughtfully. 'Although you do not look to me as though you minded danger. I do not myself. I hope you do not think that it is because I am a coward that I want you to take my place? You see, it is most important for Ostrova that I should marry and have at least two sons. After that, it does not matter what happens to me.'

'I see,' said Jane.

'And you accept?'

'Yes,' said Jane resolutely. 'I accept.'

Pauline clapped her hands vehemently several times. Princess Poporensky appeared immediately.

'I have told her all, Anna,' announced the Grand Duchess. 'She will do what we want, and she is to have

154

three thousand pounds. Tell Feodor to make a note of it. She is really very like me, is she not? I think she is better looking, though.'

The princess waddled out of the room, and returned with Count Streptitch.

'We have arranged everything, Feodor Alexandrovitch,' the Grand Duchess said.

He bowed.

'Can she play her part, I wonder?' he queried, eyeing Jane doubtfully.

'I'll show you,' said the girl suddenly. 'You permit, ma'am?' she said to the Grand Duchess.

The latter nodded delightedly.

Jane stood up.

'But this is splendid, Anna,' she said. 'I never imagined we should succeed so well. Come, let us see ourselves, side by side.'

And, as Pauline had done, she drew the other girl to the glass.

'You see? A perfect match!'

Words, manner and gesture, it was an excellent imitation of Pauline's greeting. The princess nodded her head, and uttered a grunt of approbation.

'It is good, that,' she declared. 'It would deceive most people.'

'You are very clever,' said Pauline appreciatively. 'I could not imitate anyone else to save my life.'

Jane believed her. It had already struck her that Pauline was a young woman who was very much herself.

'Anna will arrange details with you,' said the Grand

Duchess. 'Take her into my bedroom, Anna, and try some of my clothes on her.'

She nodded a gracious farewell, and Jane was conveyed away by the Princess Poporensky.

'This is what Her Highness will wear to open the bazaar,' explained the old lady, holding up a daring creation of white and black. 'This is in three days' time. It may be necessary for you to take her place there. We do not know. We have not yet received information.'

At Anna's bidding, Jane slipped off her own shabby garments, and tried on the frock. It fitted her perfectly. The other nodded approvingly.

'It is almost perfect—just a shade long on you, because you are an inch or so shorter than Her Highness.'

'That is easily remedied,' said Jane quickly. 'The Grand Duchess wears low-heeled shoes, I noticed. If I wear the same kind of shoes, but with high heels, it will adjust things nicely.'

Anna Michaelovna showed her the shoes that the Grand Duchess usually wore with the dress. Lizard skin with a strap across. Jane memorized them, and arranged to get a pair just like them, but with different heels.

'It would be well,' said Anna Michaelovna, 'for you to have a dress of distinctive colour and material quite unlike Her Highness's. Then in case it becomes necessary for you to change places at a moment's notice, the substitution is less likely to be noticed.'

Jane thought a minute.

'What about a flame-red marocain? And I might, perhaps, have plain glass pince-nez. That alters the appearance very much.'

Both suggestions were approved, and they went into further details.

Jane left the hotel with bank-notes for a hundred pounds in her purse, and instructions to purchase the necessary outfit and engage rooms at the Blitz Hotel as Miss Montresor of New York.

On the second day after this, Count Streptitch called upon her there.

'A transformation indeed,' he said, as he bowed.

Jane made him a mock bow in return. She was enjoying the new clothes and the luxury of her life very much.

'All this is very nice,' she sighed. 'But I suppose that your visit means I must get busy and earn my money.'

'That is so. We have received information. It seems possible that an attempt will be made to kidnap Her Highness on the way home from the bazaar. That is to take place, as you know, at Orion House, which is about ten miles out of London. Her Highness will be forced to attend the bazaar in person, as the Countess of Anchester, who is promoting it, knows her personally. But the following is the plan I have concocted.'

Jane listened attentively as he outlined it to her.

She asked a few questions, and finally declared that she understood perfectly the part that she had to play.

The next day dawned bright and clear—a perfect day for one of the great events of the London Season, the bazaar at Orion House, promoted by the Countess of Anchester in aid of Ostrovian refugees in this country.

Having regard to the uncertainty of the English climate, the bazaar itself took place within the spacious rooms of

Orion House, which has been for five hundred years in the possession of the Earls of Anchester. Various collections had been loaned, and a charming idea was the gift by a hundred society women of one pearl each taken from their own necklaces, each pearl to be sold by auction on the second day. There were also numerous sideshows and attractions in the grounds.

Jane was there early in the rôle of Miss Montresor. She wore a dress of flame-coloured marocain, and a small red cloche hat. On her feet were high-heeled lizard-skin shoes.

The arrival of the Grand Duchess Pauline was a great event. She was escorted to the platform and duly presented with a bouquet of roses by a small child. She made a short but charming speech and declared the bazaar open. Count Streptitch and Princess Poporensky were in attendance upon her.

She wore the dress that Jane had seen, white with a bold design of black, and her hat was a small cloche of black with a profusion of white ospreys hanging over the brim and a tiny lace veil coming half-way down the face. Jane smiled to herself.

The Grand Duchess went round the bazaar, visiting every stall, making a few purchases, and being uniformly gracious. Then she prepared to depart.

Jane was prompt to take up her cue. She requested a word with the Princess Poporensky and asked to be presented to the Grand Duchess.

'Ah, yes!' said Pauline, in a clear voice. 'Miss Montresor, I remember the name. She is an American journalist, I believe. She has done much for our cause. I should be glad to give her a short interview for her paper. Is there anywhere where we could be undisturbed?'

A small anteroom was immediately placed at the Grand Duchess's disposal, and Count Streptitch was despatched to bring in Miss Montresor. As soon as he had done so, and withdrawn again, the Princess Poporensky remaining in attendance, a rapid exchange of garments took place.

Three minutes later, the door opened and the Grand Duchess emerged, her bouquet of roses held up to her face.

Bowing graciously, and uttering a few words of farewell to Lady Anchester in French, she passed out and entered her car which was waiting. Princess Poporensky took her place beside her, and the car drove off.

'Well,' said Jane, 'that's that. I wonder how Miss Montresor's getting on.'

'No one will notice her. She can slip out quietly.'

'That's true,' said Jane. 'I did it nicely, didn't I?'

'You acted your part with great distinction.'

'Why isn't the count with us?'

'He was forced to remain. Someone must watch over the safety of Her Highness.'

'I hope nobody's going to throw bombs,' said Jane apprehensively. 'Hi! we're turning off the main road. Why's that?'

Gathering speed, the car was shooting down a side road.

Jane jumped up and put her head out of the window, remonstrating with the driver. He only laughed and increased his speed. Jane sank back into her seat again.

'Your spies were right,' she said, with a laugh. 'We're

for it all right. I suppose the longer I keep it up, the safer it is for the Grand Duchess. At all events we must give her time to return to London safely.'

At the prospect of danger, Jane's spirits rose. She had not relished the prospect of a bomb, but this type of adventure appealed to her sporting instincts.

Suddenly, with a grinding of brakes, the car pulled up in its own length. A man jumped on the step. In his hand was a revolver.

'Put your hands up,' he snarled.

The Princess Poporensky's hands rose swiftly, but Jane merely looked at him disdainfully, and kept her hands on her lap.

'Ask him the meaning of this outrage,' she said in French to her companion.

But before the latter had time to say a word, the man broke in. He poured out a torrent of words in some foreign language.

Not understanding a single thing, Jane merely shrugged her shoulders and said nothing. The chauffeur had got down from his seat and joined the other man.

'Will the illustrious lady be pleased to descend?' he asked, with a grin.

Raising the flowers to her face again, Jane stepped out of the car. The Princess Poporensky followed her.

'Will the illustrious lady come this way?'

Jane took no notice of the man's mock insolent manner, but of her own accord she walked towards a low-built, rambling house which stood about a hundred yards away from where the car had stopped. The road had been a *cul-de-sac* ending in the gateway and drive which led to this apparently untenanted building.

The man, still brandishing his pistol, came close behind the two women. As they passed up the steps, he brushed past them and flung open a door on the left. It was an empty room, into which a table and two chairs had evidently been brought.

Jane passed in and sat down. Anna Michaelovna followed her. The man banged the door and turned the key.

Jane walked to the window and looked out.

'I could jump out, of course,' she remarked. 'But I shouldn't get far. No, we'll just have to stay here for the present and make the best of it. I wonder if they'll bring us anything to eat?'

About half an hour later her question was answered.

A big bowl of steaming soup was brought in and placed on the table in front of her. Also two pieces of dry bread.

'No luxury for aristocrats evidently,' remarked Jane cheerily as the door was shut and locked again. 'Will you start, or shall I?'

The Princess Poporensky waved the mere idea of food aside with horror.

'How could I eat? Who knows what danger my mistress might not be in?'

'She's all right,' said Jane. 'It's myself I'm worrying about. You know these people won't be at all pleased when they find they have got hold of the wrong person. In fact, they may be very unpleasant. I shall keep up the haughty Grand Duchess stunt as long as I can, and do a bunk if the opportunity offers.'

The Princess Poporensky offered no reply.

Jane, who was hungry, drank up all the soup. It had a curious taste, but was hot and savoury.

Afterwards she felt rather sleepy. The Princess Poporensky seemed to be weeping quietly. Jane arranged herself on her uncomfortable chair in the least uncomfortable way, and allowed her head to droop.

She slept.

Jane awoke with a start. She had an idea that she had been a very long time asleep. Her head felt heavy and uncomfortable.

And then suddenly she saw something that jerked her faculties wide awake again.

She was wearing the flame-coloured marocain frock.

She sat up and looked around her. Yes, she was still in the room in the empty house. Everything was exactly as it had been when she went to sleep, except for two facts. The first was that the Princess Poporensky was no longer sitting on the other chair. The second was her own inexplicable change of costume.

'I can't have dreamt it,' said Jane. 'Because if I'd dreamt it, I shouldn't be here.'

She looked across at the window and registered a second significant fact. When she had gone to sleep the sun had been pouring through the window. Now the house threw a sharp shadow on the sunlit drive.

'The house faces west,' she reflected. 'It was afternoon when I went to sleep. Therefore it must be tomorrow morning now. Therefore that soup was drugged. Therefore— oh, I don't know. It all seems mad.'

She got up and went to the door. It was unlocked. She explored the house. It was silent and empty.

Jane put her hand to her aching head and tried to think.

And then she caught sight of a torn newspaper lying by the front door. It had glaring headlines which caught her eye.

'American Girl Bandit in England,' she read. 'The Girl in the Red Dress. Sensational hold-up at Orion House Bazaar.'

Jane staggered out into the sunlight. Sitting on the steps she read, her eyes growing bigger and bigger. The facts were short and succinct.

Just after the departure of the Grand Duchess Pauline, three men and a girl in a red dress had produced revolvers and successfully held up the crowd. They had annexed the hundred pearls and made a getaway in a fast racing car. Up to now, they had not been traced.

In the stop press (it was a late evening paper) were a few words to the effect that the 'girl bandit in the red dress' had been staying at the Blitz as a Miss Montresor of New York.

'I'm dished,' said Jane. 'Absolutely dished. I always knew there was a catch in it.'

And then she started. A strange sound had smote the air. The voice of a man, uttering one word at frequent intervals.

'Damn,' it said. 'Damn.' And yet again, 'Damn!'

Jane thrilled to the sound. It expressed so exactly her

own feelings. She ran down the steps. By the corner of them lay a young man. He was endeavouring to raise his head from the ground. His face struck Jane as one of the nicest faces she had ever seen. It was freckled and slightly quizzical in expression.

'Damn my head,' said the young man. 'Damn it. I—'

He broke off and stared at Jane.

'I must be dreaming,' he said faintly.

'That's what I said,' said Jane. 'But we're not. What's the matter with your head?'

'Somebody hit me on it. Fortunately it's a thick one.'

He pulled himself into a sitting position, and made a wry face.

'My brain will begin to function shortly, I expect. I'm still in the same old spot, I see.'

'How did you get here?' asked Jane curiously.

'That's a long story. By the way, you're not the Grand Duchess What's-her-name, are you?'

'I'm not. I'm plain Jane Cleveland.'

'You're not plain anyway,' said the young man, looking at her with frank admiration.

Jane blushed.

'I ought to get you some water or something, oughtn't I?' she asked uncertainly.

'I believe it is customary,' agreed the young man. 'All the same, I'd rather have whisky if you can find it.'

Jane was unable to find any whisky. The young man took a deep draught of water, and announced himself better.

'Shall I relate my adventures, or will you relate yours?' he asked.

'You first.'

'There's nothing much to mine. I happened to notice that the Grand Duchess went into that room with low-heeled shoes on and came out with high-heeled ones. It struck me as rather odd. I don't like things to be odd.

'I followed the car on my motor bicycle, I saw you taken into the house. About ten minutes later a big racing car came tearing up. A girl in red got out and three men. She had low-heeled shoes on, all right. They went into the house. Presently low heels came out dressed in black and white, and went off in the first car, with an old pussy and a tall man with a fair beard. The others went off in the racing car. I thought they'd all gone, and was just trying to get in at that window and rescue you when someone hit me on the head from behind. That's all. Now for your turn.'

Jane related her adventures.

'And it's awfully lucky for me that you did follow,' she ended. 'Do you see what an awful hole I should have been in otherwise? The Grand Duchess would have had a perfect alibi. She left the bazaar before the hold-up began, and arrived in London in her car. Would anybody ever have believed my fantastic improbable story?'

'Not on your life,' said the young man with conviction.

They had been so absorbed in their respective narratives that they had been quite oblivious of their surroundings. They looked up now with a slight start to see a tall sad-faced man leaning against the house. He nodded at them.

'Very interesting,' he commented.

'Who are you?' demanded Jane.

The sad-faced man's eyes twinkled a little.

'Detective-Inspector Farrell,' he said gently. 'I've been very interested in hearing your story and this young lady's. We might have found a little difficulty in believing hers, but for one or two things.'

'For instance?'

'Well, you see, we heard this morning that the real Grand Duchess had eloped with a chauffeur in Paris.'

Jane gasped.

'And then we knew that this American "girl bandit" had come to this country, and we expected a coup of some kind. We'll have laid hands on them very soon, I can promise you that. Excuse me a minute, will you?'

He ran up the steps into the house.

'*Well!*' said Jane. She put a lot of force into the expression.

'I think it was awfully clever of you to notice those shoes,' she said suddenly.

'Not at all,' said the young man. 'I was brought up in the boot trade. My father's a sort of boot king. He wanted me to go into the trade—marry and settle down. All that sort of thing. Nobody in particular—just the principle of the thing. But I wanted to be an artist.' He sighed.

'I'm so sorry,' said Jane kindly.

'I've been trying for six years. There's no blinking it. I'm a rotten painter. I've a good mind to chuck it and go home like the prodigal son. There's a good billet waiting for me.'

'A job is the great thing,' agreed Jane wistfully. 'Do you think you could get me one trying on boots somewhere?'

'I could give you a better one than that—if you'd take it.'

'Oh, what?'

'Never mind now. I'll tell you later. You know, until yesterday I never saw a girl I felt I could marry.'

'Yesterday?'

'At the bazaar. And then I saw her—the one and only Her!'

He looked very hard at Jane.

'How beautiful the delphiniums are,' said Jane hurriedly, with very pink cheeks.

'They're lupins,' said the young man.

'It doesn't matter,' said Jane.

'Not a bit,' he agreed. And he drew a little nearer.

# A Fruitful Sunday

'Well, really, I call this too delightful,' said Miss Dorothy Pratt for the fourth time. 'How I wish the old cat could see me now. She and her Janes!'

The 'old cat' thus scathingly alluded to was Miss Pratt's highly estimable employer, Mrs Mackenzie Jones, who had strong views upon the Christian names suitable for parlour-maids and had repudiated Dorothy in favour of Miss Pratt's despised second name of Jane.

Miss Pratt's companion did not reply at once—for the best of reasons. When you have just purchased a Baby Austin, fourth hand, for the sum of twenty pounds, and are taking it out for the second time only, your whole attention is necessarily focused on the difficult task of using both hands and feet as the emergencies of the moment dictate.

'Er—ah!' said Mr Edward Palgrove and negotiated a crisis with a horrible grinding sound that would have set a true motorist's teeth on edge.

'Well, you don't talk to a girl much,' complained Dorothy.

Mr Palgrove was saved from having to respond as at that moment he was roundly and soundly cursed by the driver of a motor omnibus.

'Well, of all the impudence,' said Miss Pratt, tossing her head.

'I only wish *he* had this foot brake,' said her swain bitterly.

'Is there anything wrong with it?'

'You can put your foot on it till kingdom comes,' said Mr Palgrove. 'But nothing happens.'

'Oh, well, Ted, you can't expect everything for twenty pounds. After all, here we are, in a real car, on Sunday afternoon going out of town the same as everybody else.'

More grinding and crashing sounds.

'Ah,' said Ted, flushed with triumph. 'That was a better change.'

'You do drive something beautiful,' said Dorothy admiringly.

Emboldened by feminine appreciation, Mr Palgrove attempted a dash across Hammersmith Broadway, and was severely spoken to by a policeman.

'Well, I never,' said Dorothy, as they proceeded towards Hammersmith Bridge in a chastened fashion. 'I don't know what the police are coming to. You'd think they'd be a bit more civil spoken seeing the way they've been shown up lately.'

'Anyway, I didn't want to go along this road,' said Edward sadly. 'I wanted to go down the Great West Road and do a bust.'

'And be caught in a trap as likely as not,' said Dorothy.

'That's what happened to the master the other day. Five pounds and costs.'

'The police aren't so dusty after all,' said Edward generously. 'They pitch into the rich all right. No favour. It makes me mad to think of these swells who can walk into a place and buy a couple of Rolls-Royces without turning a hair. There's no sense in it. I'm as good as they are.'

'And the jewellery,' said Dorothy, sighing. 'Those shops in Bond Street. Diamonds and pearls and I don't know what! And me with a string of Woolworth pearls.'

She brooded sadly upon the subject. Edward was able once more to give his full attention to his driving. They managed to get through Richmond without mishap. The altercation with the policeman had shaken Edward's nerve. He now took the line of least resistance, following blindly behind any car in front whenever a choice of thoroughfares presented itself.

In this way he presently found himself following a shady country lane which many an experienced motorist would have given his soul to find.

'Rather clever turning off the way I did,' said Edward, taking all the credit to himself.

'Sweetly pretty, I call it,' said Miss Pratt. 'And I do declare, there's a man with fruit to sell.'

Sure enough, at a convenient corner, was a small wicker table with baskets of fruit on it, and the legend EAT MORE FRUIT displayed on a banner.

'How much?' said Edward apprehensively when frenzied pulling of the handbrake had produced the desired result.

'Lovely strawberries,' said the man in charge.

He was an unprepossessing-looking individual with a leer.

'Just the thing for the lady. Ripe fruit, fresh picked. Cherries too. Genuine English. Have a basket of cherries, lady?'

'They do look nice ones,' said Dorothy.

'Lovely, that's what they are,' said the man hoarsely. 'Bring you luck, lady, that basket will.' He at last condescended to reply to Edward. 'Two shillings, sir, and dirt cheap. You'd say so if you knew what was inside the basket.'

'They look awfully nice,' said Dorothy.

Edward sighed and paid over two shillings. His mind was obsessed by calculation. Tea later, petrol—this Sunday motoring business wasn't what you'd call *cheap*. That was the worst of taking girls out! They always wanted everything they saw.

'Thank you, sir,' said the unprepossessing-looking one. 'You've got more than your money's worth in that basket of cherries.'

Edward shoved his foot savagely down and the Baby Austin leaped at the cherry vendor after the manner of an infuriated Alsatian.

'Sorry,' said Edward. 'I forgot she was in gear.'

'You ought to be careful, dear,' said Dorothy. 'You might have hurt him.'

Edward did not reply. Another half-mile brought them to an ideal spot by the banks of a stream. The Austin was left by the side of the road and Edward and Dorothy sat affectionately upon the river bank and munched cherries. A Sunday paper lay unheeded at their feet.

'What's the news?' said Edward at last, stretching himself flat on his back and tilting his hat to shade his eyes.

Dorothy glanced over the headlines.

'The Woeful Wife. Extraordinary story. Twenty-eight people drowned last week. Reported death of Airman. Startling Jewel Robbery. Ruby Necklace worth fifty thousand pounds missing. Oh, Ted! Fifty thousand pounds. Just fancy!' She went on reading. 'The necklace is composed of twenty-one stones set in platinum and was sent by registered post from Paris. On arrival, the packet was found to contain a few pebbles and the jewels were missing.'

'Pinched in the post,' said Edward. 'The posts in France are awful, I believe.'

'I'd like to see a necklace like that,' said Dorothy. 'All glowing like blood—pigeon's blood, that's what they call the colour. I wonder what it would feel like to have a thing like that hanging round your neck.'

'Well, *you're* never likely to know, my girl,' said Edward facetiously.

Dorothy tossed her head.

'Why not, I should like to know. It's amazing the way girls can get on in the world. I might go on the stage.'

'Girls that behave themselves don't get anywhere,' said Edward discouragingly.

Dorothy opened her mouth to reply, checked herself, and murmured, 'Pass me the cherries.

'I've been eating more than you have,' she remarked.

'I'll divide up what's left and—why, whatever's this at the bottom of the basket?'

She drew it out as she spoke—a long glittering chain of blood-red stones.

They both stared at it in amazement.

'In the basket, did you say?' said Edward at last.

Dorothy nodded.

'Right at the bottom—under the fruit.'

Again they stared at each other.

'How did it get there, do you think?'

'I can't imagine. It's odd, Ted, just after reading that bit in the paper—about the rubies.'

Edward laughed.

'You don't imagine you're holding fifty thousand pounds in your hand, do you?'

'I just said it was odd. Rubies set in platinum. Platinum is that sort of dull silvery stuff—like this. Don't they sparkle and aren't they a lovely colour? I wonder how many of them there are?' She counted. 'I say, Ted, there are twenty-one exactly.'

'No!'

'Yes. The same number as the paper said. Oh, Ted, you don't think—'

'It could be.' But he spoke irresolutely. 'There's some sort of way you can tell—scratching them on glass.'

'That's diamonds. But you know, Ted, that was a very odd-looking man—the man with the fruit—a nasty-looking man. And he was funny about it—said we'd got more than our money's worth in the basket.'

'Yes, but look here, Dorothy, what would he want to hand us over fifty thousand pounds for?'

173

*Agatha Christie*

Miss Pratt shook her head, discouraged.

'It doesn't seem to make sense,' she admitted. 'Unless the police were after him.'

'The police?' Edward paled slightly.

'Yes. It goes on to say in the paper—"the police have a clue".'

Cold shivers ran down Edward's spine.

'I don't like this, Dorothy. Supposing the police get after *us*.'

Dorothy stared at him with her mouth open.

'But we haven't done anything, Ted. We found it in the basket.'

'And that'll sound a silly sort of story to tell! It isn't likely.'

'It isn't very,' admitted Dorothy. 'Oh, Ted, do you really think it is IT? It's like a fairy story!'

'I don't think it sounds like a fairy story,' said Edward. 'It sounds to me more like the kind of story where the hero goes to Dartmoor unjustly accused for fourteen years.'

But Dorothy was not listening. She had clasped the necklace round her neck and was judging the effect in a small mirror taken from her handbag.

'The same as a duchess might wear,' she murmured ecstatically.

'I won't believe it,' said Edward violently. 'They're imitation. They *must* be imitation.'

'Yes, dear,' said Dorothy, still intent on her reflection in the mirror. 'Very likely.'

'Anything else would be too much of a—a coincidence.'

174

'Pigeon's blood,' murmured Dorothy.

'It's absurd. That's what I say. Absurd. Look here, Dorothy, are you listening to what I say, or are you not?'

Dorothy put away the mirror. She turned to him, one hand on the rubies round her neck.

'How do I look?' she asked.

Edward stared at her, his grievance forgotten. He had never seen Dorothy quite like this. There was a triumph about her, a kind of regal beauty that was completely new to him. The belief that she had jewels round her neck worth fifty thousand pounds had made of Dorothy Pratt a new woman. She looked insolently serene, a kind of Cleopatra and Semiramis and Zenobia rolled into one.

'You look—you look—stunning,' said Edward humbly.

Dorothy laughed, and her laugh, too, was entirely different.

'Look here,' said Edward. 'We've got to do something. We must take them to a police station or something.'

'Nonsense,' said Dorothy. 'You said yourself just now that they wouldn't believe you. You'll probably be sent to prison for stealing them.'

'But—but what else can we do?'

'Keep them,' said the new Dorothy Pratt.

Edward stared at her.

'Keep them? You're mad.'

'We found them, didn't we? Why should we think they're valuable? We'll keep them and I shall wear them.'

'And the police will pinch *you*.'

Dorothy considered this for a minute or two.

'All right,' she said. 'We'll sell them. And you can buy a

Rolls-Royce, or two Rolls-Royces, and I'll buy a diamond head-thing and some rings.'

Still Edward stared. Dorothy showed impatience.

'You've got your chance now—it's up to you to take it. We didn't steal the thing—I wouldn't hold with that. It's come to us and it's probably the only chance we'll ever have of getting all the things we want. Haven't you got any spunk at all, Edward Palgrove?'

Edward found his voice.

'Sell it, you say? That wouldn't be so jolly easy. Any jeweller would want to know where I got the blooming thing.'

'You don't take it to a jeweller. Don't you ever read detective stories, Ted? You take it to a "fence", of course.'

'And how should I know any fences? I've been brought up respectable.'

'Men ought to know everything,' said Dorothy. 'That's what they're for.'

He looked at her. She was serene and unyielding.

'I wouldn't have believed it of you,' he said weakly.

'I thought you had more spirit.'

There was a pause. Then Dorothy rose to her feet.

'Well,' she said lightly. 'We'd best be getting home.'

'Wearing that thing round your neck?'

Dorothy removed the necklace, looked at it reverently and dropped it into her handbag.

'Look here,' said Edward. 'You give that to me.'

'No.'

'Yes, you do. I've been brought up honest, my girl.'

'Well, you can go on being honest. You need have nothing to do with it.'

'Oh, hand it over,' said Edward recklessly. 'I'll do it. I'll find a fence. As you say, it's the only chance we shall ever have. We came by it honest—bought it for two shillings. It's no more than what gentlemen do in antique shops every day of their life and are proud of it.'

'That's it!' said Dorothy. 'Oh, Edward, you're splendid!'

She handed over the necklace and he dropped it into his pocket. He felt worked up, exalted, the very devil of a fellow! In this mood he started the Austin. They were both too excited to remember tea. They drove back to London in silence. Once at a cross-roads, a policeman stepped towards the car, and Edward's heart missed a beat. By a miracle, they reached home without mishap.

Edward's last words to Dorothy were imbued with the adventurous spirit.

'We'll go through with this. Fifty thousand pounds! It's worth it!'

He dreamt that night of broad arrows and Dartmoor, and rose early, haggard and unrefreshed. He had to set about finding a fence—and how to do it he had not the remotest idea!

His work at the office was slovenly and brought down upon him two sharp rebukes before lunch.

How did one find a 'fence'? Whitechapel, he fancied, was the correct neighbourhood—or was it Stepney?

On his return to the office a call came through for him on the telephone. Dorothy's voice spoke—tragic and tearful.

'Is that you, Ted? I'm using the telephone, but she may come in any minute, and I'll have to stop. Ted, you haven't done anything, have you?'

Edward replied in the negative.

'Well, look here, Ted, you mustn't. I've been lying awake all night. It's been awful. Thinking of how it says in the Bible you mustn't steal. I must have been mad yesterday— I really must. You won't do anything, will you, Ted, dear?'

Did a feeling of relief steal over Mr Palgrove? Possibly it did—but he wasn't going to admit any such thing.

'When I say I'm going through with a thing, I go through with it,' he said in a voice such as might belong to a strong superman with eyes of steel.

'Oh, but, Ted, dear, you mustn't. Oh, Lord, she's coming. Look here, Ted, she's going out to dinner tonight. I can slip out and meet you. Don't do anything till you've seen me. Eight o'clock. Wait for me round the corner.' Her voice changed to a seraphic murmur. 'Yes, ma'am, I think it was a wrong number. It was Bloomsbury 0243 they wanted.'

As Edward left the office at six o'clock, a huge headline caught his eye.

### JEWEL ROBBERY. LATEST DEVELOPMENTS

Hurriedly he extended a penny. Safely ensconced in the Tube, having dexterously managed to gain a seat, he eagerly perused the printed sheet. He found what he sought easily enough.

A suppressed whistle escaped him.

'Well—I'm—'

And then another adjacent paragraph caught his eye. He read it through and let the paper slip to the floor unheeded.

Precisely at eight o'clock, he was waiting at the rendez-vous. A breathless Dorothy, looking pale but pretty, came hurrying along to join him.

'You haven't done anything, Ted?'

'I haven't done anything.' He took the ruby chain from his pocket. 'You can put it on.'

'But, Ted—'

'The police have got the rubies all right—and the man who pinched them. And now read this!'

He thrust a newspaper paragraph under her nose. Dorothy read:

### NEW ADVERTISING STUNT

A clever new advertising dodge is being adopted by the All-English Fivepenny Fair who intend to challenge the famous Woolworths. Baskets of fruit were sold yesterday and will be on sale every Sunday. Out of every fifty baskets, one will contain an imitation necklace in different coloured stones. These necklaces are really wonderful value for the money. Great excitement and merriment was caused by them yesterday and EAT MORE FRUIT will have a great vogue next Sunday. We congratulate the Fivepenny Fair on their resource and wish them all good luck in their campaign of Buy British Goods.

'Well—' said Dorothy.

And after a pause: 'Well!'

'Yes,' said Edward. 'I felt the same.'

A passing man thrust a paper into his hand.

'Take one, brother,' he said.

'*The price of a virtuous woman is far above rubies.*'

'There!' said Edward. 'I hope that cheers you up.'

'I don't know,' said Dorothy doubtfully. 'I don't exactly want to *look* like a good woman.'

'You don't,' said Edward. 'That's why the man gave me that paper. With those rubies round your neck you don't look one little bit like a good woman.'

Dorothy laughed.

'You're rather a dear, Ted,' she said. 'Come on, let's go to the pictures.'

# Mr Eastwood's Adventure

Mr Eastwood looked at the ceiling. Then he looked down at the floor. From the floor his gaze travelled slowly up the right-hand wall. Then, with a sudden stern effort, he focused his gaze once more upon the typewriter before him.

The virgin white of the sheet of paper was defaced by a title written in capital letters.

'THE MYSTERY OF THE SECOND CUCUMBER'

so it ran. A pleasing title. Anthony Eastwood felt that anyone reading that title would be at once intrigued and arrested by it. 'The Mystery of the Second Cucumber,' they would say. 'What *can* that be about? A *cucumber*? The second *cucumber*? I must certainly read that story.' And they would be thrilled and charmed by the consummate ease with which this master of detective fiction had woven an exciting plot round this simple vegetable.

That was all very well. Anthony Eastwood knew as well as anyone what the story ought to be like—the bother was that somehow or other he couldn't get on with it. The two essentials for a story were a title and a plot—the rest was mere spade-work, sometimes the title led to a plot all by itself, as it were, and then all was plain sailing—but in this case the title continued to adorn the top of the page, and not the vestige of a plot was forthcoming.

Again Anthony Eastwood's gaze sought inspiration from the ceiling, the floor, and the wallpaper, and still nothing materialized.

'I shall call the heroine Sonia,' said Anthony, to urge himself on. 'Sonia or possibly Dolores—she shall have a skin of ivory pallor—the kind that's not due to ill-health, and eyes like fathomless pools. The hero shall be called George, or possibly John—something short and British. Then the gardener—I suppose there will have to be a gardener, we've got to drag that beastly cucumber in somehow or other—the gardener might be Scottish, and amusingly pessimistic about the early frost.'

This method sometimes worked, but it didn't seem to be going to this morning. Although Anthony could see Sonia and George and the comic gardener quite clearly, they didn't show any willingness to be active and do things.

'I could make it a banana, of course,' thought Anthony desperately. 'Or a lettuce, or a brussels sprout—brussels sprout, now, how about that? Really a cryptogram for *Brussels*—stolen bearer bonds—sinister Belgian Baron.'

For a moment a gleam of light seemed to show, but it died down again. The Belgian Baron wouldn't materialize, and Anthony suddenly remembered that early frosts and cucumbers were incompatible, which seemed to put the lid on the amusing remarks of the Scottish gardener.

'Oh! Damn!' said Mr Eastwood.

He rose and seized the *Daily Mail*. It was just possible that someone or other had been done to death in such a way as to lend inspiration to a perspiring author. But the news this morning was mainly political and foreign. Mr Eastwood cast down the paper in disgust.

Next, seizing a novel from the table, he closed his eyes and dabbed his finger down on one of the pages. The word thus indicated by Fate was 'sheep'. Immediately, with startling brilliance, a whole story unrolled itself in Mr Eastwood's brain. Lovely girl—lover killed in the war, her brain unhinged, tends sheep on the Scottish mountains—mystic meeting with dead lover, final effect of sheep and moonlight like Academy picture with girl lying dead in the snow, and *two trails of footsteps . . .*

It was a beautiful story. Anthony came out of its conception with a sigh and a sad shake of the head. He knew only too well the editor in question did not want that kind of story—beautiful though it might be. The kind of story he wanted, and insisted on having (and incidentally paid handsomely for getting), was all about mysterious dark women, stabbed to the heart, a young hero unjustly suspected, and the sudden unravelling of the mystery and fixing of the guilt on the least likely person, by the means of wholly inadequate clues—in fact, 'THE MYSTERY OF THE SECOND CUCUMBER.'

'Although,' reflected Anthony, 'ten to one, he'll alter the title and call it something rotten, like "*Murder Most Foul*" without so much as asking me! Oh, curse that telephone.'

He strode angrily to it, and took down the receiver.

Twice already in the last hour he had been summoned to it—once for a wrong number, and once to be roped in for dinner by a skittish society dame whom he hated bitterly, but who had been too pertinacious to defeat.

'Hallo!' he growled into the receiver.

A woman's voice answered him, a soft caressing voice with a trace of foreign accent.

'Is that you, beloved?' it said softly.

'Well—er—I don't know,' said Mr Eastwood cautiously. 'Who's speaking?'

'It is I. Carmen. Listen, beloved. I am pursued—in danger—you must come at once. It is life or death now.'

'I beg your pardon,' said Mr Eastwood politely. 'I'm afraid you've got the wrong—'

She broke in before he could complete the sentence.

'*Madre de Dios!* They are coming. If they find out what I am doing, they will kill me. Do not fail me. Come at once. It is death for me if you don't come. You know, 320 Kirk Street. The word is cucumber . . . Hush . . .'

He heard the faint click as she hung up the receiver at the other end.

'Well, I'm damned,' said Mr Eastwood, very much astonished.

He crossed over to his tobacco jar, and filled his pipe carefully.

'I suppose,' he mused, 'that that was some curious effect of my subconscious self. She can't have *said* cucumber. The whole thing is very extraordinary. Did she say cucumber, or didn't she?'

He strolled up and down, irresolutely.

'320 Kirk Street. I wonder what it's all about? She'll be expecting the other man to turn up. I wish I could have explained. 320 Kirk Street. The word is cucumber—oh, impossible, absurd—hallucination of a busy brain.'

He glanced malevolently at the typewriter.

'What good are you, I should like to know? I've been looking at you all the morning, and a lot of good it's done me. An author should get his plot from life—from life, do you hear? I'm going out to get one now.'

He clapped a hat on his head, gazed affectionately at his priceless collection of old enamels, and left the flat.

Kirk Street, as most Londoners know, is a long, straggling thoroughfare, chiefly devoted to antique shops, where all kinds of spurious goods are offered at fancy prices. There are also old brass shops, glass shops, decayed second-hand shops and second-hand clothes dealers.

No 320 was devoted to the sale of old glass. Glassware of all kinds filled it to overflowing. It was necessary for Anthony to move gingerly as he advanced up a centre aisle flanked by wine glasses and with lustres and chandeliers swaying and twinkling over his head. A very old lady was sitting at the back of the shop. She had a budding moustache that many an undergraduate might have envied, and a truculent manner.

She looked at Anthony and said, 'Well?' in a forbidding voice.

Anthony was a young man somewhat easily discomposed. He immediately inquired the price of some hock glasses.

'Forty-five shillings for half a dozen.'

'Oh, really,' said Anthony. 'Rather nice, aren't they? How much are these things?'

'Beautiful, they are, old Waterford. Let you have the pair for eighteen guineas.'

Mr Eastwood felt that he was laying up trouble for himself. In another minute he would be buying something, hypnotized by this fierce old woman's eye. And yet he could not bring himself to leave the shop.

'What about that?' he asked, and pointed to a chandelier.

'Thirty-five guineas.'

'Ah!' said Mr Eastwood regretfully. 'That's rather more than I can afford.'

'What do you want?' asked the old lady. 'Something for a wedding present?'

'That's it,' said Anthony, snatching at the explanation. 'But they're very difficult to suit.'

'Ah, well,' said the lady, rising with an air of determination. 'A nice piece of old glass comes amiss to nobody. I've got a couple of old decanters here—and there's a nice little liqueur set, just the thing for a bride—'

For the next ten minutes Anthony endured agonies. The lady had him firmly in hand. Every conceivable specimen of the glass-maker's art was paraded before his eyes. He became desperate.

'Beautiful, beautiful,' he exclaimed in a perfunctory manner, as he put down a large goblet that was being forced on his attention. Then blurted out hurriedly, 'I say, are you on the telephone here?'

'No, we're not. There's a call office at the post office

just opposite. Now, what do you say, the goblet—or these fine old rummers?'

Not being a woman, Anthony was quite unversed in the gentle art of getting out of a shop without buying anything.

'I'd better have the liqueur set,' he said gloomily.

It seemed the smallest thing. He was terrified of being landed with the chandelier.

With bitterness in his heart he paid for his purchase. And then, as the old lady was wrapping up the parcel, courage suddenly returned to him. After all, she would only think him eccentric, and, anyway, what the devil did it matter what she thought?

'Cucumber,' he said, clearly and firmly.

The old crone paused abruptly in her wrapping operations.

'Eh? What did you say?'

'Nothing,' lied Anthony defiantly.

'Oh! I thought you said cucumber.'

'So I did,' said Anthony defiantly.

'Well,' said the old lady. 'Why ever didn't you say that before? Wasting my time. Through that door there and upstairs. She's waiting for you.'

As though in a dream, Anthony passed through the door indicated, and climbed some extremely dirty stairs. At the top of them a door stood ajar displaying a tiny sitting-room.

Sitting on a chair, her eyes fixed on the door, and an expression of eager expectancy on her face, was a girl.

Such a girl! She really had the ivory pallor that Anthony had so often written about. And her eyes! Such eyes! She was not English, that could be seen at a glance. She had a foreign exotic quality which showed itself even in the costly simplicity of her dress.

Anthony paused in the doorway, somewhat abashed. The moment of explanations seemed to have arrived. But with a cry of delight the girl rose and flew into his arms.

'You have come,' she cried. 'You have come. Oh, the saints and the Holy Madonna be praised.'

Anthony, never one to miss opportunities, echoed her fervently. She drew away at last, and looked up in his face with a charming shyness.

'I should never have known you,' she declared. 'Indeed I should not.'

'Wouldn't you?' said Anthony feebly.

'No, even your eyes seem different—and you are ten times handsomer than I ever thought you would be.'

'Am I?'

To himself Anthony was saying, 'Keep calm, my boy, keep calm. The situation is developing very nicely, but don't lose your head.'

'I may kiss you again, yes?'

'Of course you can,' said Anthony heartily. 'As often as you like.'

There was a very pleasant interlude.

'I wonder who the devil I am?' thought Anthony. 'I hope to goodness the real fellow won't turn up. What a perfect darling she is.'

Suddenly the girl drew away from him, and a momentary terror showed in her face.

'You were not followed here?'

'Lord, no.'

'Ah, but they are very cunning. You do not know them as well as I do. Boris, he is a fiend.'

'I'll soon settle Boris for you.'

'You are a lion—yes, but a lion. As for them, they are *canaille*—all of them. Listen, *I have it*! They would have killed me had they known. I was afraid—I did not know what to do, and then I thought of you . . . Hush, what was that?'

It was a sound in the shop below. Motioning to him to remain where he was, she tiptoed out on to the stairs. She returned with a white face and staring eyes.

'*Madre de Dios!* It is the police. They are coming up here. You have a knife? A revolver? Which?'

'My dear girl, you don't expect me seriously to murder a policeman?'

'Oh, but you are mad—mad! They will take you away and hang you by the neck until you're dead.'

'They'll *what*?' said Mr Eastwood, with a very unpleasant feeling going up and down his spine.

Steps sounded on the stair.

'Here they come,' whispered the girl. 'Deny everything. It is the only hope.'

'That's easy enough,' admitted Mr Eastwood, *sotto voce*.

In another minute two men had entered the room. They were in plain clothes, but they had an official bearing that spoke of long training. The smaller of the two, a little dark man with quiet grey eyes, was the spokesman.

'I arrest you, Conrad Fleckman,' he said, 'for the murder of Anna Rosenburg. Anything you say will be used in

189

evidence against you. Here is my warrant and you will do well to come quietly.'

A half-strangled scream burst from the girl's lips. Anthony stepped forward with a composed smile.

'You are making a mistake, officer,' he said pleasantly. 'My name is Anthony Eastwood.'

The two detectives seemed completely unimpressed by his statement.

'We'll see about that later,' said one of them, the one who had not spoken before. 'In the meantime, you come along with us.'

'Conrad,' wailed the girl. 'Conrad, do not let them take you.'

Anthony looked at the detectives.

'You will permit me, I am sure, to say goodbye to this young lady?'

With more decency of feeling than he had expected, the two men moved towards the door. Anthony drew the girl into the corner by the window, and spoke to her in a rapid undertone.

'Listen to me. What I said was true. I am not Conrad Fleckman. When you rang up this morning, they must have given you the wrong number. My name is Anthony Eastwood. I came in answer to your appeal because—well, I came.'

She stared at him incredulously.

'You are not Conrad Fleckman?'

'No.'

'Oh!' she cried, with a deep accent of distress. 'And I kissed you!'

'That's all right,' Mr Eastwood assured her. 'The early Christians made a practice of that sort of thing. Jolly sensible. Now look here, I'll tool off with these people. I shall soon prove my identity. In the meantime, they won't worry you, and you can warn this precious Conrad of yours. Afterwards—'

'Yes?'

'Well—just this. My telephone number is Northwestern 1743—and mind they don't give you the wrong one.'

She gave him an enchanting glance, half-tears, half a smile.

'I shall not forget—indeed, I shall not forget.'

'That's all right then. Goodbye. I say—'

'Yes?'

'Talking of the early Christians—once more wouldn't matter, would it?'

She flung her arms round his neck. Her lips just touched his.

'I do like you—yes, I do like you. You will remember that, whatever happens, won't you?'

Anthony disengaged himself reluctantly and approached his captors.

'I am ready to come with you. You don't want to detain this young lady, I suppose?'

'No, sir, that will be quite all right,' said the small man civilly.

'Decent fellows, these Scotland Yard men,' thought Anthony to himself, as he followed them down the narrow stairway.

There was no sign of the old woman in the shop, but

Anthony caught a heavy breathing from a door at the rear, and guessed that she stood behind it, cautiously observing events.

Once out in the dinginess of Kirk Street, Anthony drew a long breath, and addressed the smaller of the two men.

'Now then, inspector—you are an inspector, I suppose?'

'Yes, sir. Detective-Inspector Verrall. This is Detective-Sergeant Carter.'

'Well, Inspector Verrall, the time has come to talk sense—and to listen to it too. I'm not Conrad What's-his-name. My name is Anthony Eastwood, as I told you, and I am a writer by profession. If you will accompany me to my flat, I think that I shall be able to satisfy you of my identity.'

Something in the matter-of-fact way Anthony spoke seemed to impress the detectives. For the first time an expression of doubt passed over Verrall's face.

Carter, apparently, was harder to convince.

'I dare say,' he sneered. 'But you'll remember the young lady was calling you "Conrad" all right.'

'Ah! that's another matter. I don't mind admitting to you both that for—er—reasons of my own, I was passing myself off upon that lady as a person called Conrad. A private matter, you understand.'

'Likely story, isn't it?' observed Carter. 'No, sir, you come along with us. Hail that taxi, Joe.'

A passing taxi was stopped, and the three men got inside. Anthony made a last attempt, addressing himself to Verrall as the more easily convinced of the two.

'Look here, my dear inspector, what harm is it going to

do you to come along to my flat and see if I'm speaking the truth? You can keep the taxi if you like—there's a generous offer! It won't make five minutes' difference either way.'

Verrall looked at him searchingly.

'I'll do it,' he said suddenly. 'Strange as it appears, I believe you're speaking the truth. We don't want to make fools of ourselves at the station by arresting the wrong man. What's the address?'

'Forty-eight Brandenburg Mansions.'

Verrall leant out and shouted the address to the taxi-driver. All three sat in silence until they arrived at their destination, when Carter sprang out, and Verrall motioned to Anthony to follow him.

'No need for any unpleasantness,' he explained, as he, too, descended. 'We'll go in friendly like, as though Mr Eastwood was bringing a couple of pals home.'

Anthony felt extremely grateful for the suggestion, and his opinion of the Criminal Investigation Department rose every minute.

In the hall-way they were fortunate enough to meet Rogers, the porter. Anthony stopped.

'Ah! Good-evening, Rogers,' he remarked casually.

'Good-evening, Mr Eastwood,' replied the porter respectfully.

He was attached to Anthony, who set an example of liberality not always followed by his neighbours.

Anthony paused with his foot on the bottom step of the stairs.

'By the way, Rogers,' he said casually. 'How long have

I been living here? I was just having a little discussion about it with these friends of mine.'

'Let me see, sir, it must be getting on for close on four years now.'

'Just what I thought.'

Anthony flung a glance of triumph at the two detectives. Carter grunted, but Verrall was smiling broadly.

'Good, but not good enough, sir,' he remarked. 'Shall we go up?'

Anthony opened the door of the flat with his latchkey. He was thankful to remember that Seamark, his man, was out. The fewer witnesses of this catastrophe the better.

The typewriter was as he had left it. Carter strode across to the table and read the headline on the paper.

'THE MYSTERY OF THE SECOND CUCUMBER'

he announced in a gloomy voice.

'A story of mine,' explained Anthony nonchalantly.

'That's another good point, sir,' said Verrall, nodding his head, his eyes twinkling. 'By the way, sir, what was it about? What *was* the mystery of the second cucumber?'

'Ah, there you have me,' said Anthony. 'It's that second cucumber that's been at the bottom of all this trouble.'

Carter was looking at him intently. Suddenly he shook his head and tapped his forehead significantly.

'Balmy, poor young fellow,' he murmured in an audible aside.

'Now, gentlemen,' said Mr Eastwood briskly. 'To business.

Here are letters addressed to me, my bankbook, communications from editors. What more do you want?'

Verrall examined the papers that Anthony thrust upon him.

'Speaking for myself, sir,' he said respectfully, 'I want nothing more. I'm quite convinced. But I can't take the responsibility of releasing you upon myself. You see, although it seems positive that you have been residing here as Mr Eastwood for some years, yet it is possible that Conrad Fleckman and Anthony Eastwood are one and the same person. I must make a thorough search of the flat, take your fingerprints, and telephone to headquarters.'

'That seems a comprehensive programme,' remarked Anthony. 'I can assure you that you're welcome to any guilty secrets of mine you may lay your hands on.'

The inspector grinned. For a detective, he was a singularly human person.

'Will you go into the little end room, sir, with Carter, whilst I'm getting busy?'

'All right,' said Anthony unwillingly. 'I suppose it couldn't be the other way about, could it?'

'Meaning?'

'That you and I and a couple of whiskies and sodas should occupy the end room whilst our friend, the Sergeant, does the heavy searching.'

'If you prefer it, sir?'

'I do prefer it.'

They left Carter investigating the contents of the desk with business-like dexterity. As they passed out of the room, they heard him take down the telephone and call up Scotland Yard.

'This isn't so bad,' said Anthony, settling himself with a whisky and soda by his side, having hospitably attended to the wants of Inspector Verrall. 'Shall I drink first, just to show you that the whisky isn't poisoned?'

The inspector smiled.

'Very irregular, all this,' he remarked. 'But we know a thing or two in our profession. I realized right from the start that we'd made a mistake. But of course one had to observe all the usual forms. You can't get away from red tape, can you, sir?'

'I suppose not,' said Anthony regretfully. 'The sergeant doesn't seem very matey yet, though, does he?'

'Ah, he's a fine man, Detective-Sergeant Carter. You wouldn't find it easy to put anything over on him.'

'I've noticed that,' said Anthony.

'By the way, inspector,' he added, 'is there any objection to my hearing something about myself?'

'In what way, sir?'

'Come now, don't you realize that I'm devoured by curiousity? Who was Anna Rosenburg, and why did I murder her?'

'You'll read all about it in the newspapers tomorrow, sir.'

'"*Tomorrow I may be Myself with Yesterday's ten thousand years*",' quoted Anthony. 'I really think you might satisfy my perfectly legitimate curiosity, inspector. Cast aside your official reticence, and tell me all.'

'It's quite irregular, sir.'

'My dear inspector, when we are becoming such fast friends?'

'Well, sir, Anna Rosenburg was a German-Jewess who lived at Hampstead. With no visible means of livelihood, she grew yearly richer and richer.'

'I'm just the opposite,' commented Anthony. 'I have a visible means of livelihood and I get yearly poorer and poorer. Perhaps I should do better if I lived in Hampstead. I've always heard Hampstead is very bracing.'

'At one time,' continued Verrall, 'she was a second-hand clothes dealer—'

'That explains it,' interrupted Anthony. 'I remember selling my uniform after the war—not khaki, the other stuff. The whole flat was full of red trousers and gold lace, spread out to best advantage. A fat man in a check suit arrived in a Rolls-Royce with a factotum complete with bag. He bid one pound ten for the lot. In the end I threw in a hunting coat and some Zeiss glasses to make up the two pounds, at a given signal the factotum opened the bag and shovelled the goods inside, and the fat man tendered me a ten-pound note and asked me for change.'

'About ten years ago,' continued the inspector, 'there were several Spanish political refugees in London—amongst them a certain Don Fernando Ferrarez with his young wife and child. They were very poor, and the wife was ill. Anna Rosenburg visited the place where they were lodging and asked if they had anything to sell. Don Fernando was out, and his wife decided to part with a very wonderful Spanish shawl, embroidered in a marvellous manner, which had been one of her husband's last presents to her before flying from Spain. When Don Fernando returned, he flew into a terrible rage on hearing the shawl had been sold, and tried vainly to recover it. When he at last succeeded in finding the second-hand clothes woman in question, she declared that she had resold the shawl to a woman whose name she did not know. Don Fernando was in despair. Two months later he was stabbed in the street and died as a result of his wounds. From that time onward, Anna Rosenburg seemed suspiciously flush of money. In the ten years that followed, her house was burgled no less than eight times. Four of the attempts were frustrated and nothing was taken, on the other four occasions, an embroidered shawl of some kind was amongst the booty.'

The inspector paused, and then went on in obedience to an urgent gesture from Anthony.

'A week ago, Carmen Ferrarez, the young daughter of Don Fernando, arrived in this country from a convent in France. Her first action was to seek out Anna Rosenburg at Hampstead. There she is reported to have had a violent scene with the old woman, and her words at leaving were overheard by one of the servants.

'"You have it still," she cried. "All these years you have grown rich on it—but I say to you solemnly that in the end it will bring you bad luck. You have no moral right to it, and the day will come when you will wish you had never seen the Shawl of the Thousand Flowers."

'Three days after that, Carmen Ferrarez disappeared mysteriously from the hotel where she was staying. In her room was found a name and address—the name of Conrad Fleckman, and also a note from a man purporting to be an antique dealer asking if she were disposed to part with a certain embroidered shawl which he believed she had in her possession. The address given on the note was a false one.

'It is clear that the shawl is the centre of the whole mystery. Yesterday morning Conrad Fleckman called upon Anna Rosenburg. She was shut up with him for an hour or more, and when he left she was obliged to go to bed, so white and shaken was she by the interview. But she gave orders that if he came to see her again he was always to be admitted. Last night she got up and went out about nine o'clock, and did not return. She was found this morning in the house occupied by Conrad Fleckman, stabbed through the heart. On the floor beside her was— what do you think?'

'The shawl?' breathed Anthony. 'The Shawl of a Thousand Flowers.'

'Something far more gruesome than that. Something which explained the whole mysterious business of the shawl and made its hidden value clear . . . Excuse me, I fancy that's the chief—'

There had indeed been a ring at the bell. Anthony contained his impatience as best he could and waited for the inspector to return. He was pretty well at ease about his own position now. As soon as they took the fingerprints they would realise their mistake.

And then, perhaps, Carmen would ring up . . .

The Shawl of a Thousand Flowers! What a strange story—just the kind of story to make an appropriate setting for the girl's exquisite dark beauty.

Carmen Ferrarez . . .

He jerked himself back from day dreaming. What a time that inspector fellow was. He rose and pulled the door open. The flat was strangely silent. Could they have gone? Surely not without a word to him.

He strode out into the next room. It was empty—so was the sitting-room. Strangely empty! It had a bare dishevelled appearance. Good heavens! His enamels—the silver!

He rushed wildly through the flat. It was the same tale everywhere. The place had been denuded. Every single thing of value, and Anthony had a very pretty collector's taste in small things, had been taken.

With a groan Anthony staggered to a chair, his head in his hands. He was aroused by the ringing of the front door bell. He opened it to confront Rogers.

'You'll excuse me, sir,' said Rogers. 'But the gentlemen fancied you might be wanting something.'

'The gentlemen?'

'Those two friends of yours, sir. I helped them with the packing as best I could. Very fortunately I happened to have them two good cases in the basement.' His eyes dropped to the floor. 'I've swept up the straw as best I could, sir.'

'You packed the things in here?' groaned Anthony.

'Yes, sir. Was that not your wishes, sir? It was the tall gentleman told me to do so, sir, and seeing as you were busy talking to the other gentleman in the little end room, I didn't like to disturb you.'

'I wasn't talking to him,' said Anthony. 'He was talking to me—curse him.'

Rogers coughed.

'I'm sure I'm very sorry for the necessity, sir,' he murmured.

'Necessity?'

'Of parting with your little treasures, sir.'

'Eh? Oh, yes. Ha, ha!' He gave a mirthless laugh. 'They've driven off by now, I suppose. Those—those friends of mine, I mean?'

'Oh, yes, sir, some time ago. I put the cases on the taxi and the tall gentleman went upstairs again, and then they both came running down and drove off at once . . . Excuse me, sir, but is anything wrong, sir?'

Rogers might well ask. The hollow groan which Anthony emitted would have aroused surmise anywhere.

'Everything is wrong, thank you, Rogers. But I see clearly that you were not to blame. Leave me, I would commune a while with my telephone.'

Five minutes later saw Anthony pouring his tale into the ears of Inspector Driver, who sat opposite to him, note-book in hand. An unsympathetic man, Inspector Driver, and not (Anthony reflected) nearly so like a real inspector! Distinctly stagey, in fact. Another striking example of the superiority of Art over Nature.

Anthony reached the end of his tale. The inspector shut up his note-book.

'Well?' said Anthony anxiously.

'Clear as paint,' said the inspector. 'It's the Patterson gang. They've done a lot of smart work lately. Big fair man, small dark man, and the girl.'

'The girl?'

'Yes, dark and mighty good looking. Acts as a decoy usually.'

'A—a Spanish girl?'

'She might call herself that. She was born in Hampstead.'

'I *said* it was a bracing place,' murmured Anthony.

'Yes, it's clear enough,' said the inspector, rising to depart. 'She got you on the phone and pitched you a tale—she guessed you'd come along all right. Then she goes along to old Mother Gibson's who isn't above accepting a tip for the use of her room for them as finds it awkward to meet in public—lovers, you understand, nothing criminal. You fall for it all right, they get you back here, and while one of them pitches you a tale, the other gets away with the swag. It's the Pattersons all right—just their touch.'

'And my things?' said Anthony anxiously.

'We'll do what we can, sir. But the Pattersons are uncommon sharp.'

'They seem to be,' said Anthony bitterly.

The inspector departed, and scarcely had the gone before there came a ring at the door. Anthony opened it. A small boy stood there, holding a package.

'Parcel for you, sir.'

Anthony took it with some surprise. He was not expecting a parcel of any kind. Returning to the sitting-room with it, he cut the string.

It was the liqueur set!

'Damn!' said Anthony.

Then he noticed that at the bottom of one of the glasses there was a tiny artificial rose. His mind flew back to the upper room in Kirk Street.

'I do like you—yes, I do like you. You will remember that whatever happens, won't you?'

That was what she had said. *Whatever happens* . . . Did she mean—

Anthony took hold of himself sternly.

'This won't do,' he admonished himself.

His eye fell on the typewriter, and he sat down with a resolute face.

### THE MYSTERY OF THE SECOND CUCUMBER

His face grew dreamy again. The Shawl of a Thousand Flowers. What was it that was found on the floor beside the dead body? The gruesome thing that explained the whole mystery?

Nothing, of course, since it was only a trumped-up tale to hold his attention, and the teller had used the old Arabian Nights' trick of breaking off at the most interesting point. But couldn't there be a gruesome thing that explained the whole mystery? couldn't there now? If one gave one's mind to it?

Anthony tore the sheet of paper from his typewriter and substituted another. He typed a headline:

### THE MYSTERY OF THE SPANISH SHAWL

He surveyed it for a moment or two in silence.

Then he began to type rapidly . . .

# The Golden Ball

George Dundas stood in the City of London meditating.

All about him toilers and money-makers surged and flowed like an enveloping tide. But George, beautifully dressed, his trousers exquisitely creased, took no heed of them. He was busy thinking what to do next.

Something had occurred! Between George and his rich uncle (Ephraim Leadbetter of the firm of Leadbetter and Gilling) there had been what is called in a lower walk of life 'words'. To be strictly accurate the words had been almost entirely on Mr Leadbetter's side. They had flowed from his lips in a steady stream of bitter indignation, and the fact that they consisted almost entirely of repetition did not seem to have worried him. To say a thing once beautifully and then let it alone was not one of Mr Leadbetter's mottos.

The theme was a simple one—the criminal folly and wickedness of a young man, who has his way to make, taking a day off in the middle of the week without even asking leave. Mr Leadbetter, when he had said everything he could think of and several things twice, paused for breath and asked George what he meant by it.

George replied simply that he had felt he wanted a day off. A holiday, in fact.

And what, Mr Leadbetter wanted to know, were Saturday afternoon and Sunday? To say nothing of Whitsuntide, not long past, and August Bank Holiday to come?

George said he didn't care for Saturday afternoons, Sundays or Bank Holidays. He meant a real day, when it might be possible to find some spot where half London was not assembled already.

Mr Leadbetter then said that he had done his best by his dead sister's son—nobody could say he hadn't given him a chance. But it was plain that it was no use. And in future George could have five real days with Saturday and Sunday added to do with as he liked.

'The golden ball of opportunity has been thrown up for you, my boy,' said Mr Leadbetter in a last touch of poetical fancy. 'And you have failed to grasp it.'

George said it seemed to him that that was just what he *had* done, and Mr Leadbetter dropped poetry for wrath and told him to get out.

Hence George—meditating. Would his uncle relent or would he not? Had he any secret affection for George, or merely a cold distaste?

It was just at that moment that a voice—a most unlikely voice—said, 'Hello!'

A scarlet touring car with an immense long bonnet had drawn up to the curb beside him. At the wheel was that beautiful and popular society girl, Mary Montresor. (The description is that of the illustrated papers who produced a portrait of her at least four times a month.) She was smiling at George in an accomplished manner.

'I never knew a man could look so like an island,' said Mary Montresor. 'Would you like to get in?'

'I should love it above all things,' said George with no hesitation, and stepped in beside her.

They proceeded slowly because the traffic forbade anything else.

'I'm tired of the city,' said Mary Montresor. 'I came to see what it was like. I shall go back to London.'

Without presuming to correct her geography, George said it was a splendid idea. They proceeded sometimes slowly, sometimes with wild bursts of speed when Mary Montresor saw a chance of cutting in. It seemed to George that she was somewhat optimistic in the latter view, but he reflected that one could only die once. He thought it best, however, to essay no conversation. He preferred his fair driver to keep strictly to the job in hand.

It was she who reopened the conversation, choosing the moment when they were doing a wild sweep round Hyde Park Corner.

'How would you like to marry me?' she inquired casually.

George gave a gasp, but that may have been due to a large bus that seemed to spell certain destruction. He prided himself on his quickness in response.

'I should love it,' he replied easily.

'Well,' said Mary Montresor, vaguely. 'Perhaps you may some day.'

They turned into the straight without accident, and at

that moment George perceived large new bills at Hyde Park Corner tube station. Sandwiched between GRAVE POLITICAL SITUATION and COLONEL IN DOCK, one said SOCIETY GIRL TO MARRY DUKE and the other DUKE OF EDGEHILL AND MISS MONTRESOR.

'What's this about the Duke of Edgehill?' demanded George sternly.

'Me and Bingo? We're engaged.'

'But then—what you said just now—'

'Oh, *that*,' said Mary Montresor. 'You see, I haven't made up my mind who I shall actually *marry*.'

'Then why did you get engaged to him?'

'Just to see if I could. Everybody seemed to think it would be frightfully difficult, and it wasn't a bit!'

'Very rough luck on—er—Bingo,' said George, mastering his embarrassment at calling a real live duke by a nickname.

'Not at all,' said Mary Montresor. 'It will be good for Bingo if anything *could* do him good—which I doubt.'

George made another discovery—again aided by a convenient poster.

'Why, of course, it's cup day at Ascot. I should have thought that was the one place you were simply bound to be today.'

Mary Montresor sighed.

'I wanted a holiday,' she said plaintively.

'Why, so did I,' said George, delighted. 'And as a result my uncle has kicked me out to starve.'

'Then in case we marry,' said Mary, 'my twenty thousand a year may come in useful?'

'It will certainly provide us with a few home comforts,' said George.

'Talking of homes,' said Mary, 'let's go in the country and find a home we would like to live in.'

It seemed a simple and charming plan. They negotiated Putney Bridge, reached the Kingston by-pass and with a sigh of satisfaction Mary pressed her foot down on the accelerator. They got into the country very quickly. It was half an hour later that with a sudden exclamation Mary shot out a dramatic hand and pointed.

On the brow of a hill in front of them there nestled a house of what house-agents describe (but seldom truthfully) as 'old-world' charm. Imagine the description of most houses in the country really come true for once, and you get an idea of this house.

Mary drew up outside a white gate.

'We'll leave the car and go up and look at it. It's our house!'

'Decidedly, it's our house,' agreed George. 'But just for the moment other people seem to be living in it.'

Mary dismissed the other people with a wave of her hand. They walked up the winding drive together. The house appeared even more desirable at close quarters.

'We'll go and peep in at all the windows,' said Mary.

George demurred.

'Do you think the other people—?'

'I shan't consider them. It's our house—they're only living in it by a sort of accident. Besides, it's a lovely day and they're sure to be out. And if anyone does catch us, I shall say—I shall say—that I thought it was Mrs—Mrs

Pardonstenger's house, and that I *am* so sorry I made a mistake.'

'Well, that ought to be safe enough,' said George reflectively.

They looked in through windows. The house was delightfully furnished. They had just got to the study when footsteps crunched on the gravel behind them and they turned to face a most irreproachable butler.

'Oh!' said Mary. And then putting on her most enchanting smile, she said, 'Is Mrs Pardonstenger in? I was looking to see if she was in the study.'

'Mrs Pardonstenger is at home, madam,' said the butler. 'Will you come this way, please.'

They did the only thing they could. They followed him. George was calculating what the odds against this happening could possibly be. With a name like Pardonstenger he came to the conclusion it was about one in twenty thousand. His companion whispered, 'Leave it to me. It will be all right.'

George was only too pleased to leave it to her. The situation, he considered, called for feminine finesse.

They were shown into a drawing-room. No sooner had the butler left the room than the door almost immediately reopened and a big florid lady with peroxide hair came in expectantly.

Mary Montresor made a movement towards her, then paused in well-simulated surprise.

'Why!' she exclaimed. 'It *isn't* Amy! What an extraordinary thing!'

'It *is* an extraordinary thing,' said a grim voice.

A man had entered behind Mrs Pardonstenger, an enormous man with a bulldog face and a sinister frown. George thought he had never seen such an unpleasant brute. The man closed the door and stood with his back against it.

'A very extraordinary thing,' he repeated sneeringly. 'But I fancy we understand your little game!' He suddenly produced what seemed an outsize in revolvers. 'Hands up. Hands up, I say. Frisk 'em, Bella.'

George in reading detective stories had often wondered what it meant to be frisked. Now he knew. Bella (alias Mrs P.) satisfied herself that neither he nor Mary concealed any lethal weapons on their persons.

'Thought you were mighty clever, didn't you?' sneered the man. 'Coming here like this and playing the innocents. You've made a mistake this time—a bad mistake. In fact, I very much doubt whether your friends and relations will ever see you again. Ah! you would, would you?' as George made a movement. 'None of your games. I'd shoot you as soon as look at you.'

'Be careful, George,' quavered Mary.

'I shall,' said George with feeling. 'Very careful.'

'And now march,' said the man. 'Open the door, Bella. Keep your hands above your heads, you two. The lady first—that's right. I'll come behind you both. Across the hall. Upstairs . . .'

They obeyed. What else could they do? Mary mounted the stairs, her hands held high. George followed. Behind them came the huge ruffian, revolver in hand.

Mary reached the top of the staircase and turned the

corner. At the same moment, without the least warning, George lunged out in a fierce backward kick. He caught the man full in the middle and he capsized backwards down the stairs. In a moment George had turned and leaped down after him, kneeling on his chest. With his right hand, he picked up the revolver which had fallen from the other's hand as he fell.

Bella gave a scream and retreated through a baize door. Mary came running down the stairs, her face as white as paper.

'George, you haven't killed him?'

The man was lying absolutely still. George bent over him.

'I don't think I've killed him,' he said regretfully. 'But he's certainly taken the count all right.'

'Thank God.' She was breathing rapidly.

'Pretty neat,' said George with permissible self-admiration. 'Many a lesson to be learnt from a jolly old mule. Eh, what?'

Mary pulled at his hand.

'Come away,' she cried feverishly. 'Come away quick.'

'If we had something to tie this fellow up with,' said George, intent on his own plans. 'I suppose you couldn't find a bit of rope or cord anywhere?'

'No, I couldn't,' said Mary. 'And come away, please— please—I'm so frightened.'

'You needn't be frightened,' said George with manly arrogance. '*I'm* here.'

'Darling George, please—for my sake. I don't want to be mixed up in this. *Please* let's go.'

The exquisite way in which she breathed the words 'for my sake' shook George's resolution. He allowed himself to be led forth from the house and hurried down the drive to the waiting car. Mary said faintly: 'You drive. I don't feel I can.' George took command of the wheel.

'But we've got to see this thing through,' he said. 'Heaven knows what blackguardism that nasty-looking fellow is up to. I won't bring the police into it if you don't want me to—but I'll have a try on my own. I ought to be able to get on their track all right.'

'No, George, I don't want you to.'

'We have a first-class adventure like this, and you want me to back out of it? Not on my life.'

'I'd no idea you were so bloodthirsty,' said Mary tearfully.

'I'm not bloodthirsty. I didn't begin it. The damned cheek of the fellow—threatening us with an outsize revolver. By the way—why on earth didn't that revolver go off when I kicked him downstairs?'

He stopped the car and fished the revolver out of the side-pocket of the car where he had placed it. After examining it, he whistled.

'Well, I'm damned! The thing isn't loaded. If I'd known that—' He paused, wrapped in thought. 'Mary, this is a very curious business.'

'I know it is. That's why I'm begging you to leave it alone.'

'Never,' said George firmly.

Mary uttered a heartrending sigh.

'I see,' she said, 'that I shall have to tell you. And the

worst of it is that I haven't the least idea how you'll take it.'

'What do you mean—tell me?'

'You see, it's like this.' She paused. 'I feel girls should stick together nowadays—they should insist on knowing something about the men they meet.'

'Well?' said George, utterly fogged.

'And the most important thing to a girl is how a man will behave in an emergency—has he got presence of mind—courage—quick wittedness? That's the kind of thing you can hardly ever know—until it's too late. An emergency mightn't arise until you'd been married for years. All you do know about a man is how he dances and if he's good at getting taxis on a wet night.'

'Both very useful accomplishments,' George pointed out.

'Yes, but one wants to feel a man is a man.'

'The great wide-open spaces where men *are* men.' George quoted absently.

'Exactly. But we have no wide-open spaces in England. So one has to create a situation artificially. That's what I did.'

'Do you mean—?'

'I do mean. That house, as it happens, actually *is* my house. We came to it by design—not by chance. And the man—that man that you nearly killed—'

'Yes?'

'He's Rube Wallace—the film actor. He does prizefighters, you know. The dearest and gentlest of men. I engaged him. Bella's his wife. That's why I was so terrified that you'd killed him. Of course the revolver wasn't loaded. It's a stage property. Oh, George, are you very angry?'

'Am I the first person you have—er—tried this test on?'

'Oh, no. There have been—let me see—nine and a half!'

'Who was the half?' inquired George with curiosity.

'Bingo,' replied Mary coldly.

'Did any of them think of kicking like a mule?'

'No—they didn't. Some tried to bluster and some gave in at once, but they all allowed themselves to be marched upstairs and tied up, and gagged. Then, of course, I managed to work myself loose from my bonds—like in books—and I freed them and we got away—finding the house empty.'

'And nobody thought of the mule trick or anything like it?'

'No.'

'In that case,' said George graciously, 'I forgive you.'

'Thank you, George,' said Mary meekly.

'In fact,' said George, 'the only question that arises is: where do we go now? I'm not sure if it's Lambeth Palace or Doctor's Commons, wherever that is.'

'What *are* you talking about?'

'The licence. A special licence, I think, is indicated. You're too fond of getting engaged to one man and then immediately asking another one to marry you.'

'I didn't ask you to marry me!'

'You did. At Hyde Park Corner. Not a place I should choose for a proposal myself, but everyone has their idiosyncrasies in these matters.'

'I did nothing of the kind. I just asked, as a joke, whether you would care to marry me? It wasn't intended seriously.'

'If I were to take counsel's opinion, I am sure that he would say it constituted a genuine proposal. Besides, you know you want to marry me.'

'I don't.'

'Not after nine and a half failures? Fancy what a feeling of security it will give you to go through life with a man who can extricate you from any dangerous situation.'

Mary appeared to weaken slightly at this telling argument. But she said firmly: 'I wouldn't marry any man unless he went on his knees to me.'

George looked at her. She was adorable. But George had other characteristics of the mule beside its kick. He said with equal firmness:

'To go on one's knees to any woman is degrading. I will not do it.'

Mary said with enchanting wistfulness: 'What a pity.'

They drove back to London. George was stern and silent. Mary's face was hidden by the brim of her hat. As they passed Hyde Park Corner, she murmured softly:

'Couldn't you go on your knees to me?'

George said firmly: 'No.'

He felt he was being a superman. She admired him for his attitude. But unluckily he suspected her of mulish tendencies herself. He drew up suddenly.

'Excuse me,' he said.

He jumped out of the car, retraced his steps to a fruit barrow they had just passed and returned so quickly that the policeman who was bearing down upon them to ask what they meant by it, had not had time to arrive.

George drove on, lightly tossing an apple into Mary's lap.

'Eat more fruit,' he said. 'Also symbolical.'

'Symbolical?'

'Yes. Originally Eve gave Adam an apple. Nowadays Adam gives Eve one. See?'

'Yes,' said Mary rather doubtfully.

'Where shall I drive you?' inquired George formally.

'Home, please.'

He drove to Grosvenor Square. His face was absolutely impassive. He jumped out and came round to help her out. She made a last appeal.

'Darling George—couldn't you? Just to please me?'

'Never,' said George.

And at that moment it happened. He slipped, tried to recover his balance and failed. He was kneeling in the mud before her. Mary gave a squeal of joy and clapped her hands.

'Darling George! Now I will marry you. You can go straight to Lambeth Palace and fix up with the Archbishop of Canterbury about it.'

'I didn't mean to,' said George hotly. 'It was a bl—er—a banana skin.' He held the offender up reproachfully.

'Never mind,' said Mary. 'It happened. When we quarrel and you throw it in my teeth that I proposed to you, I can retort that you had to go on your knees to me before I would marry you. And all because of that blessed banana skin! It *was* a blessed banana skin you were going to say?'

'Something of the sort,' said George.

*

At five-thirty that afternoon, Mr Leadbetter was informed that his nephew had called and would like to see him.

'Called to eat humble pie,' said Mr Leadbetter to himself. 'I dare say I was rather hard on the lad, but it was for his own good.'

And he gave orders that George should be admitted.

George came in airily.

'I want a few words with you, uncle,' he said. 'You did me a grave injustice this morning. I should like to know whether, at my age, you could have gone out into the street, disowned by your relatives, and between the hours of eleven-fifteen and five-thirty acquire an income of twenty thousand a year. This is what I have done!'

'You're mad, boy.'

'Not mad, resourceful! I am going to marry a young, rich, beautiful society girl. One, moreover, who is throwing over a duke for my sake.'

'Marrying a girl for her money? I'd not have thought it of you.'

'And you'd have been right. I would never have dared to ask her if she hadn't—very fortunately—asked me. She retracted afterwards, but I made her change her mind. And do you know, uncle, how all this was done? By a judicious expenditure of twopence and a grasping of the golden ball of opportunity.'

'Why the tuppence?' asked Mr Leadbetter, financially interested.

'One banana—off a barrow. Not everyone would have thought of that banana. Where do you get a marriage licence? Is it Doctor's Commons or Lambeth Palace?'

# The Rajah's Emerald

With a serious effort James Bond bent his attention once more on the little yellow book in his hand. On its outside the book bore the simple but pleasing legend, 'Do you want your salary increased by £300 per annum?' Its price was one shilling. James had just finished reading two pages of crisp paragraphs instructing him to look his boss in the face, to cultivate a dynamic personality, and to radiate an atmosphere of efficiency. He had now arrived at a subtler matter. 'There is a time for frankness, there is a time for discretion,' the little yellow book informed him. 'A strong man does not always blurt out *all* he knows.' James let the little book close, and raising his head, gazed out over a blue expanse of ocean. A horrible suspicion assailed him, that he was *not* a strong man. A strong man would have been in command of the present situation, not a victim to it. For the sixtieth time that morning James rehearsed his wrongs.

This was his holiday. His holiday? Ha, ha! Sardonic laughter. Who had persuaded him to come to that fashionable seaside resort, Kimpton-on-Sea? Grace. Who had urged him into an expenditure of more than he could afford? Grace. And he had fallen in with the plan eagerly. She had got him here, and what was the result? Whilst he was staying in an obscure boarding-house about a mile and a half from the sea-front, Grace who should have been in a similar boarding-house (not the same one—the proprieties of James's circle were very strict) had flagrantly deserted him, and was staying at no less than the Esplanade Hotel upon the sea-front.

It seemed that she had friends there. Friends! Again James laughed sardonically. His mind went back over the last three years of his leisurely courtship of Grace. Extremely pleased she had been when he first singled her out for notice. That was before she had risen to heights of glory in the millinery salons at Messrs Bartles in the High Street. In those early days it had been James who gave himself airs, now alas! the boot was on the other leg. Grace was what is technically known as 'earning good money'. It had made her uppish. Yes, that was it, thoroughly uppish. A confused fragment out of a poetry book came back to James's mind, something about 'thanking heaven fasting, for a good man's love'. But there was nothing of that kind of thing observable about Grace. Well fed on an Esplanade Hotel breakfast, she was ignoring a good man's love utterly. She was indeed accepting the attentions of a poisonous idiot called Claud Sopworth, a man, James felt convinced, of no moral worth whatsoever.

James ground a heel into the the earth, and scowled darkly at the horizon. Kimpton-on-Sea. What had possessed him to come to such a place? It was pre-eminently a resort of the rich and fashionable, it possessed two large hotels, and several miles of picturesque bungalows belonging to fashionable actresses, rich Jews and those members of the English aristocracy who had married wealthy wives. The rent, furnished, of the smallest bungalow was twenty-five guineas a week. Imagination boggled at what the rent of the large ones might amount to. There was one of these palaces immediately behind James's seat. It belonged to that famous sportsman Lord Edward Campion, and there were staying there at the moment a houseful of distinguished guests including the Rajah of Maraputna, whose wealth was fabulous. James had read all about him in the local weekly newspaper that morning: the extent of his Indian possessions, his palaces, his wonderful collection of jewels, with a special mention of one famous emerald which the papers declared enthusiastically was the size of a pigeon's egg. James, being town bred, was somewhat hazy about the size of a pigeon's egg, but the impression left on his mind was good.

'If I had an emerald like that,' said James, scowling at the horizon again, 'I'd show Grace.'

The sentiment was vague, but the enunciation of it made James feel better. Laughing voices hailed him from behind, and he turned abruptly to confront Grace. With her was Clara Sopworth, Alice Sopworth, Dorothy Sopworth and—alas! Claud Sopworth. The girls were arm-in-arm and giggling.

'Why, you are quite a stranger,' cried Grace archly.

'Yes,' said James.

He could, he felt, have found a more telling retort. You

cannot convey the impression of a dynamic personality by the use of the one word 'yes'. He looked with intense loathing at Claud Sopworth. Claud Sopworth was almost as beautifully dressed as the hero of a musical comedy. James longed passionately for the moment when an enthusiastic beach dog should plant wet, sandy forefeet on the unsullied whiteness of Claud's flannel trousers. He himself wore a serviceable pair of dark-grey flannel trousers which had seen better days.

'Isn't the air beau-tiful?' said Clara, sniffing it appreciatively. 'Quite sets you up, doesn't it?'

She giggled.

'It's ozone,' said Alice Sopworth. 'It's as good as a tonic, you know.' And she giggled also.

James thought:

'I should like to knock their silly heads together. What is the sense of laughing all the time? They are not saying anything funny.'

The immaculate Claud murmured languidly:

'Shall we have a bathe, or is it too much of a fag?'

The idea of bathing was accepted shrilly. James fell into line with them. He even managed, with a certain amount of cunning, to draw Grace a little behind the others.

'Look here!' he complained, 'I am hardly seeing anything of you.'

'Well, I am sure we are all together now,' said Grace, 'and you can come and lunch with us at the hotel, at least—'

She looked dubiously at James's legs.

'What is the matter?' demanded James ferociously. 'Not smart enough for you, I suppose?'

221

'I do think, dear, you might take a little more pains,' said Grace. 'Everyone is so fearfully smart here. Look at Claud Sopworth!'

'I have looked at him,' said James grimly. 'I have never seen a man who looked a more complete ass than he does.'

Grace drew herself up.

'There is no need to criticize my friends, James, it's not manners. He's dressed just like any other gentleman at the hotel is dressed.'

'Bah!' said James. 'Do you know what I read the other day in "Society Snippets"? Why, that the Duke of—the Duke of, I can't remember, but one duke, anyway, was the worst dressed man in England, there!'

'I dare say,' said Grace, 'but then, you see, he is a duke.'

'Well?' demanded James. 'What is wrong with my being a duke some day? At least, well, not perhaps a duke, but a peer.'

He slapped the yellow book in his pocket, and recited to her a long list of peers of the realm who had started life much more obscurely than James Bond. Grace merely giggled.

'Don't be so soft, James,' she said. 'Fancy you Earl of Kimpton-on-Sea!'

James gazed at her in mingled rage and despair. The air of Kimpton-on-Sea had certainly gone to Grace's head.

The beach at Kimpton is a long, straight stretch of sand. A row of bathing-huts and boxes stretches evenly along it for about a mile and a half. The party had stopped before a row of six huts all labelled imposingly, 'For visitors to the Esplanade Hotel only.'

'Here we are,' said Grace brightly; 'but I'm afraid you

can't come in with us, James, you'll have to go along to the public tents over there. We'll meet you in the sea. So long!'

'So long!' said James, and he strode off in the direction indicated.

Twelve dilapidated tents stood solemnly confronting the ocean. An aged mariner guarded them, a roll of blue paper in his hand. He accepted a coin of the realm from James, tore him off a blue ticket from his roll, threw him over a towel, and jerked one thumb over his shoulder.

'Take your turn,' he said huskily.

It was then that James awoke to the fact of competition. Others besides himself had conceived the idea of entering the sea. Not only was each tent occupied, but outside each tent was a determined-looking crowd of people glaring at each other. James attached himself to the smallest group and waited. The strings of the tent parted, and a beautiful young woman, sparsely clad, emerged on the scene settling her bathing-cap with the air of one who had the whole morning to waste. She strolled down to the water's edge, and sat down dreamily on the sands.

'That's no good,' said James to himself, and attached himself forthwith to another group.

After waiting five minutes, sounds of activity were apparent in the second tent. With heavings and strainings, the flaps parted asunder and four children and a father and mother emerged. The tent being so small, it had something of the appearance of a conjuring trick. On the instant two women sprang forward each grasping one flap of the tent.

'Excuse me,' said the first young woman, panting a little.

'Excuse *me*,' said the other young woman, glaring.

'I would have you know I was here quite ten minutes before you were,' said the first young woman rapidly.

'I have been here a good quarter of an hour, as anyone will tell you,' said the second young woman defiantly.

'Now then, now then,' said the aged mariner, drawing near.

Both young women spoke to him shrilly. When they had finished, he jerked his thumb at the second young woman, and said briefly:

'It's yours.'

Then he departed, deaf to remonstrances. He neither knew nor cared which had been there first, but his decision, as they say in newspaper competitions, was final. The despairing James caught at his arm.

'Look here! I say!'

'Well, mister?'

'How long is it going to be before I get a tent?'

The aged mariner threw a dispassionate glance over the waiting throng.

'Might be an hour, might be an hour and a half, I can't say.'

At that moment James espied Grace and the Sopworth girls running lightly down the sands towards the sea.

'Damn!' said James to himself. 'Oh, damn!'

He plucked once more at the aged mariner.

'Can't I get a tent anywhere else? What about one of these huts along here? They all seem empty.'

'The huts,' said the ancient mariner with dignity, 'are
PRIVATE.'

Having uttered this rebuke, he passed on. With a bitter
feeling of having been tricked, James detached himself from
the waiting groups, and strode savagely down the beach.
It was the limit! It was the absolute, complete limit! He
glared savagely at the trim bathing-boxes he passed. In that
moment from being an Independent Liberal, he became a
red-hot Socialist. Why should the rich have bathing-boxes
and be able to bathe any minute they chose without waiting
in a crowd? 'This system of ours,' said James vaguely, 'is
all *wrong*.'

From the sea came the coquettish screams of the splashed.
Grace's voice! And above her squeaks, the inane 'Ha, ha,
ha,' of Claud Sopworth.

'Damn!' said James, grinding his teeth, a thing which he
had never before attempted, only read about in works of
fiction.

He came to a stop, twirling his stick savagely, and turning
his back firmly on the sea. Instead, he gazed with concen-
trated hatred upon Eagle's Nest, Buena Vista, and Mon
Desir. It was the custom of the inhabitants of Kimpton-
on-Sea to label their bathing-huts with fancy names. Eagle's
Nest merely struck James as being silly, and Buena Vista
was beyond his linguistic accomplishments. But his knowledge of French was sufficient to make him realize the
appositeness of the third name.

'Mong Desire,' said James. 'I should jolly well think it
was.'

And on that moment he saw that while the doors of

the other bathing-huts were tightly closed, that of Mon Desir was ajar. James looked thoughtfully up and down the beach; this particular spot was mainly occupied by mothers of large families, busily engaged in superintending their offspring. It was only ten o'clock, too early as yet for the aristocracy of Kimpton-on-Sea to have come down to bathe.

'Eating quails and mushrooms in their beds as likely as not, brought to them on trays by powdered footmen, pah! Not one of them will be down here before twelve o'clock,' thought James.

He looked again towards the sea. With the obedience of a well-trained 'leitmotif', the shrill scream of Grace rose upon the air. It was followed by the 'Ha, ha, ha,' of Claud Sopworth.

'I will,' said James between his teeth.

He pushed open the door of Mon Desir and entered. For the moment he had a fright, as he caught sight of sundry garments hanging from pegs, but he was quickly reassured. The hut was partitioned into two, on the right-hand side, a girl's yellow sweater, a battered panama hat and a pair of beach shoes were depending from a peg. On the left-hand side an old pair of grey flannel trousers, a pullover, and a sou'wester proclaimed the fact that the sexes were segregated. James hastily transferred himself to the gentlemen's part of the hut, and undressed rapidly. Three minutes later, he was in the sea puffing and snorting importantly, doing extremely short bursts of professional-looking swimming—head under the water, arms lashing the sea—that style.

'Oh, there you are!' cried Grace. 'I was afraid you wouldn't be in for ages with all that crowd of people waiting there.'

'Really?' said James.

He thought with affectionate loyalty of the yellow book. 'The strong man can on occasions be discreet.' For the moment his temper was quite restored. He was able to say pleasantly but firmly to Claud Sopworth, who was teaching Grace the overarm stroke:

'No, no, old man, you have got it all wrong. *I'll* show her.'

And such was the assurance of his tone, that Claud withdrew discomfited. The only pity of it was, that his triumph was short-lived. The temperature of our English waters is not such as to induce bathers to remain in them for any length of time. Grace and the Sopworth girls were already displaying blue chins and chattering teeth. They raced up the beach, and James pursued his solitary way back to Mon Desir. As he towelled himself vigorously and slipped his shirt over his head, he was pleased with himself. He had, he felt, displayed a dynamic personality.

And then suddenly he stood still, frozen with terror. Girlish voices sounded from outside, and voices quite different from those of Grace and her friends. A moment later he had realized the truth, the rightful owners of Mon Desir were arriving. It is possible that if James had been fully dressed, he would have waited their advent in a dignified manner, and attempted an explanation. As it was he acted on panic. The windows of Mon Desir were modestly screened by dark green curtains. James flung himself on the door and held the knob in a desperate clutch. Hands tried ineffectually to turn it from outside.

'It's locked after all,' said a girl's voice. 'I thought Peg said it was open.'

'No, Woggle said so.'

'Woggle is the limit,' said the other girl. 'How perfectly foul, we shall have to go back for the key.'

James heard their footsteps retreating. He drew a long, deep breath. In desperate haste he huddled on the rest of his garments. Two minutes later saw him strolling negligently down the beach with an almost aggressive air of innocence. Grace and the Sopworth girls joined him on the beach a quarter of an hour later. The rest of the morning passed agreeably in stone throwing, writing in the sand and light badinage. Then Claud glanced at his watch.

'Lunch-time,' he observed. 'We'd better be strolling back.'

'I'm terribly hungry,' said Alice Sopworth.

All the other girls said that they were terribly hungry too.

'Are you coming, James?' asked Grace.

Doubtless James was unduly touchy. He chose to take offence at her tone.

'Not if my clothes are not good enough for you,' he said bitterly. 'Perhaps, as you are so particular, I'd better not come.'

That was Grace's cue for murmured protestations, but the seaside air had affected Grace unfavourably. She merely replied:

'Very well. Just as you like, see you this afternoon then.'

James was left dumbfounded.

'Well!' he said, staring after the retreating group. 'Well, of all the—'

He strolled moodily into the town. There were two cafés in Kimpton-on-Sea, they are both hot, noisy and overcrowded. It was the affair of the bathing-huts once more, James had to wait his turn. He had to wait longer than his turn, an unscrupulous matron who had just arrived forestalling him when a vacant seat did present itself. At last he was seated at a small table. Close to his left ear three raggedly bobbed maidens were making a determined hash of Italian opera. Fortunately James was not musical. He studied the bill of fare dispassionately, his hands thrust deep into his pockets. He thought to himself:

'Whatever I ask for it's sure to be "off". That's the kind of fellow I am.'

His right hand, groping in the recesses of his pocket, touched an unfamiliar object. It felt like a pebble, a large round pebble.

'What on earth did I want to put a stone in my pocket for?' thought James.

His fingers closed round it. A waitress drifted up to him.

'Fried plaice and chipped potatoes, please,' said James.

'Fried plaice is "off",' murmured the waitress, her eyes fixed dreamily on the ceiling.

'Then I'll have curried beef,' said James.

'Curried beef is "off".'

'Is there anything on this beastly menu that isn't "off"?' demanded James.

The waitress looked pained, and placed a pale-grey fore-finger against haricot mutton. James resigned himself to the inevitable and ordered haricot mutton. His mind still seething with resentment against the ways of cafés, he drew his hand out of his pocket, the stone still in it. Unclosing his fingers, he looked absentmindedly at the object in his palm. Then with a shock all lesser matters passed from his mind, and he stared with all his eyes. The thing he held was not a pebble, it was—he could hardly doubt it—an emerald, an enormous green emerald. James stared at it horror-stricken. No, it couldn't be an emerald, it must be coloured glass. There couldn't be an emerald of that size, unless—printed words danced before James's eyes, 'The Rajah of Maraputna—famous emerald the size of a pigeon's egg.' Was it—could it be—*that* emerald at which he was now looking? The waitress returned with the haricot mutton, and James closed his fingers spasmodically. Hot and cold shivers chased themselves up and down his spine. He had the sense of being caught in a terrible dilemma. If this was the emerald—but was it? Could it be? He unclosed his fingers and peeped anxiously. James was no expert on precious stones, but the depth and the glow of the jewel convinced him this was the real thing. He put both elbows on the table and leaned forward staring with unseeing eyes at the haricot mutton slowly congealing on the dish in front of him. He had got to think this out. If this was the Rajah's emerald, what was he going to do about it? The word 'police' flashed into his mind. If you found anything of value you took it to the police station. Upon this axiom had James been brought up.

Yes, but—how on earth had the emerald got into his trouser pocket? That was doubtless the question the police would ask. It was an awkward question, and it was moreover a question to which he had at the moment no answer. How had the emerald got into his trouser pocket? He looked despairingly down at his legs, and as he did so a misgiving shot through him. He looked more closely. One pair of old grey flannel trousers is very much like another pair of old grey flannel trousers, but all the same, James had an instinctive feeling that these were not his trousers after all. He sat back in his chair stunned with the force of the discovery. He saw now what had happened, in the hurry of getting out of the bathing-hut, he had taken the wrong trousers. He had hung his own, he remembered, on an adjacent peg to the old pair hanging there. Yes, that explained matters so far, he had taken the wrong trousers. But all the same, what on earth was an emerald worth hundreds and thousands of pounds doing there? The more he thought about it, the more curious it seemed. He could, of course, explain to the police—

It was awkward, no doubt about it, it was decidedly awkward. One would have to mention the fact that one had deliberately entered someone else's bathing-hut. It was not, of course, a serious offence, but it started him off wrong.

'Can I bring you anything else, sir?'

It was the waitress again. She was looking pointedly at the untouched haricot mutton. James hastily dumped some of it on his plate and asked for his bill. Having obtained it, he paid and went out. As he stood undecidedly in the street, a poster opposite caught his eye. The adjacent town of Harchester possessed an evening paper, and it was the contents bill of this paper that James was looking at. It announced a simple, sensational fact: 'THE RAJAH'S EMERALD STOLEN.' 'My God,' said James faintly, and leaned against a pillar. Pulling himself together he fished out a penny and purchased a copy of the paper. He was not long in finding what he sought. Sensational items of local news were few and far between. Large headlines adorned the front page. 'Sensational Burglary at Lord Edward Campion's. Theft of Famous Historical Emerald. Rajah of Maraputna's Terrible Loss.' The facts were few and simple. Lord Edward Campion had entertained several friends the evening before. Wishing to show the stone to one of the ladies present, the Rajah had gone to fetch it and had found it missing. The police had been called in. So far no clue had been obtained. James let the paper fall to the ground. It was still not clear to him how the emerald had come to be reposing in the pocket of an old pair of flannel trousers in a bathing-hut, but it was borne in upon him every minute that the police would certainly regard his own story as suspicious. What on earth was he to do? Here he was, standing in the principal street of Kimpton-on-Sea with stolen booty worth a king's ransom reposing idly in his pocket, whilst the entire police force of the district were busily searching for just that same booty. There were two courses open to him. Course number one, to go straight to the police station and tell his story—but it must be admitted that James funked that course badly. Course number two, somehow or other to get rid of the emerald. It occurred to him to do it up in a neat little parcel and post it back to the Rajah. Then he shook his head, he had read too many detective stories for that sort of thing. He knew how your super-sleuth could get busy with a magnifying glass and every kind of patent device. Any detective worth his salt would get busy on James's parcel and would in half an hour or so have discovered the sender's profession, age, habits and personal appearance. After that it would be a mere matter of hours before he was tracked down.

It was then that a scheme of dazzling simplicity suggested itself to James. It was the luncheon hour, the beach would be comparatively deserted, he would return to Mon Desir, hang up the trousers where he had found them, and regain his own garments. He started briskly towards the beach.

Nevertheless, his conscience pricked him slightly. The emerald *ought* to be returned to the Rajah. He conceived the idea that he might perhaps do a little detective work—once, that is, that he had regained his own trousers and replaced the others. In pursuance of this idea, he directed his steps towards the aged mariner, whom he rightly regarded as being an inexhaustible source of Kimpton information.

'Excuse me!' said James politely; 'but I believe a friend of mine has a hut on this beach, Mr Charles Lampton. It is called Mon Desir, I fancy.'

The aged mariner was sitting very squarely in a chair, a pipe in his mouth, gazing out to sea. He shifted his pipe a little, and replied without removing his gaze from the horizon:

'Mon Desir belongs to his lordship, Lord Edward Campion, everyone knows that. I never heard of Mr Charles Lampton, he must be a newcomer.'

'Thank you,' said James, and withdrew.

The information staggered him. Surely the Rajah could not himself have slipped the stone into the pocket and forgotten it. James shook his head, the theory did not satisfy him, but evidently some member of the house-party must be the thief. The situation reminded James of some of his favourite works of fiction.

Nevertheless, his own purpose remained unaltered. All fell out easily enough. The beach was, as he hoped it would be, practically deserted. More fortunate still, the door of Mon Desir remained ajar. To slip in was the work of a moment, Edward was just lifting his own trousers from the hook, when a voice behind him made him spin round suddenly.

'So I have caught you, my man!' said the voice.

James stared open-mouthed. In the doorway of Mon Desir stood a stranger; a well-dressed man of about forty years of age, his face keen and hawk-like.

'So I have caught you!' the stranger repeated.

'Who—who are you?' stammered James.

'Detective-Inspector Merrilees from the Yard,' said the other crisply. 'And I will trouble you to hand over that emerald.'

'The—the emerald?'

James was seeking to gain time.

'That's what I said, didn't I?' said Inspector Merrilees.

He had a crisp, business-like enunciation. James tried to pull himself together.

'I don't know what you are talking about,' he said with an assumption of dignity.

'Oh, yes, my lad, I think you do.'

'The whole thing,' said James, 'is a mistake. I can explain it quite easily—' He paused.

A look of weariness had settled on the face of the other.

'They always say that,' murmured the Scotland Yard man dryly. 'I suppose you picked it up as you were strolling along the beach, eh? That is the sort of explanation.'

It did indeed bear a resemblance to it, James recognized the fact, but still he tried to gain time.

'How do I know you are what you say you are?' he demanded weakly.

Merrilees flapped back his coat for a moment, showing a badge. Edward stared at him with eyes that popped out of his head.

'And now,' said the other almost genially, 'you see what you are up against! You are a novice—I can tell that. Your first job, isn't it?'

James nodded.

'I thought as much. Now, my boy, are you going to hand over that emerald, or have I got to search you?'

James found his voice.

'I—I haven't got it on me,' he declared.

He was thinking desperately.

'Left it at your lodgings?' queried Merrilees.

James nodded.

'Very well, then,' said the detective, 'we will go there together.'

He slipped his arm through James's.

'I am taking no chances of your getting away from me,' he said gently. 'We will go to your lodgings, and you will hand that stone over to me.'

James spoke unsteadily.

'If I do, will you let me go?' he asked tremulously.

Merrilees appeared embarrassed.

'We know just how that stone was taken,' he explained, 'and about the lady involved, and, of course, as far as that goes—well, the Rajah wants it hushed up. You know what these native rulers are?'

James, who knew nothing whatsoever about native rulers, except for one *cause célèbre*, nodded his head with an appearance of eager comprehension.

'It will be most irregular, of course,' said the detective; 'but you *may* get off scot-free.'

Again James nodded. They had walked the length of the Esplanade, and were now turning into the town. James intimated the direction, but the other man never relinquished his sharp grip on James's arm.

Suddenly James hesitated and half-spoke. Merrilees looked up sharply, and then laughed. They were just passing the police station, and he noticed James's agonized glances at it.

'I am giving you a chance first,' he said good-humouredly.

It was at that moment that things began to happen. A loud bellow broke from James, he clutched the other's arm, and yelled at the top of his voice:

'Help! thief. Help! thief.'

A crowd surrounded them in less than a minute. Merrilees was trying to wrench his arm from James's grasp.

'I charge this man,' cried James. 'I charge this man, he picked my pocket.'

'What are you talking about, you fool?' cried the other.

A constable took charge of matters. Mr Merrilees and James were escorted into the police station. James reiterated his complaint.

'This man has just picked my pocket,' he declared excitedly. 'He has got my note-case in his right-hand pocket, there!'

'The man is mad,' grumbled the other. 'You can look for yourself, inspector, and see if he is telling the truth.'

At a sign from the inspector, the constable slipped his hand deferentially into Merrilees's pocket. He drew something out and held it up with a gasp of astonishment.

'My God!' said the inspector, startled out of professional decorum. 'It must be the Rajah's emerald.'

Merrilees looked more incredulous than anyone else.

'This is monstrous,' he spluttered, 'monstrous. The man must have put it into my pocket himself as we were walking along together. It's a plant.'

The forceful personality of Merrilees caused the inspector to waver. His suspicions swung round to James. He whispered something to the constable, and the latter went out.

'Now then, gentlemen,' said the inspector, 'let me have your statements please, one at a time.'

'Certainly,' said James. 'I was walking along the beach, when I met this gentleman, and he pretended he was acquainted with me. I could not remember having met him before, but I was too polite to say so. We walked along together. I had my suspicions of him, and just when we got opposite the police station, I found his hand in my pocket. I held on to him and shouted for help.'

The inspector transferred his glance to Merrilees.

'And now you, sir.'

Merrilees seemed a little embarrassed.

'The story is very nearly right,' he said slowly; 'but not quite. It was not I who scraped acquaintance with him, but he who scraped acquaintance with me. Doubtless he was trying to get rid of the emerald, and slipped it into my pocket while we were talking.'

The inspector stopped writing.

'Ah!' he said impartially. 'Well, there will be a gentleman here in a minute who will help us to get to the bottom of the case.'

Merrilees frowned.

'It is really impossible for me to wait,' he murmured, pulling out his watch. 'I have an appointment. Surely, inspector, you can't be so ridiculous as to suppose I'd steal the emerald and walk along with it in my pocket?'

'It is not likely, sir, I agree,' the inspector replied. 'But you will have to wait just a matter of five or ten minutes till we get this thing cleared up. Ah! here is his lordship.'

A tall man of forty strode into the room. He was wearing a pair of dilapidated trousers and an old sweater.

'Now then, inspector, what is all this?' he said. 'You have got hold of the emerald, you say? That's splendid, very smart work. Who are these people you have got here?'

His eyes ranged over James and came to rest on Merrilees. The forceful personality of the latter seemed to dwindle and shrink.

'Why—Jones!' exclaimed Lord Edward Campion.

'You recognize this man, Lord Edward?' asked the inspector sharply.

'Certainly I do,' said Lord Edward dryly. 'He is my valet, came to me a month ago. The fellow they sent down from London was on to him at once, but there was not a trace of the emerald anywhere among his belongings.'

'He was carrying it in his coat pocket,' the inspector declared. 'This gentleman put us on to him.' He indicated James.

In another minute James was being warmly congratulated and shaken by the hand.

'My dear fellow,' said Lord Edward Campion. 'So you suspected him all along, you say?'

'Yes,' said James. 'I had to trump up the story about my pocket being picked to get him into the police station.'

'Well, it is splendid,' said Lord Edward, 'absolutely splendid. You must come back and lunch with us, that is if you haven't lunched. It is late, I know, getting on for two o'clock.'

'No,' said James; 'I haven't lunched—but—'

'Not a word, not a word,' said Lord Edward. 'The Rajah, you know, will want to thank you for getting back his emerald for him. Not that I have quite got the hang of the story yet.'

They were out of the police station by now, standing on the steps.

'As a matter of fact,' said James, 'I think I should like to tell you the true story.'

He did so. His lordship was very much entertained.

'Best thing I ever heard in my life,' he declared. 'I see it all now. Jones must have hurried down to the bathing-hut as soon as he had pinched the thing, knowing that the police would make a thorough search of the house. That old pair of trousers I sometimes put on for going out fishing, nobody was likely to touch them, and he could recover the jewel at his leisure. Must have been a shock to him when he came today to find it gone. As soon as you appeared, he realized that you were the person who had removed the stone. I still don't quite see how you managed to see through that detective pose of his, though!'

'A strong man,' thought James to himself, 'knows when to be frank and when to be discreet.'

He smiled deprecatingly whilst his fingers passed gently over the inside of his coat lapel feeling the small silver badge of that little-known club, the Merton Park Super Cycling Club. An astonishing coincidence that the man Jones should also be a member, but there it was!

'Hallo, James!'

He turned. Grace and the Sopworth girls were calling to him from the other side of the road. He turned to Lord Edward.

'Excuse me a moment?'

He crossed the road to them.

'We are going to the pictures,' said Grace. 'Thought you might like to come.'

'I am sorry,' said James. 'I am just going back to lunch with Lord Edward Campion. Yes, that man over there in the comfortable old clothes. He wants me to meet the Rajah of Maraputna.'

He raised his hat politely and rejoined Lord Edward.

# *Swan Song*

It was eleven o'clock on a May morning in London. Mr Cowan was looking out of the window, behind him was the somewhat ornate splendour of a sitting-room in a suite at the Ritz Hotel. The suite in question had been reserved for Mme Paula Nazorkoff, the famous operatic star, who had just arrived in London. Mr Cowan, who was Madame's principal man of business, was awaiting an interview with the lady. He turned his head suddenly as the door opened, but it was only Miss Read, Mme Nazorkoff's secretary, a pale girl with an efficient manner.

'Oh, so it's you, my dear,' said Mr Cowan. 'Madame not up yet, eh?'

Miss Read shook her head.

'She told me to come round at ten o'clock,' Mr Cowan said. 'I have been waiting an hour.'

He displayed neither resentment nor surprise. Mr Cowan was indeed accustomed to the vagaries of the artistic temperament. He was a tall man, clean-shaven, with a frame rather too well covered, and clothes that were rather too faultless. His hair was very black and shining, and his teeth were agressively white. When he spoke, he had a way of slurring his 's's' which was not quite a lisp, but came perilously near to it. It required no stretch of imagination to realize that his father's name had probably been Cohen. At that minute a door at the other side of the room opened, and a trim, French girl hurried through.

'Madame getting up?' inquired Cowan hopefully. 'Tell us the news, Elise.'

Elise immediately elevated both hands to heaven.

'Madame she is like seventeen devils this morning, nothing pleases her! The beautiful yellow roses which monsieur sent to her last night, she says they are all very well for New York, but that it is *imbecile* to send them to her in London. In London, she says, red roses are the only things possible, and straight away she opens the door, and precipitates the yellow roses into the passage, where they descend upon a monsieur, *très comme il faut*, a military gentleman, I think, and he is justly indignant, that one!'

Cowan raised his eyebrows, but displayed no other signs of emotion. Then he took from his pocket a small memorandum book and pencilled in it the words 'red roses'.

Elise hurried out through the other door, and Cowan turned once more to the window. Vera Read sat down at the desk, and began opening letters and sorting them. Ten minutes passed in silence, and then the door of the bedroom burst open, and Paula Nazorkoff flamed into the room. Her immediate effect upon it was to make it seem smaller; Vera Read appeared more colourless, and Cowan retreated into a mere figure in the background.

'Ah, ha! My children,' said the prima donna. 'Am I not punctual?'

She was a tall woman, and for a singer not unduly fat. Her arms and legs were still slender, and her neck was a beautiful column. Her hair, which was coiled in a great roll half-way down her neck, was of a dark, glowing red. If it owed some at least of its colour to henna, the result was none the less effective. She was not a young woman, forty at least, but the lines of her face were still lovely, though the skin was loosened and wrinkled round the flashing, dark eyes. She had the laugh of a child, the digestion of an ostrich, and the temper of a fiend, and she was acknowledged to be the greatest dramatic soprano of her day. She turned directly upon Cowan.

'Have you done as I asked you? Have you taken that abominable English piano away, and thrown it into the Thames?'

'I have got another for you,' said Cowan, and gestured towards where it stood in the corner.

Nazorkoff rushed across to it, and lifted the lid.

'An Erard,' she said, 'that is better. Now let us see.'

The beautiful soprano voice rang out in an arpeggio, then it ran lightly up and down the scale twice, then took a soft little run up to a high note, held it, its volume swelling louder and louder, then softened again till it died away in nothingness.

'Ah!' said Paula Nazorkoff in naïve satisfaction. 'What a beautiful voice I have! Even in London I have a beautiful voice.'

'That is so,' agreed Cowan in hearty congratulation.

'And you bet London is going to fall for you all right, just as New York did.'

'You think so?' queried the singer.

There was a slight smile on her lips, and it was evident that for her the question was a mere commonplace.

'Sure thing,' said Cowan.

Paula Nazorkoff closed the piano lid down and walked across to the table, with that slow undulating walk that proved so effective on the stage.

'Well, well,' she said, 'let us get to business. You have all the arrangements there, my friend?'

Cowan took some papers out of the portfolio he had laid on a chair.

'Nothing has been altered much,' he remarked. 'You will sing five times at Covent Garden, three times in *Tosca*, twice in *Aida*.'

'*Aida!* Pah,' said the prima donna; 'it will be unutterable boredom. *Tosca*, that is different.'

'Ah, yes,' said Cowan. '*Tosca* is *your* part.'

Paula Nazorkoff drew herself up.

'I am the greatest Tosca in the world,' she said simply.

'That is so,' agreed Cowan. 'No one can touch you.'

'Roscari will sing "Scarpia", I suppose?'

Cowan nodded.

'And Emile Lippi.'

'What?' shrieked Nazorkoff. 'Lippi, that hideous little barking frog, croak—croak—croak. I will not sing with him, I will bite him, I will scratch his face.'

'Now, now,' said Cowan soothingly.

'He does not sing, I tell you, he is a mongrel dog who barks.'

'Well, we'll see, we'll see,' said Cowan.

He was too wise ever to argue with temperamental singers.

'The Cavaradossi?' demanded Nazorkoff.

'The American tenor, Hensdale.'

The other nodded.

'He is a nice little boy, he sings prettily.'

'And Barrère is to sing it once, I believe.'

'He is an artist,' said Madame generously. 'But to let that croaking frog Lippi be Scarpia! Bah—I'll not sing with him.'

'You leave it to me,' said Cowan soothingly.

He cleared his throat, and took up a fresh set of papers.

'I am arranging for a special concert at the Albert Hall.'

Nazorkoff made a grimace.

'I know, I know,' said Cowan, 'but everybody does it.'

'I will be good,' said Nazorkoff, 'and it will be filled to the ceiling, and I shall have much money. *Ecco!*'

Again Cowan shuffled papers.

'Now here is quite a different proposition,' he said, 'from Lady Rustonbury. She wants you to go down and sing.'

'Rustonbury?'

The prima donna's brow contracted as if in the effort to recollect something.

'I have read that name lately, very lately. It is a town—or a village, isn't it?'

'That's right, pretty little place in Hertfordshire. As for Lord Rustonbury's place, Rustonbury Castle, it's a real dandy old feudal seat, ghosts and family pictures, and secret staircases, and a slap-up private theatre. Rolling in money they are, and always giving some private show. She suggests that we give a complete opera, preferably *Butterfly*.'

'*Butterfly?*'

Cowan nodded.

'And they are prepared to pay. We'll have to square Covent Garden, of course, but even after that it will be well worth your while financially. In all probability, royalty will be present. It will be a slap-up advertisement.'

Madame raised her still beautiful chin.

'Do I need advertisement?' she demanded proudly.

'You can't have too much of a good thing,' said Cowan, unabashed.

'Rustonbury,' murmured the singer, 'where did I see—?'

She sprang up suddenly, and running to the centre table, began turning over the pages of an illustrated paper which lay there. There was a sudden pause as her hand stopped, hovering over one of the pages, then she let the periodical slip to the floor and returned slowly to her seat. With one of her swift changes of mood, she seemed now an entirely different personality. Her manner was very quiet, almost austere.

'Make all arrangements for Rustonbury, I would like to sing there, but there is one condition—the opera must be *Tosca*.'

Cowan looked doubtful.

'That will be rather difficult—for a private show, you know, scenery and all that.'

'*Tosca* or nothing.'

Cowan looked at her very closely. What he saw seemed to convince him, he gave a brief nod and rose to his feet.

'I will see what I can arrange,' he said quietly.

Nazorkoff rose too. She seemed more anxious than was usual, with her, to explain her decision.

'It is my greatest rôle, Cowan. I can sing that part as no other woman has ever sung it.'

'It is a fine part,' said Cowan. 'Jeritza made a great hit in it last year.'

'Jeritza?' cried the other, a flush mounting in her cheeks. She proceeded to give him at great length her opinion of Jeritza.

Cowan, who was used to listening to singers' opinions of other singers, abstracted his attention till the tirade was over; he then said obstinately:

'Anyway, she sings "Vissi D'Arte" lying on her stomach.'

'And why not?' demanded Nazorkoff. 'What is there to prevent her? I will sing it on my back with my legs waving in the air.'

Cowan shook his head with perfect seriousness.

'I don't believe that would go down any,' he informed her. 'All the same, that sort of thing takes on, you know.'

'No one can sing "Vissi D'Arte" as I can,' said Nazorkoff confidently. 'I sing it in the voice of the convent—as the good nuns taught me to sing years and years ago. In the voice of a choir boy or an angel, without feeling, without passion.'

'I know,' said Cowan heartily. 'I have heard you, you are wonderful.'

'That is art,' said the prima donna, 'to pay the price, to

248

suffer, to endure, and in the end not only to have all knowledge, but also the power to go back, right back to the beginning and recapture the lost beauty of the heart of a child.'

Cowan looked at her curiously. She was staring past him with a strange, blank look in her eyes, and something about that look of hers gave him a creepy feeling. Her lips just parted, and she whispered a few words softly to herself. He only just caught them.

'At last,' she murmured. 'At last—*after all these years.*'

Lady Rustonbury was both an ambitious and an artistic woman, she ran the two qualities in harness with complete success. She had the good fortune to have a husband who cared for neither ambition nor art and who therefore did not hamper her in any way. The Earl of Rustonbury was a large, square man, with an interest in horseflesh and in nothing else. He admired his wife, and was proud of her, and was glad that his great wealth enabled her to indulge all her schemes. The private theatre had been built less than a hundred years ago by his grandfather. It was Lady Rustonbury's chief toy—she had already given an Ibsen drama in it, and a play of the ultra new school, all divorce and drugs, also a poetical fantasy with Cubist scenery. The forthcoming performance of *Tosca* had created widespread interest. Lady Rustonbury was entertaining a very distinguished house-party for it, and all London that counted was motoring down to attend.

Mme Nazorkoff and her company had arrived just before

luncheon. The new young American tenor, Hensdale, was to sing 'Cavaradossi', and Roscari, the famous Italian baritone, was to be Scarpia. The expense of the production had been enormous, but nobody cared about that. Paula Nazorkoff was in the best of humours, she was charming, gracious, her most delightful and cosmopolitan self. Cowan was agreeably surprised, and prayed that this state of things might continue.

After luncheon the company went out to the theatre, and inspected the scenery and various appointments. The orchestra was under the direction of Mr Samuel Ridge, one of England's most famous conductors. Everything seemed to be going without a hitch, and strangely enough, that fact worried Mr Cowan. He was more at home in an atmosphere of trouble, this unusual peace disturbed him.

'Everything is going a darned sight too smoothly,' murmured Mr Cowan to himself. 'Madame is like a cat that has been fed on cream, it's too good to last, something is bound to happen.'

Perhaps as the result of his long contact with the operatic world, Mr Cowan had developed the sixth sense, certainly his prognostications were justified. It was just before seven o'clock that evening when the French maid, Elise, came running to him in great distress.

'Ah, Mr Cowan, come quickly, I beg of you come quickly.'

'What's the matter?' demanded Cowan anxiously. 'Madame got her back up about anything—ructions, eh, is that it?'

'No, no, it is not Madame, it is Signor Roscari, he is ill, he is dying!'

'Dying? Oh, come now.'

Cowan hurried after her as she led the way to the stricken Italian's bedroom. The little man was lying on his bed, or rather jerking himself all over it in a series of contortions that would have been humorous had they been less grave. Paula Nazorkoff was bending over him; she greeted Cowan imperiously.

'Ah! there you are. Our poor Roscari, he suffers horribly. Doubtless he has eaten something.'

'I am dying,' groaned the little man. 'The pain—it is terrible. Ow!'

He contorted himself again, clasping both hands to his stomach, and rolling about on the bed.

'We must send for a doctor,' said Cowan.

Paula arrested him as he was about to move to the door.

'The doctor is already on his way, he will do all that can be done for the poor suffering one, that is arranged for, but never never will Roscari be able to sing tonight.'

'I shall never sing again, I am dying,' groaned the Italian.

'No, no, you are not dying,' said Paula. 'It is but an indigestion, but all the same, impossible that you should sing.'

'I have been poisoned.'

'Yes, it is the ptomaine without doubt,' said Paula. 'Stay with him, Elise, till the doctor comes.'

The singer swept Cowan with her from the room.

'What are we to do?' she demanded.

Cowan shook his head hopelessly. The hour was so far advanced that it would not be possible to get anyone from London to take Roscari's place. Lady Rustonbury, who had just been informed of her guest's illness, came hurrying along the corridor to join them. Her principal concern, like Paula Nazorkoff's, was the success of *Tosca*.

'If there were only someone near at hand,' groaned the prima donna.

'Ah!' Lady Rustonbury gave a sudden cry. 'Of course! Bréon.'

'Bréon?'

'Yes, Edouard Bréon, you know, the famous French baritone. He lives near here, there was a picture of his house in this week's *Country Homes*. He is the very man.'

'It is an answer from heaven,' cried Nazorkoff. 'Bréon as Scarpia, I remember him well, it was one of his greatest rôles. But he has retired, has he not?'

'I will get him,' said Lady Rustonbury. 'Leave it to me.'

And being a woman of decision, she straightaway ordered out the Hispano Suiza. Ten minutes later, M. Edouard Bréon's country retreat was invaded by an agitated countess. Lady Rustonbury, once she had made her mind up, was a very determined woman, and doubtless M. Bréon realized that there was nothing for it but to submit. Himself a man of very humble origin, he had climbed to the top of his profession, and had consorted on equal terms with dukes and princes, and the fact never failed to gratify him. Yet, since his retirement to this old-world English spot, he had known discontent. He missed the life of adulation and applause, and the English county had not been as prompt to recognize him as he thought they should have been. So he was greatly flattered and charmed by Lady Rustonbury's request.

'I will do my poor best,' he said, smiling. 'As you know, I have not sung in public for a long time now. I do not even take pupils, only one or two as a great favour. But there— since Signor Roscari is unfortunately indisposed—'

'It was a terrible blow,' said Lady Rustonbury.

'Not that he is really a singer,' said Bréon.

He told her at some length why this was so. There had been, it seemed, no baritone of distinction since Edouard Bréon retired.

'Mme Nazorkoff is singing "Tosca",' said Lady Rustonbury. 'You know her, I dare say?'

'I have never met her,' said Bréon. 'I heard her sing once in New York. A great artist—she has a sense of drama.'

Lady Rustonbury felt relieved—one never knew with these singers—they had such queer jealousies and antipathies.

She re-entered the hall at the castle some twenty minutes later waving a triumphant hand.

'I have got him,' she cried, laughing. 'Dear M. Bréon has really been too kind, I shall never forget it.'

Everyone crowded round the Frenchman, and their gratitude and appreciation were as incense to him. Edouard Bréon, though now close on sixty, was still a fine-looking man, big and dark, with a magnetic personality.

'Let me see,' said Lady Rustonbury. 'Where is Madame—? Oh! there she is.'

Paula Nazorkoff had taken no part in the general welcoming of the Frenchman. She had remained quietly sitting in a high oak chair in the shadow of the fireplace. There was, of course, no fire, for the evening was a warm one and the singer was slowly fanning herself with an immense palm-leaf fan. So aloof and detached was she, that Lady Rustonbury feared she had taken offence.

'M. Bréon.' She led him up to the singer. 'You have never yet met Madame Nazorkoff, you say.'

With a last wave, almost a flourish, of the palm leaf, Paula Nazorkoff laid it down, and stretched out her hand to the Frenchman. He took it and bowed low over it, and a faint sigh escaped from the prima donna's lips.

'Madame,' said Bréon, 'we have never sung together. That is the penalty of my age! But Fate has been kind to me, and come to my rescue.'

Paula laughed softly.

'You are too kind, M. Bréon. When I was still but a poor little unknown singer, I have sat at your feet. Your "Rigoletto"—what art, what perfection! No one could touch you.'

'Alas!' said Bréon, pretending to sigh. 'My day is over. Scarpia, Rigoletto, Radames, Sharpless, how many times have I not sung them, and now—no more!'

'Yes—tonight.'

'True, Madame—I forgot. Tonight.'

'You have sung with many "Toscas",' said Nazorkoff arrogantly; 'but never with *me*!'

The Frenchman bowed.

'It will be an honour,' he said softly. 'It is a great part, Madame.'

'It needs not only a singer, but an actress,' put in Lady Rustonbury.

'That is true,' Bréon agreed. 'I remember when I was a

young man in Italy, going to a little out of the way theatre in Milan. My seat cost me only a couple of lira, but I heard as good singing that night as I have heard in the Metropolitan Opera House in New York. Quite a young girl sang "Tosca", she sang it like an angel. Never shall I forget her voice in "Vissi D'Arte", the clearness of it, the purity. But the dramatic force, that was lacking.'

Nazorkoff nodded.

'That comes later,' she said quietly.

'True. This young girl—Bianca Capelli, her name was—I interested myself in her career. Through me she had the chance of big engagements, but she was foolish—regrettably foolish.'

He shrugged his shoulders.

'How was she foolish?'

It was Lady Rustonbury's twenty-four-year-old daughter, Blanche Amery, who spoke. A slender girl with wide blue eyes.

The Frenchman turned to her at once politely.

'Alas! Mademoiselle, she had embroiled herself with some low fellow, a ruffian, a member of the Camorra. He got into trouble with the police, was condemned to death; she came to me begging me to do something to save her lover.'

Blanche Amery was staring at him.

'And did you?' she asked breathlessly.

'Me, Mademoiselle, what could I do? A stranger in the country.'

'You might have had influence?' suggested Nazorkoff, in her low vibrant voice.

'If I had, I doubt whether I should have exerted it. The man was not worth it. I did what I could for the girl.'

He smiled a little, and his smile suddenly struck the English girl as having something peculiarly disagreeable about it. She felt that, at that moment, his words fell far short of representing his thoughts.

'You did what you could,' said Nazorkoff. 'That was kind of you, and she was grateful, eh?'

The Frenchman shrugged his shoulders.

'The man was executed,' he said, 'and the girl entered a convent. Eh, *voila*! The world has lost a singer.'

Nazorkoff gave a low laugh.

'We Russians are more fickle,' she said lightly.

Blanche Amery happened to be watching Cowan just as the singer spoke, and she saw his quick look of astonishment, and his lips that half-opened and then shut tight in obedience to some warning glance from Paula.

The butler appeared in the doorway.

'Dinner,' said Lady Rustonbury, rising. 'You poor things, I am so sorry for you, it must be dreadful always to have to starve yourself before singing. But there will be a very good supper afterwards.'

'We shall look forward to it,' said Paula Nazorkoff. She laughed softly. '*Afterwards!*'

Inside the theatre, the first act of *Tosca* had just drawn to a close. The audience stirred, spoke to each other. The royalties, charming and gracious, sat in the three velvet chairs in the front row. Everyone was whispering and murmuring to each other, there was a general feeling that in the first act Nazorkoff had hardly lived up to her great reputation. Most of the audience did not realize that in this the singer showed her art, in the first act she was saving her voice and herself. She made of La Tosca a light, frivolous figure, toying with love, coquettishly jealous and exciting. Bréon, though the glory of his voice was past its prime, still struck a magnificent figure as the cynical Scarpia. There was no hint of the decrepit roué in his conception of the part. He made of Scarpia a handsome, almost benign figure, with just a hint of the subtle malevolence that underlay the outward seeming. In the last passage, with the organ and the procession, when Scarpia stands lost in thought, gloating over his plan to secure Tosca, Bréon had displayed a wonderful art. Now the curtain rose up on the second act, the scene in Scarpia's apartments.

This time, when Tosca entered, the art of Nazorkoff at once became apparent. Here was a woman in deadly terror playing her part with the assurance of a fine actress. Her easy greeting of Scarpia, her nonchalance, her smiling replies to him! In this scene, Paula Nazorkoff acted with her eyes, she carried herself with deadly quietness, with an impassive, smiling face. Only her eyes that kept darting glances at Scarpia betrayed her true feelings. And so the story went on, the torture scene, the breaking down of Tosca's composure, and her utter abandonment when she fell at Scarpia's feet imploring him vainly for mercy. Old Lord Leconmere, a connoisseur of music, moved appreciatively, and a foreign ambassador sitting next to him murmured:

'She surpasses herself, Nazorkoff, tonight. There is no

other woman on the stage who can let herself go as she does.'

Leconmere nodded.

And now Scarpia has named his price, and Tosca, horrified, flies from him to the window. Then comes the beat of drums from afar, and Tosca flings herself wearily down on the sofa. Scarpia standing over her, recites how his people are raising up the gallows—and then silence, and again the far-off beat of drums. Nazorkoff lay prone on the sofa, her head hanging downwards almost touching the floor, masked by her hair. Then, in exquisite contrast to the passion and stress of the last twenty minutes, her voice rang out, high and clear, the voice, as she had told Cowan, of a choir boy or an angel.

*'Vissi d'arte, vissi d'amore, non feci mai male ad anima viva! Con man furtiva quante miserie conobbi, aiutai.'*

It was the voice of a wondering, puzzled child. Then she is once more kneeling and imploring, till the instant when Spoletta enters. Tosca, exhausted, gives in, and Scarpia utters his fateful words of double-edged meaning. Spoletta departs once more. Then comes the dramatic moment, whe Tosca, raising a glass of wine in her trembling hand, catches sight of the knife on the table, and slips it behind her.

Bréon rose up, handsome, saturnine, inflamed with passion. *'Tosca, finalmente mia!'* The lightning stabs with the knife, and Tosca's hiss of vengeance:

*'Questo è il baccio di Tosca!'* ('It is thus that Tosca kisses.')
Never had Nazorkoff shown such an appreciation of

Tosca's act of vengeance. That last fierce whispered '*Muori dannato,*' and then in a strange, quiet voice that filled the theatre:

'*Or gli perdono!*' ('Now I forgive him!')

The soft death tune began as Tosca set about her ceremonial, placing the candles each side of his head, the crucifix on his breast, her last pause in the doorway looking back, the roll of distant drums, and the curtain fell.

This time real enthusiasm broke out in the audience, but it was short-lived. Someone hurried out from behind the wings, and spoke to Lord Rustonbury. He rose, and after a minute or two's consultation, turned and beckoned to Sir Donald Calthorp, who was an eminent physician. Almost immediately the truth spread through the audience. Something had happened, an accident, someone was badly hurt. One of the singers appeared before the curtain and explained that M. Bréon had unfortunately met with an accident—the opera could not proceed. Again the rumour went round, Bréon had been stabbed, Nazorkoff had lost her head, she had lived in her part so completely that she had actually stabbed the man who was acting with her. Lord Leconmere, talking to his ambassador friend, felt a touch on his arm, and turned to look into Blanche Amery's eyes.

'It was not an accident,' the girl was saying. 'I am sure it was not an accident. Didn't you hear, just before dinner, that story he was telling about the girl in Italy? That girl was Paula Nazorkoff. Just after, she said something about being Russian, and I saw Mr Cowan look amazed. She may have taken a Russian name, but he knows well enough that she is Italian.'

*Agatha Christie*

'My dear Blanche,' said Lord Leconmere.

'I tell you I am sure of it. She had a picture paper in her bedroom opened at the page showing M. Bréon in his English country home. She knew before she came down here. I believe she gave something to that poor little Italian man to make him ill.'

'But why?' cried Lord Leconmere. 'Why?'

'Don't you see? It's the story of Tosca all over again. He wanted her in Italy, but she was faithful to her lover, and she went to him to try to get him to save her lover, and he pretended he would. Instead he let him die. And now at last her revenge has come. Didn't you hear the way she hissed "*I am Tosca*"? And I saw Bréon's face when she said it, *he knew then*—he recognized her!'

In her dressing-room, Paula Nazorkoff sat motionless, a white ermine cloak held round her. There was a knock at the door.

'Come in,' said the prima donna.

Elise entered. She was sobbing.

'Madame, Madame, he is dead! And—'

'Yes?'

'Madame, how can I tell you? There are two gentlemen of the police there, they want to speak to you.'

Paula Nazorkoff rose to her full height.

'I will go to them,' she said quietly.

She untwisted a collar of pearls from her neck, and put them into the French girl's hands.

'Those are for you, Elise, you have been a good girl. I shall not need them now where I am going. You understand, Elise? *I shall not sing "Tosca" again.*'

She stood a moment by the door, her eyes sweeping over the dressing-room, as though she looked back over the past thirty years of her career.

Then softly between her teeth, she murmured the last line of another opera:

'*La commedia è finita!*'

# The *Agatha Christie* Collection

## THE MISS MARPLE MYSTERIES

### Join the legendary spinster sleuth from St Mary Mead in solving murders far and wide.

*The Murder at the Vicarage*

*The Thirteen Problems*

*The Body in the Library*

*The Moving Finger*

*A Murder is Announced*

*They Do It With Mirrors*

*A Pocket Full of Rye*

*4.50 from Paddington*

*The Mirror Crack'd from Side to Side*

*A Caribbean Mystery*

*At Bertram's Hotel*

*Nemesis*

*Sleeping Murder*

*Miss Marple's Final Cases*

## THE TOMMY & TUPPENCE MYSTERIES

### Jump on board with the entertaining crime-solving couple from Young Adventurers Ltd.

*The Secret Adversary*

*Partners in Crime*

*N or M?*

*By the Pricking of My Thumbs*

*Postern of Fate*

---

Find out all about the Queen of Crime
and her stories at **www.agathachristie.com**

Keep up to date with launches and news from the world
of Agatha Christie and discuss all things Agatha on the forum!

Shop online for books, audiobooks, DVDs and other merchandise

For a touch of
Christie mystery,
scan the code!

 /agathachristie      /officialagathachristie      /QueenofCrime

# The *Agatha Christie* Collection

## THE HERCULE POIROT MYSTERIES
### Match your wits with the famous Belgian detective.

*The Mysterious Affair at Styles*

*The Murder on the Links*

*Poirot Investigates*

*The Murder of Roger Ackroyd*

*The Big Four*

*The Mystery of the Blue Train*

*Black Coffee*

*Peril at End House*

*Lord Edgware Dies*

*Murder on the Orient Express*

*Three Act Tragedy*

*Death in the Clouds*

*The ABC Murders*

*Murder in Mesopotamia*

*Cards on the Table*

*Murder in the Mews*

*Dumb Witness*

*Death on the Nile*

*Appointment With Death*

*Hercule Poirot's Christmas*

*Sad Cypress*

*One, Two, Buckle My Shoe*

*Evil Under the Sun*

*Five Little Pigs*

*The Hollow*

*The Labours of Hercules*

*Taken at the Flood*

*Mrs McGinty's Dead*

*After the Funeral*

*Hickory Dickory Dock*

*Dead Man's Folly*

*Cat Among the Pigeons*

*The Adventure of the Christmas Pudding*

*The Clocks*

*Third Girl*

*Hallowe'en Party*

*Elephants Can Remember*

*Poirot's Early Cases*

*Curtain: Poirot's Last Case*

# The *Agatha Christie* Collection

**Don't miss a single one of Agatha Christie's classic novels and short story collections.**

# *Agatha Christie*
## Short stories for your E-reader

<table>
<tr><td>

## MISS MARPLE

*The Tuesday Night Club*

*The Idol House of Astarte*

*Ingots of Gold*

*The Blood-Stained Pavement*

*Motive v. Opportunity*

*The Thumb Mark of St Peter*

*The Blue Geranium*

*The Companion*

*The Four Suspects*

*A Christmas Tragedy*

*The Herb of Death*

*The Affair at the Bungalow*

*Death by Drowning*

*Miss Marple Tells a Story*

*Strange Jest*

*Tape-Measure Murder*

*The Case of the Caretaker*

*The Case of the Perfect Maid*

</td><td>

## MYSTERY

*Sanctuary*

*The Girl in the Train*

*The Red Signal*

*The Mystery of the Blue Jar*

*Jane in Search of a Job*

*Mr Eastwood's Adventure*

*Philomel Cottage*

*The Manhood of Edward Robinson*

*The Witness for the Prosecution*

*Wireless*

*The Fourth Man*

*S.O.S.*

*The Rajah's Emerald*

*The Gipsy*

*The Lamp*

*The Strange Case of Sir Arthur Carmichael*

*The Call of Wings*

*In a Glass Darkly*

</td></tr>
</table>

# Agatha Christie

## Short stories for your E-reader